Dear Reader,

Sometimes love comes along when we least expect it to, and as we see in these two classic romances from bestselling author Nora Roberts, we need to be ready and willing to let it into our lives when it does.

In *The Best Mistake,* former model turned single mom Zoe Fleming could really use a tenant to help pay the bills, but longtime bachelor J. Cooper McKinnon isn't exactly who she had in mind. Sure, Coop's great with her son, but the last thing Zoe needs is another man in her life, even if he is extremely charming. It seems as though inviting Coop into her home might turn out to be the best mistake she's ever made.

In *Local Hero,* Hester Wallace wants nothing more than to provide a good life for her nine-year-old son, Radley. But when Rad starts showing an interest in their neighbor Mitch Dempsey, Hester realizes there's one thing she can never be—a male role model. Hester would do anything for Rad, but there's something dangerously alluring about Mitch, and she worries that if he gets too close, Rad won't be the only one who gets attached....

We hope you enjoy these charmed tales of two couples who can't deny that when love comes along, it's best to welcome it with open arms—and an open heart.

The Editors

Silhouette Books

NORA ROBERTS

Love Comes Along

Silhouette Books

Published by Silhouette Books

America's Publisher of Contemporary Romance

SILHOUETTE BOOKS

LOVE COMES ALONG

ISBN-13: 978-0-373-28179-4

Recycling programs
for this product may
not exist in your area.

Copyright © 2014 by Harlequin Books S.A.

The publisher acknowledges the copyright holder
of the individual works as follows:

THE BEST MISTAKE
Copyright © 1994 by Nora Roberts

LOCAL HERO
Copyright © 1987 by Nora Roberts

Visit Silhouette Books at www.Harlequin.com

Printed in U.S.A.

THE BEST MISTAKE

Chapter 1

No one answered the door. Coop glanced at the scrawled note in his hand to make sure he had the right address. It checked out, and since the tidy two-story Tudor in the neat, tree-lined neighborhood was precisely what he was after, he knocked again. Loudly.

There was a car in the drive, an aging station wagon that could use a good wash and a little bodywork. Somebody was in there, he thought, scowling up at the second-floor window, where music pumped out—high-volume rock with a thumping backbeat. He stuffed the note and his hands in his pockets and took a moment to survey the surroundings.

The house was trim, set nicely off the road behind clipped bayberry hedges. The flower garden, in which spring blossoms were beginning to thrive, was both colorful and just wild enough not to look static.

Not that he was a big flower lover, but there *was* something to be said for ambience.

There was a shiny red tricycle beside the driveway, and that made him a little uneasy. He wasn't particularly fond of kids. Not that he disliked them. It was just that they always seemed a kind of foreign entity to him, like aliens from an outlying planet: they spoke a different language, had a different culture. And, well, they were short, and usually sticky.

Still, the ad had talked of quiet, privacy, and a convenient distance from Baltimore. That was exactly what he was looking for.

He knocked again, only to have a thundering wave of music wash out the window over him. The rock didn't bother him. At least he understood it. But he wasn't a man to kick his heels outside a closed door for long, so he tried the knob.

When it turned, he pushed the door open and walked in. In an old habit, he pushed back the dark hair that fell over his forehead and scanned the none-too-neat living room he'd entered.

There was a lot of clutter, and he, a bachelor who'd spent a great deal of his thirty-two years living alone, wondered over it. He wasn't fussy or obsessive, he often told himself. It was simply that everything had a place, and it was easier to find if it had been put there. Obviously his prospective landlord didn't agree.

There were toys that went along with the tricycle outside, piles of magazines and newspapers, a pint-size fielder's cap that declared for the O's.

At least the kid had taste, Coop decided, and moved on.

There was a small powder room done in an amazing

combination of purple and green, and a den that had been converted into a makeshift office. File drawers were open, papers spilling out. In the kitchen dishes waited in the sink to be washed, and lurid drawings, created by a child with a wild imagination, decorated the front of the refrigerator.

Maybe, he thought, it was just as well no one had answered the door.

He considered backtracking and wandering upstairs. As long as he was here, it made sense to check the rest of the place out. Instead, he stepped outside to get the lay of the land. He spotted open wooden steps leading to a short deck. The private entrance the ad had mentioned, he mused, and climbed.

The glass door was open, and the music rolling through it was overwhelming. He caught the smell of fresh paint, one he'd always enjoyed, and stepped inside.

The open area combined kitchen and living space cleverly enough. The appliances weren't new, but they were gleaming. The tile floor had been scrubbed recently enough for him to identify pine cleaner beneath the scent of paint.

Feeling more hopeful, he followed the music, snooping a bit as he went. The bathroom was as scrupulously clean as the kitchen, and, fortunately, a plain glossy white. Beside the sink was a book on home repair, open to the plumbing section. Wary, Coop turned on the tap. When the water flowed out fast and clear, he nodded, satisfied.

A small room with definite office potential and a nice view of the yard was across the hall. The ad had claimed two bedrooms.

The music led him to it, a fair-sized room that fronted

the house, with space enough for his California king. The floor, which seemed to be a random-width oak in good condition, was covered with splattered drop cloths. There were paint cans, trays, brushes, extra rollers. A laborer in baggy overalls and bare feet completed the picture. Despite the hair-concealing cap and oversize denim, Coop recognized a woman when he saw one.

She was tall, and the bare feet on the stepladder were long and narrow and decorated with paint splotches and hot-pink toenails. She sang, badly, along with the music.

Coop rapped on the doorjamb. "Excuse me."

She went on painting, her hips moving rhythmically as she started on the ceiling border. Stepping across the drop cloths, Coop tapped her on the back.

She screamed, jumped and turned all at once. Though he was quick on his feet, he wasn't fast enough to avoid the slap of the paintbrush across his cheek.

He swore and jerked backward, then forward again to catch her before she tumbled off the ladder. He had a quick, and not unpleasant, impression of a slim body, a pale, triangular face dominated by huge, long-lashed brown eyes, and the scent of honeysuckle.

Then he was grunting and stumbling backward, clutching the stomach her elbow had jammed into. She yelled something while he fought to get his breath back.

"Are you crazy?" he managed, then shot up a hand as she hefted a can, slopping paint over the sides as she prepared to use it as a weapon. "Lady, if you throw that at me, I'm going to have to hurt you."

"What?" she shouted.

"I said, don't throw that. I'm here about the ad."

"What?" she shouted again. Her eyes were still wide and full of panic, and she looked capable of anything.

"The ad, damn it." Still rubbing his stomach, Coop marched to the portable stereo and shut it off. "I'm here about the ad," he repeated, his voice loud in the sudden silence.

The big brown eyes narrowed with suspicion. "What ad?"

"The apartment." He swiped a hand over his cheek, studied the smear of white on it, and swore again. "The apartment."

"Really?" She kept her eyes glued to his. He looked tough, she thought. Like a brawler with those broad shoulders, lean athletic build and long legs. His eyes, a light, almost translucent green, looked anything but friendly, and the faded Baltimore Orioles T-shirt and battered jeans didn't contribute any sense of respectability. She figured she could outrun him, and she could certainly outscream him. "The ad doesn't start to run until tomorrow."

"Tomorrow?" Nonplussed, he reached into his pocket for his scribbled note. "This is the right address. The ad was for this place."

She stood her ground. "It doesn't run until tomorrow, so I don't see how you could know about it."

"I work at the paper." Moving cautiously, he held out the note. "Since I've been looking for a place, I asked one of the girls in Classifieds to keep an eye out." He glanced down at his note again. "Two-bedroom apartment on second floor, private entrance, quiet neighborhood convenient for commuters."

She only continued to frown at him. "That's right."

Realizing his inside track wasn't strictly ethical, he winced. "Look, I guess she got a little overenthusiastic. I gave her a couple of tickets to a game, and she must've figured she'd do me a favor and pass the information along a little early."

When he saw that her grip on the can had relaxed, he tried a smile. "I knocked, then I came around back." Probably best not to mention he'd wandered through the house first.

"The ad didn't run the address."

"I work at the paper," he repeated. He was taking a good look at her now. There was something vaguely familiar about her face. And what a face it was. All slashing cheekbones and liquid eyes, that creamy porcelain skin women's face cream ads always raved about. Her mouth was wide, with an alluringly full lower lip. At the moment, the face continued to frown.

"They had the address for billing," he continued. "Since I had a couple of hours, I thought I'd come by and check it out. Look, I can come back tomorrow, if you'd feel more comfortable. But I'm here now." He shrugged. "I can show you my press pass."

He pulled it out for her, and was pleased when she narrowed her eyes to study it. "I do a column. J. Cooper McKinnon on sports. 'All in the Game'?"

"Oh." It meant nothing to her. The sports page wasn't her choice of reading material. But the smile had appeased her. He didn't look so much like a thug when he smiled. And the smear of paint decorating the lean, tanned face added just enough comedy to soothe her. "I guess it's all right, then. I wasn't expecting to show the apartment for a couple of days yet. It's not ready." She held up the can, set it down again. "I'm still painting."

"I noticed."

She laughed at that. It was a full-throated, smoky sound that went with the natural huskiness of her voice.

"Guess you did. I'm Zoe Fleming." She crouched down to dampen a rag with paint remover.

"Thanks." He rubbed the rag over his cheek. "The ad said immediate occupancy."

"Well, I figured I'd be finished in here by tomorrow, when the ad was scheduled to run. Are you from the area?"

"I've got a place downtown. I'm looking for something with a little more space, a little more atmosphere."

"This is a pretty good-sized apartment. It was converted about eight years ago. The guy who owned it had it done for his son, and when he died, the son sold it and moved to California. He wanted to write sitcoms."

Coop walked over to check out the view. He moved fluidly, Zoe thought, like a man who knew how to stay light and ready on his feet. She'd had the impression of wiry strength when her body tumbled into his. And good strong hands. Quick ones, too. She pursed her lips. It might be handy to have a man around.

"Is it just you, Mr. McKinnon?" She thought wistfully how nice it would be if he had a family—another child for Keenan to play with.

"Just me." The place felt right, he decided. It would be good to get out of a box that was just one more box in a building of boxes, to smell grass now and then. Barbecue smoke. "I can move in over the weekend."

She hadn't thought it would be so easy, and she nibbled her lip as she thought it through. She'd never been a landlady before, but she'd been a tenant, and she figured she knew the ropes. "I'll need first and last months' rent."

"Yeah."

"And, ah, references."

"I'll give you the number of the management company that handles my building. You can call Personnel at the paper. Have you got a lease for me to sign?"

She didn't. She'd checked out a book from the library, and she'd meant to type up a scaled-down copy of a lease from it the next morning. "I'll have it tomorrow. Don't you want to look at the rest of the apartment, ask any questions?" She'd been practicing her landlady routine for days.

"I've seen it. It's fine."

"Well." That deflated her a bit. "I guess I can cancel the ad."

There was a sound like a herd of rampaging elephants. Zoe glanced toward the open door and crouched to intercept the missile that hurtled through.

It was a boy, Coop saw when she scooped the child up. He had glossy golden hair, red sneakers, and jeans that were streaked with some unidentifiable substance that looked like it would easily transfer to other surfaces. He carried a plastic lunch box with a picture of some apocalyptic space battle on it, and a sheet of drawing paper that was grimy at the edges.

"I drew the ocean," he announced. "And a million people got ate by sharks."

"Gruesome." Zoe shuddered obligingly before accepting his sloppy kiss. She set him down to admire the drawing. "These are really big sharks," she said, cagily distinguishing the shark blobs from the people blobs.

"They're monster sharks. Mutant monster sharks. They have teeth."

"So I see. Keenan, this is Mr. McKinnon. Our new tenant."

Keenan wrapped one arm around Zoe's leg for security as he eyed the stranger. His eyes were working their way up to Coop's face when they lit on the T-shirt. "That's baseball. I'm gonna learn. Mama's getting a book so's she can teach me."

A book. Coop barely checked a snort. As if you could learn the greatest game invented by Man from a book. What kind of nerd did the kid have for a father?

"Great." It was all Coop intended to say. He'd always thought it wise to avoid entangling himself in a conversation with anyone under sixteen.

Keenan had other ideas. "If you're going to live here, you have to pay rent. Then we can pay the mortgage and stuff and go to Disney World."

What *was* the kid? An accountant?

"Okay, old man." Zoe laughed and ruffled his hair. "I can handle it from here. Go on down and put your stuff away."

"Is Beth coming to play with me tonight?"

"Yes, Beth's coming. Now scoot. I'll be down in a minute."

"'Kay." He made a dash for the door, stopping when his mother called him. It only took one look, the raised brow for him to remember. He looked back at Coop, flashed a quick, sunny grin. "Bye, mister."

The herd of elephants rampaged again, then there was the crash of a door slamming. "He makes an entrance," Zoe said as she turned back to Coop. "The dramatic flair comes from my mother. She's an actress, off-off-Broadway." Tilting her head, Zoe rested one bare foot on the bottom rung of the stepladder. "You look like you're ready to change your mind. You have a problem with children?"

"No." The kid might have thrown him off, but Coop

doubted it would be a problem. The boy would hardly be beating a path to his door. And if he did, Coop thought, he could send him off again quickly enough. "No, he's, ah, cute."

"Yes, he is. I won't claim he's an angel, but he won't make a nuisance of himself. If he gives you any trouble, just let me know."

"Sure. Look, I'll come by tomorrow to sign the lease and give you a check. I'll pick up the keys then."

"That'll be fine."

"Any special time good for you?"

She looked blank for a moment. "What's tomorrow?"

"Friday."

"Friday." She closed her eyes and flipped through her messy internal calendar. "I'm working between ten and two. I think." She opened her eyes again, smiled. "Yeah, I'm pretty sure. Anytime after two-thirty?"

"Fine. Nice meeting you, Mrs. Fleming."

She took his offered hand. "It's Miss," she said easily. "I'm not married. And since we'll be living together, so to speak, you can make it Zoe."

Chapter 2

No one answered the door. Again. Coop checked his watch and saw that it was quarter to three. He didn't like to think he was a man obsessed with time, but as his living centered around deadlines, he did respect it. There was no rusting station wagon in the driveway this time, but he walked around the back of the house, hoping. Before he could start up the stairs to the apartment, he was hailed from across the chain-link fence.

"Young man! Yoo-hoo, young man!" Across the yard next door came a flowered muumuu, topped with a curling thatch of brightly hennaed hair that crowned a wide face. The woman hurried to the fence in a whirl of color. It wasn't just the dress and the improbable hair, Coop noted. The face itself was a rainbow of rich red lipstick, pink cheeks and lavender eye shadow.

When she reached the fence, she pressed a many-ringed hand over the wide shelf of her breasts. "Not as young as I used to be," she said. "I'm Mrs. Finkleman."

"Hi."

"You're the young man who's going to live upstairs." Mrs. Finkleman, a born flirt, patted her curls. "Zoe didn't tell me you were so handsome. Single, are you?"

"Yeah," Coop said cautiously. "Miss Fleming was supposed to meet me. She doesn't seem to be home."

"Well, that's Zoe, flying here, flying there." Mrs. Finkleman beamed and leaned comfortably on the fence, as if she were settling in for a nice cozy gossip. "Got a dozen things on her plate at once, that girl does. Having to raise that sweet little boy all alone. Why, I don't know what I'd have done without my Harry when our young ones were coming up."

Coop was a reporter, after all. That, added to the fact that he was curious about his landlady, put him in interview mode. "The kid's father doesn't help out any?"

Mrs. Finkleman snorted. "Don't see hide nor hair of him. From what I'm told, he lit out the minute he found out Zoe was expecting. Left her high and dry, and her hardly more than a child herself. Far as I know, he's never so much as seen the boy. The little sweetheart."

Coop assumed she was referring to Keenan. "Nice kid. What's he, five, six?"

"Just four. Bright as a button. They grow them smarter these days. Teach them faster, too. The little love's in preschool now. He'll be home any minute."

"His mother went to pick him up, then?"

"Oh, no, not her week for car pool. Alice Miller— that's the white house with blue trim, down the block? —it's her week. She has a boy and a girl. Little darlings.

The youngest, Steffie, is Keenan's age. Now her oldest, Brad, there's a pistol for you."

As she began to fill Coop in on the neighborhood rascal, he decided it was time to draw the interview to a close. "Maybe you could tell Miss Fleming I was by? I can leave a number where she can reach me when—"

"Oh, goodness." Mrs. Finkleman waved a hand. "I do run on. Nearly forgot why I came out here in the first place. Zoe called and asked me to look out for you. Got held up at the flower shop. She works there three days a week. That's Floral Bouquet, down in Ellicott City? Nice place, but expensive. Why, it's a crime to charge so much for a daisy."

"She got held up," Coop prompted.

"Her relief had car trouble, so Zoe's going to be a little late. Said you could go right on into the kitchen there, where she left the lease and the keys."

"That's fine. Thanks."

"No problem at all. This is a friendly neighborhood. Always somebody to lend a helping hand. I don't think Zoe mentioned what you did for a living."

"I'm a sportswriter for the *Dispatch*."

"You don't say? Why, my Harry's just wild for sports. Can't budge him from in front of the TV when a game's on."

"That's what makes this country great."

Mrs. Finkleman laughed and gave Coop's arm an affectionate bat that might have felled a lesser man. "You men are all the same. You can come over and talk sports with Harry anytime. Me, if it's not baseball, it isn't worth talking about."

Coop, who'd been about to retreat, brightened. "You like baseball?"

"Son, I'm a Baltimore native." As if that said it all. "Our boys are going to go all the way this year. Mark my word."

"They could do it, if they heat those bats up. The pitching rotation's gold this year, and the infield's tight as a drum. What they need—"

Coop was interrupted by a cheerful toot. He glanced over to see Keenan burst out of a red sedan and rocket across the side yard.

"Hi, mister. Hi, Mrs. Finkleman. Carly Myers fell down, and there was blood." The big brown eyes gleamed wickedly. "Lots and lots of it, and she screamed and cried." He demonstrated, letting go with a piercing yell that had Coop's ears ringing. "Then she got a Band-Aid with stars on it." Keenan thought it would have been worth losing some blood for such a neat badge of honor. "Where's Mama?"

"Little lamb." Mrs. Finkleman leaned over the fence to pinch Keenan's cheek. "She's working a little late. She said you could come stay with me until she gets home."

"Okay." Keenan liked his visits next door, since they always included cookies and a rock on Mrs. Finkleman's wonderfully soft lap. "I gotta put my lunch box away."

"Such a good boy," Mrs. Finkleman cooed. "You come on over when you're done. Why don't you show the nice man inside so he can wait for your mother?"

"Okay."

Before Coop could take evasive action, his hand was clutched by Keenan's. He'd been right, he thought with a wince. It was sticky.

"We've got cookies," Keenan told him, cannily deducing that he could have double his afternoon's treat if he played his cards right.

"Great."

"We baked them ourselves, on our night off." Keenan sent Coop a hopeful look. "They're really good."

"I bet." Coop caught the back door before it could slam shut.

"There." Keenan pointed to a ceramic cookie jar in the shape of a big yellow bird on the counter. "In Big Bird."

"Okay, okay." Since it seemed like the best way to appease the kid, Coop reached in and pulled out a handful of cookies. When he dumped them on the table, Keenan's eyes went as wide as saucers. He could hardly believe his luck.

"You can have one, too." He stuffed an entire chocolate chip deluxe in his mouth and grinned.

"That good, huh?" With a shrug, Coop sampled one himself. The kid, Coop decided after the first bite, knew his cookies. "You'd better get next door."

Keenan devoured another cookie, stalling. "I gotta wash out my thermos, 'cause if you don't, it smells."

"Right." Cooper sat at the table to read through the lease while the boy dragged a stool in front of the sink.

Keenan squirted dishwashing liquid in the thermos, and then, when he noticed Coop wasn't paying any attention, he squirted some more. And more. He turned the water up high and giggled when soap began to bubble and spew. With his tongue caught between his teeth, he jiggled the stopper into the sink and began to play dishwasher.

Coop forgot about him, reading quickly. The lease seemed standard enough, he decided. Zoe had already signed both copies. He dashed his signature across from hers, folded his copy, then set the check he'd already written on the table. He'd picked up the keys and rose to tuck his copy in his pocket when he spotted Keenan.

"Oh, God."

The boy was drenched, head to foot. Soap bubbles dotted his face and hair. A good-sized puddle was forming on the tile at the base of the stool.

"What are you doing?"

Keenan looked over his shoulder, smiled innocently. "Nothing."

"Look, you've got water everywhere." Coop looked around for a towel.

"Everywhere," Keenan agreed, and, testing the opposition, he slapped his hands in the sink. Water and suds geysered.

"Cut it out! Jeez! Aren't you supposed to be somewhere else?" He grabbed a dish towel and advanced, only to be slapped in the face by the next geyser. His eyes narrowed. "Look, kid—"

He heard the front door slam. Like mother, like son, he thought.

"Keenan?" Zoe called out. "I hope you haven't been into those cookies."

Coop looked at the crumbs on the table, on the floor, floating in the soapy water.

"Oh, hell," he muttered.

"Oh, hell," Keenan echoed, beaming at him. He giggled and danced on his stool. "Hi, Mom."

Zoe, her arms full of day-old irises, took in the scene with one glance. Her son was as wet as a drowned dog, her kitchen looked as though a small hurricane had blown through. Hurricane Keenan, she thought. And her new tenant looked damp, frazzled, and charmingly sheepish.

Like a boy caught with his hand in the cookie jar, she noted, glancing at the telltale crumbs.

"Been playing dishwasher again?" With a calm that baffled Coop, she set the flowers down. "I'm just not sure it's the right career choice, Keen-man."

Keenan fluttered his long, wet lashes. "He wanted cookies."

Coop started to defend himself, then simply scowled at the boy.

"I'm sure he did. Go on into the laundry room and get out of those wet clothes."

"Okay." He jumped from the stool, splashing more water before he zoomed away. He stopped only long enough to give his mother a wet kiss before he disappeared into an adjoining room.

"Sorry I'm late," Zoe said easily, yanking the stopper out of the sink then walking to a cupboard to get a vase.

Coop opened his mouth. He started to explain what had gone on in the past ten minutes, but realized he wasn't at all sure. "I signed the lease."

"I see that. Would you mind putting some water in this?" She held out the vase. "I need to get a mop."

"Sure."

She was probably going to wallop the kid with it, Coop thought, and felt a quick tug of regret and guilt. But the sounds from the laundry room where she'd disappeared weren't those he associated with corporal punishment. They were a young boy's giggles, a woman's lusty laugh. Coop stood, a vase of water in his hands, and wondered at it.

"You're standing in a puddle," Zoe commented when she came back with a mop and pail.

"Oh, right." Coop glanced down at his wet hightops, shifted. "Here's your vase."

"Thanks." She tended to her flowers first. "You met Mrs. Finkleman, I hear."

"News travels fast."

"Around here it does." When she handed him a dishcloth to dry his face with, he caught her scent—much more potent, much more colorful, than the flowers. She was wearing jeans and a baggy T-shirt with Floral Bouquet across the chest. Her hair, he noted, was some elusive shade between brown and blond. She wore it tied back in a jaunty ponytail.

When she lifted her brows, he realized he'd been staring. "Sorry. I mean—I'm sorry about the mess."

"Were you playing dishwasher, too?"

"Not exactly." It was impossible not to smile back, to ignore the quick pull of attraction.

It wouldn't be so bad, he mused, having a pretty landlady, sharing the house with her, maybe an occasional meal. Or an occasional—

"Mama!" Keenan stood in the doorway, wearing nothing but skin. "I can't find my pants."

"In the basket by the washing machine," she told him, without taking her eyes from Coop's.

He'd forgotten about the kid, let himself fantasize a little before remembering she didn't come as a single. He took a long mental step backward and jingled the keys to his new apartment.

"I've got some boxes out in the car," he told her. "I'm going to move some things in this afternoon."

"That's fine." It was silly to feel disappointed, Zoe

thought. Foolish to have felt that fast feminine flutter when she recognized interest in his eyes. More foolish to feel let down because the interest had blanked out when her child called her. "Do you need any help?"

"No, I can handle it. I've got a game to cover tonight, so I'm going to move the rest in tomorrow." He backed toward the door. "Thanks."

"Welcome aboard, Mr. McKinnon."

"Coop," he said as he stepped outside. "It's Coop."

Coop, she thought, leaning on the mop handle. It had seemed like such a good idea to make use of the apartment upstairs. The extra income would take some of the pressure off, and maybe add a few bonuses. Like that trip to Disney World that Keenan wanted so badly.

It had been a risk to buy the house, but she'd wanted her son to grow up in a nice neighborhood, with a yard, maybe a dog when he was a little older. The rental income would take away some of the risk.

But she hadn't realized it could add another, more personal risk. She hadn't realized how awkward it might be to have a tenant who was male, single, and absolutely gorgeous.

She laughed at herself. Dream on, Zoe, she thought. J. Cooper McKinnon was just like the rest, who ran like a hound when they heard the patter of little feet.

Something crashed in the laundry room. She just shook her head.

"Come on, sailor," she called to Keenan. "It's time to swab the deck."

Chapter 3

"Pretty good digs, Coop. Really, pretty good." Ben Robbins, a staff reporter for the *Dispatch,* sipped a cold one while surveying Coop's apartment. "I didn't think much of it when we hauled all your junk up here, but it ain't half-bad."

It was a lot better than not half-bad, and Coop knew it. He had everything exactly where he wanted it. The living room was dominated by his long, low-slung sofa of burgundy leather and his big-screen television, so perfect for viewing games. A couple of brass lamps, a nicely worn coffee table scuffed from the heels of the dozens of shoes that had rested on it and a single generous chair completed the formal section of the room.

There was an indoor basketball hoop, small-scaled, for practice—and because shooting a little round ball helped him think. A used pinball machine called Home

Run, a stand that held two baseball bats, his tennis racket and a hockey stick, a pair of old boxing gloves hanging on the wall and a scarred Fooz Ball table made up the recreation area.

Coop wouldn't have called them toys. They were tools.

He'd chosen blinds, rather than curtains, for the windows. Blinds, he thought, that would close out the light if a man decided to treat himself to an afternoon nap.

The bedroom held little other than his bed, a nightstand and another TV. The room was for sleeping—or, if he got lucky, another type of sport.

But it was his office that pleased him most. He could already imagine himself spending hours there at his computer, a game playing on his desktop TV. He'd outfitted it with a big swivel chair, a desk that had just the right number of scars and burns, a fax, a dual-line phone and a VCR—to play back those controversial calls or heart-stopping plays.

With all the plaques and photos and sports memorabilia scattered about, it was home.

His home.

"Looks like the neighborhood bar," Ben said, and stretched out his short, hairy legs. "Where the jocks hang out."

Coop considered that the highest of compliments. "It suits me."

"To the ground," Ben agreed, and toasted Coop with his bottle of beer. "A place where a man can relax, be himself. You know, since I started living with Sheila, I've got little china things all over, and underwear hanging in the bathroom. The other day she comes home with a new bedspread. It's got *flowers* all over. Pink flowers." He winced as he drank. "It's like sleeping in a meadow."

"Hey." With all the smug righteousness of the unencumbered, Coop propped his feet on the coffee table. "Your choice, pal."

"Yeah, yeah. Too bad I'm nuts about her. And her an Oakland fan, too."

"Takes all kinds. Talk is the A's are trading Remirez."

Ben snorted. "Yeah, yeah, pull the other one, champ."

"That's the buzz." Coop shrugged, took a pull on his own beer. "Sending him to K.C. for Dunbar, and that rookie fielder, Jackson."

"They got to be crazy. Remirez hit .280 last season."

".285," Coop told him. "With twenty-four baggers. Led the team in errors, too."

"Yeah, but with a bat like that... And Dunbar, what's he? Maybe he hit .220?"

"It was .218, but he's like a vacuum cleaner at second. Nothing gets by him. And the kid's got potential. Big, strapping farm boy with an arm like a bullet. They need new blood. Most of the starting lineup's over thirty."

They argued baseball and finished their beers in complete male harmony.

"I've got a game to cover."

"Tonight? I thought the O's were in Chicago until tomorrow."

"They are." Coop pocketed his tape recorder, his pad, a pencil. "I'm covering the college game. There's a hot third baseman who's got the scouts drooling. Thought I'd take a look, cop an interview."

"What a job." Ben hauled himself to his feet. "Going to games, hanging around locker rooms."

"Yeah, it's a rough life." He slung an arm over Ben's

shoulders as they headed out. "So, how's the story on neutering pets going?"

"Stuff it, Coop."

"Hey, some of us hang around the pound, some of us hang around the ballpark."

And a hell of a day it was for it, too, Coop thought. Balmy and clear-skied. He could almost smell roasting peanuts and hot dogs.

"While you're hanging around a bunch of sweaty college boys in jockstraps, I'll be snuggled up with a woman."

"Under a flowered bedspread."

"Yeah, but she says flowers make her feel sexy. And I'm here to tell you— My, oh, my…"

When Ben's small, square face went lax, Coop turned. He felt his own jaw drop. And, if he wasn't mistaken, his tongue landed on his shoes.

She was wearing what had to be the shortest skirt ever devised by man. Beneath it were a pair of endless legs that were molded into black fishnet hose. She swayed when she walked. How could she help it, when she stood in black skyscraper heels?

A tiny white bustier exposed a delicious amount of cleavage. Around her neck was a shiny black bow tie that, for reasons utterly inexplicable to Coop, made every male cell in his body sizzle.

Her hair was down, falling straight as a pin to her shoulders in a melding of tones that made him think of wild deer leaping through a sunlit forest.

She stopped, smiled, said something, but his mind had checked out the moment his eyes landed on her legs.

"…if you've settled in okay."

"Ah…" He blinked like a man coming out of a coma. "What?"

"I said I haven't had a chance to check and see if you've settled in okay."

"Fine." He folded his tongue back in his mouth and got a grip on himself. "Just fine."

"Good. Keenan came down with a cold, so things have been hectic. I caught a glimpse of you hauling things up the steps a couple of days ago."

"Hauling," he repeated. "Yeah. Ben," he said when his friend jabbed him. "This is Ben. He's been giving me a hand moving."

"Hi, Ben. I'm Zoe."

"Hi, Zoe," Ben said stupidly. "I'm Ben."

She just smiled. It was the outfit, she knew. As much as she hated it, she couldn't help but be amused by how it affected certain members of the species. "Do you work at the paper, too?"

"Yeah, I'm, ah, doing a story on neutering pets."

"Really?" She almost felt sorry for him, the way his Adam's apple was bobbing. "I'll be sure to look for it. I'm glad you're settling in okay. I've got to get to work."

"You're going out?" Coop said. "In that?"

Her lips twitched. "Well, this isn't my usual outfit when I'm carpooling, but I thought I'd wear it to work tonight. At Shadows? I'm a waitress. Nice meeting you, Ben."

She walked to her car. No, Coop thought, swayed to it, in those long, lazy strides. They were both still staring when she pulled out of the drive and cruised down the street.

"Your landlady," Ben said in a reverential whisper. "That was your landlady."

"I think it was." She hadn't looked like that when he signed the lease. Beautiful, yes—she'd been beautiful, but in a wholesome, unthreatening sort of way. She hadn't looked so…so… Words failed him. She was a mother, for God's sake, he reminded himself. She wasn't supposed to look like that. "She's got a kid."

"Yeah? What kind?"

"Human, I think."

"Come on."

"A boy," Coop said absently. "This high." He held a hand, palm down, about three feet from the ground.

"She may have a kid, but she's also got legs. This high." Ben waved a hand in front of his own throat. "You got a charmed life, Coop. My landlord's got arms like cinder blocks, and a tattoo of a lizard. You got one who looks like a centerfold."

"She's a mother," Coop said under his breath.

"Well, I wouldn't mind coming home to her for milk and cookies. See you at the sweatshop."

"Sure." Coop stood where he was, frowning at the quiet street. Mothers weren't supposed to look like that, he thought again. They were supposed to look…motherly. Safe. Comfortable. He blew out a breath, willed away the knot in his stomach.

She wasn't *his* mother, he reminded himself.

By midnight, Zoe's feet were screaming. Her back ached, and her arms felt as though she'd been hauling boulders rather than drink trays. She'd deflected six propositions, two of them good-hearted enough to amuse, one of them insulting enough to earn the gentleman in question a bruised instep, courtesy of one of her stiletto heels. The others had been the usual, and easily ignored.

It went with the territory, and it didn't bother her overmuch.

The lounge earned its name from the shadowy effect of neon and all the dim corners. The decor was fifties tacky, and the waitresses were dolled up like old-fashioned mindless floozies to match.

But the tips were excellent, and the clientele, for the most part, harmless.

"Two house wines, white, a Black Russian and a coffee, light." After calling out her order to the bartender, Zoe took a moment to roll her shoulders.

She hoped Beth had gotten Keenan to bed without any fuss. He'd been cranky all day—which meant he was nearly over his sniffles. He'd put up quite a fuss that morning, Zoe remembered, when she'd nixed the idea of him going to school.

Didn't get that from me, she thought. She'd never fussed about not going to school. Now, at twenty-five, she deeply regretted letting her education slide. If she'd applied herself, tried for college, she could have developed a skill, had a career.

Instead, she had a high school diploma she'd barely earned, and was qualified for little more than serving drinks to men whose eyes tried to crawl down her cleavage.

But she wasn't one for regrets. She'd done what she'd done, and she had the greatest prize of all. Keenan. In a couple of years, she figured, she'd have saved enough that she could turn in her bustier and take a night course. Once she had a few business courses under her belt, she could open her own flower shop. And she wouldn't have to leave Keenan with sitters at night.

She served her drinks, took an order from another table and thanked God her break was coming up in five minutes.

When she saw Coop walk in, her first thought was Keenan. But the sick alarm passed almost as quickly as it had come. Coop was relaxed, obviously scoping the place out. When his eyes met hers, he nodded easily and made his way through the scattered tables.

"I thought I'd stop in for a drink."

"This is the place for it. Do you want to sit at the bar, or do you want a table?"

"A table. Got a minute?"

"At quarter after I've got fifteen of them. Why?"

"I'd like to talk to you."

"Okay. What can I get you?"

"Coffee, black."

"Coffee, black. Have a seat."

He watched her head toward the bar and tried not to dwell on how attractive she looked walking away. He hadn't come in because he wanted a drink, but because she seemed like a nice woman in a tight skirt—spot, he corrected. A tight spot.

Get hold of yourself, Coop, he warned himself. He knew better than to let a pair of long legs cloud his judgment. He'd only come in to ask a few questions, get the full story. That was what he did, and he was good at it. Just as he was good at dissecting a game, any game, and finding those small triumphs and small mistakes that influenced the outcome.

"We've been busy tonight." Zoe set two coffees on the table before sliding onto a chair across from Coop.

She let out a long, heartfelt sigh, then smiled. "This is the first time I've been off my feet in four hours."

"I thought you worked in a flower shop."

"I do, three days a week." She slid her cramped feet out of her shoes. "Around Mother's Day, Christmas, Easter—you know, the big flower days, I can squeeze in more." She sipped the coffee she'd loaded with sugar and let it pump into her system. "It's just a small shop, and Fred—that's the owner—only keeps on a couple of part-timers. That way he doesn't have to pay any of the bennies, like hospitalization, sick leave."

"That's lousy."

"Hey, it's a job. I like it. It's just Fred and Martha—she's his wife. They've taught me a lot about flowers and plants."

Someone pumped quarters into the jukebox. The room heated up with music. Coop leaned over the table so that she could hear him. For a moment he lost the thread somewhere in her big brown eyes.

"Have I met you somewhere before?" he asked her.

"In the apartment."

"No, I mean…" He shook his head, let it go. "Uh, why here?"

"Why here what?"

"Why do you work here?"

She blinked, those long lashes fluttering down, then up. "For a paycheck."

"It doesn't seem like you should be working in a bar."

"Excuse me?" Zoe wasn't sure if she should be amused or insulted. She chose the former simply because it was her nature. "Do you have a problem with cocktail waitresses?"

"No, no. It's just that, you're a mother."

"Yes, I am. I have a son to prove it." She laughed and leaned her chin on her fist. "Are you thinking it would be more appropriate for me to be home baking cookies or knitting a scarf?"

"No." Though it embarrassed him that he did. "It's that outfit," he blurted out. "And the way all these men look at you."

"If a woman's going to wear something like this, men are going to look. Looking's all they do," she added. "If it makes you feel better, I don't dress like this for PTA meetings."

He was feeling more ridiculous every second. "Look, it's none of my business. I just have a habit of asking questions. Seems to me you could do better than this. I mean, you've got the flower job, and the rent—"

"And I have a mortgage, a son who seems to outgrow his clothes and shoes every other week, a car payment, grocery bills, doctor bills."

"Doctor? Is the kid sick?"

Zoe rolled her eyes. Just when she was starting to get irritated, he deflated her. "No. Kids Keenan's age are always bringing some germ or other home from school. He needs regular checkups with his pediatrician, with the dentist. Those things aren't free."

"No, but there are programs. Assistance." He stopped, because those big brown eyes had turned fierce.

"I'm perfectly capable of earning a living, and of taking care of my child."

"I didn't mean—"

"Maybe I don't have a college degree or any fancy skills, but I can pay my own way, and my son doesn't lack for anything." She jammed her feet into the back-breaking heels and stood. "We've been doing just fine on our own, and I don't need some nosy jock reporter coming in here and telling me how to be a mother. Coffee's on the house, you jerk."

He winced as she stormed away from the table, then let out a long breath. Handled that one *real* well, Coop.

He wondered if there would be an eviction notice on his door in the morning.

Chapter 4

She didn't kick him out. She had thought of it, but had decided the satisfaction she'd gain didn't quite equal the rental income. Besides, she'd heard it all before.

One of the reasons she'd moved from New York was that she'd grown impossibly weary of friends and family telling her how to run her life. How to raise her son.

Baltimore had been a clean slate.

She'd had enough money put aside to afford a nice two-bedroom apartment and invest the rest. And because she was willing to work at any job, and work hard, she'd rarely been unemployed. It had been difficult for her to put Keenan in day care. But he'd thrived. He had his mother's knack for making friends.

Now, two years after the move, she had a house, and a yard, in the kind of neighborhood she wanted for her son. And she'd paid for every bit of it on her own.

Too many people had told her she was crazy, that she was too young, that she was throwing her life and her chances away. With a grunt, Zoe shoved the lawn mower around and began to cut another strip of grass. *Her* grass, she thought with clenched teeth.

She'd proved them wrong. She'd had her baby, kept her baby, and she was making a decent life for him. She and Keenan weren't statistics. They were a family.

They didn't need anyone to feel sorry for them, or to offer handouts. She was taking care of everything, one step at a time. And she had plans. Good, solid plans.

The tap on her shoulder made her jump. When she whipped her head around and looked at Coop, her hands tightened on the mower. "What?"

"I want to apologize," he shouted. When she only continued to glare at him, he reached down and shut off the engine. "I want to apologize," he repeated. "I was out of line last night."

"Really?"

"I'm sort of addicted to poking into other people's business."

"Maybe you should go cold turkey." She reached down to grab the pull cord. His hand closed over hers. She stared at it a moment. He had big hands, rough-palmed. She remembered the impression she'd gotten of strength and energy. Now the hand was gentle and hard to resist.

She hadn't felt a man's hands—hadn't wanted to feel a man's hands—in a very long time.

"Sometimes I push the wrong buttons," Coop continued. He was staring at their hands, as well, thinking how small hers felt under his. How soft. "It's earned me a fist in the face a time or two." He tried a smile when her gaze slid up to his.

"That doesn't surprise me."

She didn't smile back, but he sensed a softening. The roar of the mower had awakened him. When he'd looked out and seen her marching along behind it in baggy shorts, a T-shirt and a ridiculous straw hat, he'd wanted to go back to bed. But he'd been compelled to seek her out.

It was only a flag of truce, he told himself. After all, he had to live with her. More or less.

"I didn't mean to be critical. I was curious about you. And the kid," he added quickly. "And maybe seeing you in that outfit last night pushed a few of my buttons."

She lifted a brow. That was honest enough, she thought. "All right. No permanent damage."

It had been easier than he'd expected. Coop decided to press his luck. "Listen, I've got to cover the game this afternoon. Maybe you'd like to come along. It's a nice day for baseball."

She supposed it was. It was warm and sunny, with a nice, freshening breeze. There were worse ways to spend the day than in a ballpark with an attractive man who was doing his best to pry his foot out of his mouth.

"It sounds like fun—if I didn't have to work. But Keenan would love it." She watched his jaw drop, and smothered a smile.

"Keenan? You want me to take him?"

"I can't think of anything he'd rather do. Some of the kids play in their yards, and they let him chase the ball. But he's never seen the real thing, except on TV." She smiled now, guilelessly, and held back a hoot of laughter. She could all but see Coop's mind working.

"I don't know too much about kids," he said, back-pedaling cautiously.

"But you know about sports. It'll be great for Keenan to experience his first real game with an expert. When are you leaving?"

"Ah…a couple of hours."

"I'll make sure he's ready. This is awfully nice of you." While he stood staring, she leaned over and kissed his cheek. After one hard tug, she had the mower roaring again.

Coop stood planted like a tree when she strolled away. What the hell was he supposed to do with a kid all afternoon?

He bought popcorn, hot dogs and enormous cups of soft drinks. Coop figured food would keep the kid quiet. Keenan had bounced on the seat of the car throughout the drive to Camden Yards, and since they had arrived he'd goggled at everything.

Coop had heard "What's that?" and "How come?" too many times to count. Nervous as a cat, he settled into the press box with his laptop.

"You can watch through the window here," he instructed Keenan. "And you can't bother anybody, because they're working."

"Okay." Almost bursting with excitement, Keenan clutched his hot dog.

There were lots of people in the press box, some with neat computers, like Coop, others with headphones. A few of them had smiled at him, and all of them had said hello to Coop. Keenan knew Coop was important. As his mother had instructed, he kept close and didn't ask for any presents. Even though there had been really neat stuff at the stands. His mother had given him five whole dollars and told him he could buy a souvenir. But there'd been so many he didn't know which to pick. And Coop had walked so fast he'd hardly been able to look.

But it didn't matter, because he was at a real ball game.

Wide-eyed, he stared down at the field. It was bigger than anything he'd imagined. He knew where the pitcher would stand, and he recognized home plate, but he wasn't sure of anything else.

The big scoreboard exploded with pictures, and words he couldn't read. Circling it all were the stands, filled with more people than he'd ever seen.

When they announced the lineup, he looked down at the players with naked admiration. The national anthem began, and, recognizing it, Keenan stood up, as he'd been taught.

Coop glanced over, saw the boy standing, with a hot dog in one hand and a big, dazzling grin on his face. Suddenly he remembered his first time at a ballpark. His eager hand gripping his father's, his eyes trying to see everything at once, and his heart so full of the excitement, of the game, of just being a boy.

As the players took the field, Coop reached over and tugged on Keenan's bright hair. "Pretty cool, huh?"

"It's the best ever. Those are our guys, right?"

"Those are our guys. They're gonna kick butt."

Keenan giggled and leaned closer to the glass to watch the first pitch. "Kick butt," he said with relish.

He didn't, as Coop had expected, fidget, whine or make a general nuisance of himself. Because he was accustomed to working under noisy and confusing conditions, Keenan's constant questions didn't annoy him overmuch. At least, he thought, the kid had the good sense to ask.

Between innings, Keenan peered over Coop's shoulder and sounded out the words that were popping up on the computer screen, and he did transfer some mustard from his hands onto Coop's sleeve. But it wasn't the disaster Coop had envisioned.

Coop even felt a quick tug of pride when the play-by-play announcer called Keenan over and let the boy sit in his lap for an inning.

Most kids would've been running around the booth begging for more candy. But this one, Coop thought, had come for the game.

"How come he didn't run all the way? How come he didn't?" Keenan shifted from foot to foot. His bladder was past full, but he couldn't bear to miss a minute.

"The throw went to second, so he was forced out," Coop explained. "See, the second baseman caught the ball and stepped on the bag to retire the side."

"Retire the side," Keenan repeated reverently. "But we're still winning?"

"The O's are up by one going into the top of the ninth. Looking at the batting order, I'd say they'll put in a southpaw."

"Southpaw," Keenan repeated, as if it were gospel.

"A left-handed reliever. Probably Scully." He glanced over and noted that Keenan was holding his crotch. "Uh, got a problem?"

"Nuh-uh."

"Let's hit the john—the bathroom." He took Keenan's hand and hoped it wasn't too late. As they passed through the door, Scully was announced as the relief.

"Just like you said." Keenan looked up at Coop with dazzling admiration. "You're smarter than anybody."

Coop felt a grin break out over his face. "Let's just say I know the game."

When they arrived home, Keenan was wearing a new Orioles jersey and carrying an autographed baseball in a pint-size baseball glove. He waved a pennant in his other hand as he scrambled up the steps.

"Look! Look what Coop got me!" He barreled into his mother who'd barely walked in the door herself. "We went into the locker room with the real Orioles, and they signed the baseball for me. To keep."

"Let's see." She took the ball and examined it. "This is really special, Keenan."

"I'm gonna keep it forever. And I got this shirt, too, like they wear. And a glove. It even fits."

Emotion backed up in her throat. "It certainly does. Looks like you're all ready to play ball."

"I'm gonna play third base, 'cause it's the...the..."

"Hot corner," Coop supplied.

"Yeah. Can I go show Mr. Finkleman? Can I show him my baseball?"

"Sure."

"He's gonna be surprised." He turned and threw his arms around Coop's legs. "Thanks, thanks for taking me. I liked it best of anything. Can we go again, and take Mama?"

"Uh, yeah, I guess. Sure." Feeling awkward again, he patted Keenan's head.

"Okay!" Giving Coop one last squeeze, Keenan raced out the door to show off his treasures.

"You didn't have to buy him all that stuff," Zoe began. "Taking him was enough."

"No big deal. He didn't ask for it, or anything." Coop stuck his hands in his pockets. "He got such a charge out of meeting the players, and one thing kind of led to another."

"I know. I hear our team won."

"Yeah. Clipped them by one. I had to stop by the paper and file the story, or we'd have been here sooner."

"I just got in myself." On impulse, she walked over, wrapped her arms around him and hugged. Coop's hands stayed paralyzed in his pockets. "I owe you. You gave him a great day. He won't forget it." She drew back. "Neither will I."

"It's no big deal. He just hung out in the press box."

"It's a very big deal, especially since I trapped you into it." She laughed and tossed back her hair. "You were so transparent this morning, Coop. The idea of having a four-year-old tagging along terrified you. But you did good, real good. Anyway— Sorry," she said when the phone rang. "Hello? Oh, hi, Stan. Tonight? I'm not scheduled." Letting out a breath, she sat on the arm of a chair. "I'll have to let you know. No, Stan, I can't tell you now. I have to see if I can find a sitter. An hour, then. Yes, I understand you're in a jam. I'll call you back."

"Problem?"

"Hmmm… Two of the waitresses called in sick for tonight. They're short-staffed." She was already dialing the phone. "Hi, Mrs. Finkleman. Yeah, I know. He had a great time. Mm-hmm…" Zoe's gaze flicked up to Coop as Mrs. Finkleman told her how important it was for a boy to have a man in his life. "I'm sure you're right. I was wondering if you're busy tonight. Oh. That's right, I forgot. No, it's nothing. Have a good time."

Zoe hung up and pursed her lips. "It's their bingo night," she told Coop. "Beth's got a date. Maybe Alice." She reached for the phone again, shook her head. "No, she's having her in-laws over for dinner." Her eyes lit on Coop and narrowed in speculation. "You didn't have any problem with Keenan today."

"No," Coop said slowly, wary of another trap. "He was cool."

"Stan doesn't need me in until nine. Keenan goes to bed at eight, so you wouldn't have to do anything but hang around, watch television or whatever."

"Hang around here, while you work?" He took a step back. "Just me and the kid—like a babysitter? Listen…"

"I'll pay you. Beth gets two an hour, but I can up the ante."

"I don't want your money, Zoe."

"That's so sweet." She smiled, took his hand and squeezed. "Really, so sweet of you. If you could come down about eight-thirty."

"I never said—"

"You can help yourself to anything in the kitchen. I'll make some brownies, if I have time. I'd better call Stan back before he pulls out what's left of his hair." She picked up the phone, beamed at Coop. "Now I owe you two."

"Yeah, right." He hurried out before she could find some way to owe him three.

Chapter 5

For the next couple of hours, Coop immersed himself in "All in the Game," his weekly syndicated column. The kid had given him the hook, he thought. The first visit to a ball game, the passing on of tradition, and the bond that was forged over the cheers, the crack of the bat, the peanut shells.

It was a good piece, Coop decided, and wrote easily. He supposed since he owed the idea to Keenan the least he could do was hang around downstairs and eat brownies while the kid slept.

He wandered back down just as Zoe came through the kitchen door.

She hadn't been sure he'd come. She knew she'd hustled him, and after she'd finished being amused by it, she felt guilty. But here he was, right on time, standing at the foot of the steps.

"I pushed you into a corner...." she began.

"Yeah, you did." She looked so somber, he had to smile. "You've got a real talent for it."

She shrugged her shoulders and smiled back at him. "Sometimes being pushy's the only way to get things done, but I always feel bad about it after. I did bake brownies."

"I could smell them all the way upstairs." When she didn't move, he tilted his head. Funny, though she was wearing that sexy waitress rig again, she didn't seem so outrageous. Except for that bow tie, he thought. Something about that black tie around that slim white throat shot straight to his libido.

"You going to let me in, or do you want me to stand out here?"

"I have this guilt thing," she explained, "whenever I have to ask anyone for a favor. And it was so sweet of you to take Keenan to the game, especially when..."

"When I'd been asking you out?"

She shrugged her shoulders again, let them fall. He was looking at her that way again, and something in her body was reacting helplessly. Better, she thought, to set the rules quickly. "I don't go out with men. I should have told you straight out."

He had to force himself not to lift a hand to that neat little bow and tug. "At all?"

"It's just easier not to. They're not interested in Keenan, or they pretend they are so they can talk me into bed." When he rocked back on his heels and cleared his throat, she laughed. "What they don't know is that they're clear as cellophane. You see, Keenan and I are a team. As a sportswriter, you should know what that means."

"Sure. I get it."

"Anyway, you gave him a really wonderful day, and I feel like I'm twisting your arm about tonight."

He decided, after a moment, that she wasn't doing it on purpose. There was just too much sincerity in that glorious face for a con. And if there was a twinge of guilt because he had given considerable thought to talking her into bed, that was his problem.

"Look, he's asleep, right?"

"Yes. All the excitement wore him out."

"So, I'll eat your brownies and watch your TV. No big deal."

Her smile came easily now, beautifully, and made his mouth water. "I left the number of the club by the phone, just in case. The Finklemans should be home by eleven. She'd come over and relieve you if you want."

"We'll play it by ear."

"Thanks, really." She stepped back into the kitchen to let him in. "My shift ends at two, at closing."

"Long day for you."

"I've got tomorrow off." After grabbing her purse, she took a quick look around. "Make yourself at home, okay?"

"I will. See you."

She hurried out, those incredibly sexy heels clicking across the tile. Coop let out a long breath and told himself to settle down. The lady had just set the ground rules. Fun and games were out.

She had the face of a siren, the body of a goddess, and legs designed to make a strong man whimper—but deep in her heart she was Betty Crocker.

Coop took a deep sniff and decided to content himself with a plate of double fudge brownies.

* * *

The storm rolled in just before midnight. Coop had taken Zoe at her word and made himself at home. He was stretched out on her couch, sunk deep in the cushions, with his feet propped comfortably on her coffee table. He was dozing in front of an old war movie, his only regret being that he hadn't thought to bring a couple of beers down with him.

Zoe's selection ran to milk, juice and some unidentified green liquid.

He'd poked around a little—it was simply in his nature. The clutter ran throughout the house, but he began to see a pattern to it. Obviously she wasn't a detail person, but the general lack of order made the house comfortable, even cozy. Coop wasn't sure if the result was by design or simply because she was a woman who worked two jobs and had a kid to raise.

And from the library books he'd found stacked here and there, it seemed she spent most of her free time reading up on flowers, car repair, tax laws and time management.

He couldn't help but think it was a waste of a perfectly stunning woman, this voluntary burial of self in books and nowhere part-time jobs.

But it wasn't his problem.

The crash of thunder from outside harmonized nicely with the artillery barrage on the TV screen. Coop had just decided that this baby-sitting racket was a snap.

Then he heard the wailing.

Marines didn't wail, he thought fuzzily, especially when they were battling Nazi scum. He yawned, circled his neck until it cracked, then spotted Keenan.

The boy stood at the base of the stairs in Batman pajamas, a battered stuffed dog clutched in one arm and tears pouring down his face.

"Mama!" His voice sharpened like an ice pick, then hitched. "Where's my mama?"

"She's at work." Coop straightened on the sofa and stared helplessly. "Something wrong?"

A flash of lightning lit the room. By the time the thunder rolled in answer, Keenan screamed like a banshee and launched himself into Coop's lap.

"I'm scared. There's monsters outside. They're coming to get me."

"Hey…" Coop gave the head buried in his chest an inadequate pat. "Hey, it's just a thunderstorm."

"Monsters," Keenan sobbed. "I want Mama."

"Well, she's—" He started to swear, caught himself. The poor kid was shaking. With an instinct he didn't recognize, Coop cuddled Keenan in his lap. "You don't like storms, huh?" All Keenan could do was shake his head and burrow deeper. "They're just like fireworks. You know, on the Fourth of July, or after your team wins the pennant? They probably just had a big game up there. They're celebrating."

"Monsters," Keenan repeated, but he'd calmed enough to lift his head and look at Coop. "Big black monsters with sharp teeth." He jolted at the next clap of thunder. Fresh tears started to roll. "They want to eat me."

"Nah." Experimentally, Coop tested Keenan's biceps. "You're too tough."

"I am?"

"You bet. Any monsters who looked in here would see you and run for their lives. They'd never take on Coop and the Keen-man."

Keenan sniffled, rubbed a fist over his eyes. "Really?"

"Absolutely." Coop saw Keenan's lower lip tremble when thunder grumbled. "Home run," he said, and Keenan's trembling mouth curved in a hesitant smile.

"Can I stay out here with you?"

"Sure. I guess."

Keenan, an expert in such matters, settled himself comfortably in Coop's lap, laid his head against Coop's heart and sighed.

Zoe was swaying with fatigue by the time she let herself in. It was nearly 3:00 a.m., and she'd been up and going for twenty hours straight. All she wanted was to fall facedown on her bed and sleep.

She saw them in the gray light of the snowy television screen. They were curled together on the couch, the boy snuggled deep against the man. Something shifted inside her at the sight of them, both sleeping deeply, Keenan's tousled golden hair beneath Coop's broad, tanned hand.

She set her purse and her keys aside without taking her eyes off them.

How small her son looked, and how safe.

She slipped out of her shoes and walked to them on stockinged feet. In a natural gesture, she brushed a hand over Coop's hair before gently lifting her son. Keenan stirred, then settled against her.

"Mama."

"Yes, baby," she murmured. She nuzzled him as she carried him away, caught the scent of man mixed with boy.

"The monsters came, but we scared them away."

"Of course you did."

"Coop said the thunder's just fireworks. I like fire-works."

"I know." She laid him in his bed, smoothing the sheets, his hair, kissing his soft cheeks. "Go back to sleep now."

But he already had. She watched him a moment lon-ger in the faint glow of his night-light, then turned and went back downstairs to Coop.

He was sitting up now, his head in his hands, the heels rubbing against his eyes. She switched off the buzzing television set, then sat on the arm of the couch. Any man who could sleep so comfortably with a child, to her mind, had unlimited potential.

She wondered, just for an instant, what it would feel like to curl up beside him.

"The storm woke him?"

"Yeah." His voice was rusty. He cleared it. "He was pretty spooked."

"He said you chased the monsters away."

"Seemed like the right thing to do." He turned his head to look at her. Those big brown eyes were sleepy and smiling. The quick hitch in his heartbeat warned him to be on his way. But he lingered. "He's okay now?"

"He's fine. You'd make a good daddy."

"Oh, well…" That had him moving. He stood, work-ing out the kinks. "That's not my line. But it was no big deal."

"It was to me." She'd embarrassed him, she noted, and she hadn't meant to. "Why don't I fix you break-fast tomorrow?"

"Huh?"

"Pay you back with pancakes. Mrs. Finkleman tells

me you bring in a lot of pizza and Chinese, so I don't imagine you cook. Do you like pancakes?"

"Who doesn't?"

"Then let me know when you're up and around. I'll flip some for you." She lifted a hand, brushed the hair from his brow. "Thanks for helping me out."

"No problem." He took a step away, swore under his breath and turned back. "Listen, I've just got to do this, okay?"

Before she could respond, he took her face in his hands and closed his mouth over hers.

The kiss was quick, and it was light, and it sent sparks snapping down her nerve ends.

When she didn't move a muscle, he lifted his head, looked at her. She was staring at him, her eyes heavy and dark. He thought he saw the same stunned reaction in them that was curling somewhere in his gut. She opened her mouth as if to speak, but he shook his head and kissed her again. Longer, deeper, until he felt her bones begin to melt. Until he heard the small whimper of pleasure purr in her throat.

Her hands slid up his arms, gripped, then moved up to tangle in his hair. They stood there, locked against each other.

One of them quivered, perhaps both. It didn't seem to matter as the warm taste of her seeped into his mouth, into his blood. It was like a dream that he hadn't yet shaken off, one that tempted him to sink back in, to forget reality.

She'd forgotten it. All she knew for one glorious moment was that she was being held in strong arms, that her mouth was being savored wonderfully, and that needs, so long dormant, were swimming to the surface and breaking into life.

Touch me. She wondered if she said it, or if the words simply whirled hazily in her head. But his hand, hard and sure, ran once down her body, kindling fires.

She remembered what it was to burn, and what it was like when the flames died out and left you alone.

"Coop." Oh, she wanted, so badly, just to let it happen. But she wasn't a young, reckless girl this time. And she had more to think of than herself. "Coop. No."

His mouth clung to hers for another moment, his teeth nipping. But he drew back. He was, he realized, as breathless as a man who'd slid headfirst into home plate.

"Now I'm supposed to say I'm sorry."

She shook her head. "No, you're not. I'm not."

"Good." The hands that were resting on her shoulders kneaded once, then slipped away into his pockets. "Me neither. I've been thinking about doing that since I first saw your feet."

Her brows rose. Surely she'd heard him wrong. "My what?"

"Your feet. You were standing on the ladder, painting. You weren't wearing any shoes. You've got tremendously sexy feet."

"Really?" It amazed her that he could tie her into helpless knots one minute, then make her laugh the next. "Thanks. I think."

"I guess I'd better go."

"Yeah, you'd better."

He nodded, started out. This time, when he stopped, she braced, and she yearned. But he simply turned and looked at her. "I'm not going to try to talk you into bed. But I want you there. I figured I should let you know."

"I appreciate it," she said in a shaky voice.

When the door closed behind him, she let her weak legs fold and sat down on the couch. What, she asked herself, was she supposed to do now?

Chapter 6

When Coop dragged himself out of bed, it was nearly noon. He stumbled into the shower and nearly drowned himself before both of his eyes opened. Wet and out of sorts, he rubbed himself down, gave a moment's thought to shaving, then dismissed the idea.

He tugged on gym shorts and a T-shirt before heading directly to the coffeemaker. While it brewed, he opened his front door and let the full power of the sun shock him the rest of the way awake.

They were in the yard, Zoe and Keenan, laughing as mother tried to help son hit fungoes with a plastic bat. The kid wasn't having much luck, Coop noted. But he was sure having fun. He started to step back inside before either of them spotted him. But the jock in him had him kibitzing.

"He'll never hit anything standing that way," Coop

called out, and had two pairs of big brown eyes looking up in his direction.

"Hi, Coop. Hi. I'm playing baseball." Thrilled to have an audience, Keenan waved his bat and nearly caught his mother on the chin.

"Watch it, champ," she said, and shifted out of range. "Good morning," she called out. "Want your breakfast?"

"Yeah, maybe."

Keenan took another pathetic swing and had Coop muttering under his breath. Swung like a girl. Somebody had to show the kid how to hold a bat, didn't they? he asked himself as he started down.

"You're choking it too much."

Zoe's brows drew together. "The book I got said—"

"Book." He cursed automatically. Keenan echoed him. "Sorry," he muttered when Zoe gave him a narrow-eyed look. "Now listen, you learn how to add and subtract from books. You don't learn baseball. Just like a girl." He crouched down and adjusted Keenan's hands.

Zoe had been ready to concede to the expert, but the last statement stopped her. "Excuse me? Are you implying that females can't play sports?"

"Not what I said. Swing from the shoulders," he told Keenan. Coop might have been grouchy, but he wasn't stupid. "There are plenty of terrific female athletes. Keep your eye on the ball, kid." He kept one hand around Keenan's and lightly tossed the ball up in the air with the other. The bat connected with a hollow thud.

"I hit it! I hit it really, really hard!"

"Major league stuff." Coop slid his eyes back up to Zoe's. "I thought you were making pancakes."

"I was— I am." She blew out a breath. "I guess you're taking over."

"Well, I don't know diddly about pancakes, and you don't know squat about baseball. Why don't we both do what we know?"

"Like it's a big deal to hit a stupid ball with a stupid bat," she muttered as she strode to the back door.

"You can't do it."

She stopped dead in her tracks, eyes narrowed, turned. "I certainly can."

"Yeah, right. Okay, Keenan, let's try it again."

"I believe it's my turn." Challenge in her every movement, Zoe slipped the bat from her son's hands.

"Are you going to hit it, Mama? Are you?"

"You bet I am." She held out a hand for the ball Coop was holding. She tossed it up, swung, and batted the ball to the chain-link fence bordering the side yard. Keenan let out a cheer and raced to retrieve it.

Coop sniffed, smiled. "Not bad, for a girl. But anybody can hit a fungo."

"Keenan's too young for anything but a plastic ball."

"No, a fungo's when you toss it up yourself and hit it."

"Oh."

"I'm gonna throw it, Coop. You catch."

"Sure, zip it in here."

It took Keenan three tries, running in closer each time, to send the ball anywhere near Coop.

"I suppose you don't think I could hit it if you threw it at me…." Zoe began.

"Pitch it to you," Coop said patiently. "I would pitch it to you."

"All right, pitch it to me, then." She raised the bat.

"Fine, but you might want to turn a little more to the side. That's it," he said, backing away. "Zoe, you're holding the bat like you're going to use it to hammer a nail. Okay, here it comes."

He tossed the ball soft and underhand, but she still had to grit her teeth to keep herself from jerking away. Because her pride and her son's respect for women were at stake, she swung hard. No one was more stunned than Zoe when she connected. Coop snatched the ball an instant before it could smash his nose.

"Well." Zoe handed the bat back to a wide-eyed Keenan, dusted her hands. "I'll go see about those pancakes."

"She hit it really hard," Keenan said admiringly.

"Yeah." Coop watched the back door swing shut behind her. "Your mother's really...something, kid."

"Will you pitch to me, Coop? Will you?"

"Sure. But let's work on that stance, huh? You gotta look like a ballplayer."

When Zoe finished flipping the last pancake on the stack, she looked out the window and saw her son swing the bat. The ball didn't go far, but Coop made a pretense of a diving catch, missing, while Keenan danced gleefully in place.

"Too hot to handle," Coop claimed, and Keenan jumped on top of him. "Hey, there's no tackling in baseball. Football's out of season." He scooped the wriggling boy up and held him upside down. Somewhere along the line, his sour mood had vanished.

It became a habit to spend time with the boy. Nothing planned, just playing a little catch in the yard or showing Keenan how to dunk baskets in the apartment. It wasn't as though he were attached to the kid, Coop assured himself. But when he had some free time and the boy wanted to hang around, what was the harm? Maybe it was sort of nice to see those big eyes all full of hero worship. And maybe it wasn't so much of a hardship to listen to that rollicking belly laugh Keenan burst into when something struck his fancy.

If the boy sometimes came along with the bonus of his mother, it wasn't exactly a hardship.

The fact was, he had seen a great deal more of Keenan than Zoe since the night of the thunderstorm. She was friendly enough, but she'd been careful—or so it seemed to Coop—not to be alone with him.

That was something he was going to fix, he decided as he shut down his computer.

He grabbed a couple of miniature race cars, some of the flotsam and jetsam of boyhood that Keenan had left in his apartment. If Coop knew Zoe as he thought he was beginning to, the toys would be an easier entry than a bouquet of long-stemmed roses.

Jiggling the cars in his hand, he strode down the steps to knock on her kitchen door.

In the laundry room, Zoe slammed down the lid on the washer. "Who is it?"

"It's Coop."

She hesitated, started the machine. "Come on in. I'll be right out." She hefted a basket of clean laundry, as much out of defense as out of necessity, and went into the kitchen.

God, he looked good. She had really, really tried not to dwell on how good the man looked. So damn male, she thought, the rangy, athletic body, the muscles, the dark, untidy hair, and those wonderful pale green eyes. She wished her heart wouldn't always stutter when he aimed one of his cocky grins in her direction.

"Hi." She plopped the basket on the kitchen table and immediately began busying her hands folding socks.

"Hi." The kitchen was cluttered, as always. She really needed someone to help her organize, he thought. God, she smelled fantastic. "Keenan left these upstairs." Coop set the cars on the table. "I thought he might be looking for them."

"Thanks."

"So where is he?"

"In school."

"Oh, right." Coop knew Keenan's schedule as well as he knew yesterday's box scores. "You just get in from the flower shop?"

"Mmm-hmm… Business is picking up. We've got a couple of weddings. Actually, I could work full-time for the next three weeks, but it just doesn't fit Keenan's schedule."

"What do you mean?" Idly he plucked a shirt from the basket.

"Well, the spring weddings. The arrangements take a lot of extra hands, so Fred asked if I could put in full days for a while."

"So, that's good, right?"

"The school Keenan goes to is really more of a preschool than day care. It doesn't stay open after three. And I have the car pool next week, anyway. Plus, I promised to take him and some of the other kids swimming at the community center on Friday. He's really looking forward to it."

"Yeah, he mentioned it." About twenty times, Coop recalled.

"I don't want to let him down."

"So, I'll do it."

She looked back up, socks dangling from her hands. "What?"

He couldn't believe he'd said that. He stared at her for another moment, then shrugged. "I said I'd do it. It's no big deal. He can hang with me when he gets home from school."

She tilted her head. "Don't you have a job?"

"That's what I call it, since they pay me." He smiled, finding the idea went down easily. "I do most of my writing here, and he could tag along when I go in to the paper or on an interview. He'd probably get a kick out of it."

"I'm sure he would." She narrowed her eyes. Why couldn't she get a handle on J. Cooper McKinnon? "But why would you?"

He wasn't sure he had the answer to that, so he punted. "Why not? He's not that much of a pest."

With a laugh, she went back to her laundry. "Maybe he's not, but you forgot the car pool."

"I can drive. What's the big deal about hauling a bunch of kids to school and back?"

"I can't begin to tell you," she murmured. It was, perhaps, something every adult should experience for himself. "And the swimming."

"I was captain of the swim team in college. All-state."

She glanced up at that. "I thought you played baseball. Uh, Keenan mentioned it."

"Yeah, I did. Two hundred and twelve RBIs my last season. I played basketball, too, averaged forty-two points a game." He was bragging, Coop realized. Like some gawky teenager trying to impress the head cheerleader. He frowned down at the little cars, began to slide one over the table.

"Keenan says you make great engine noises."

"Yeah, it's a talent."

He'd embarrassed himself, Zoe realized, and she wanted to hug him. "Tell you what. Why don't we take it a day at a time? If you decide you can't handle it—"

His eyes flashed up at that. "I think I can handle one scrawny kid and a few of his pals."

"Okay. If you decide you don't *want* to handle it, no hard feelings."

"Fine. When do you want to start?"

"Tomorrow would be great."

"Okay." That was settled. Now, he thought, it was on to other business. "How about dinner?"

Her eyes widened in surprise. "Um…sure. We're just going to have chicken. I'll probably fry it."

"No." He stepped closer. She stepped back. "I mean, why don't we have dinner? Out. You and me."

"Oh, well…" Good answer, she thought foolishly. Very succinct. She took another step in retreat. "I have to work tonight."

"Tomorrow."

"I don't really go out."

"I've noticed. What are you backing away from, Zoe?"

"You." Annoyed with herself, she held up a hand. And found it pressed against his chest. "I don't want to date anyone. Start anything. I have very good reasons."

"You'll have to tell me about them sometime." He reached up, combed a hand through her hair and loosened the band that held it back.

"You're not going to kiss me again."

"Sure I am." He touched his lips to hers to prove it. His eyes remained open as he drew her lower lip into his mouth, as he used his tongue, his teeth, to tease and seduce. "You've got an incredible mouth."

She couldn't get her breath. Even as she gasped for it, her vision dimmed. It was all she wanted. It seemed her life depended on keeping her lips against his. This wasn't fair, she thought dimly as she began to sink into the glory of sensation. Too long, she told herself. Surely she was reacting this way only because it had been so terribly long since she'd allowed herself to feel only as a woman.

She was melting against him like wax. He hadn't known how painfully erotic it would be to feel that long, lean body go fluid. He'd only meant to kiss her, to test them both, but his hands were already reaching, stroking, exploring.

His touch, those hard, callused hands against her bare skin, all but brought her to her knees.

"I have to think."

"Think later." He pressed his mouth to her throat.

Oh, it was glorious, glorious to ache again. But she knew too well what came from soothing that ache. "Coop, we can't do this."

"Yes, we can. I'll show you."

With a laugh that came out half moan, she turned her head away. "My head's spinning. You have to stop. God, do you have any idea what you're doing to me?"

"I haven't even started. Come upstairs, come upstairs with me, Zoe. I want to feel you under me. I want to feel myself inside you."

"I want to." She trembled, the needs exploding inside her like firebombs. "Coop, I need to think first. I have to think. I haven't been with anyone in five years."

His mouth stopped its desperate journey over her

throat. Slowly he drew back to look at her. Her eyes were clouded, and her mouth was swollen and ripe. "No one?"

"No." She swallowed and prayed for her system to level before she gave in to the urge to rip off his clothes and cut loose. "Since before Keenan was born. I feel like all those needs dried up—like old leaves. You've set a match to them, and I don't know how to handle it."

"The kid's father," Coop said carefully. "You're still in love with him."

"No." She might have laughed at that, if she weren't so shaken. "He has nothing to do with it. Well, of course he does, but... I have to sit down." She walked unsteadily to a chair. "I knew this was going to happen. I think I knew it the first time I saw you. There's been no one, because I didn't want anyone. Because Keenan was all that mattered to me. I have plans." That came out as an accusation, and her eyes darkened. "Damn it, I have plans. I want to go back to school. I want to have my own flower shop one day." Her voice began to catch, alarming him.

"Zoe—"

But she barreled right over him. "And everything was going along fine. I got the house. I wanted him to have a house, and a yard, and neighbors. Everyone said I was crazy, that I'd never be able to do it, that I'd be sorry I'd given everything up to raise a child on my own. But I'm not sorry. He's the best thing that ever happened to me. And I've done a good job. Keenan's happy, and he's bright and funny and wonderful. We have a good life, and I know I can make it even better. I haven't needed anyone. And... Oh, God, I'm in love with you."

The hand he'd lifted awkwardly to pat her head froze. "What?"

"Oh, what a mess. What a mess." She plucked a tiny sock out of the laundry basket and wiped her eyes. "Maybe it's just hormones. It could be, you know. But I walked in and you were sleeping with him on the couch. It was so sweet. Then you were kissing me and everything went crazy. Then you're out in the yard looking so smug and male, showing Keenan how to hit that silly ball. And you're eating pancakes and looking at me. I can hardly breathe when you're looking at me."

Somewhere along the line, his mind had gone blank. "I think I missed a step."

"No, you didn't." She sniffled and struggled to get herself under control. "I've just taken too many. It's my fault. You've been nice to Keenan, and you've been honest with me." She sighed, dropped the damp sock in her lap. "Believe me, I know my emotions are my responsibility." Because he was still staring at her, like a man who'd just had the friendly family dog lunge for his throat, she smiled. "I'm sorry, Coop. I shouldn't have dumped all that on you. I didn't even know it was all bottled up."

This time he took a step back. "Zoe, I like the kid. Who wouldn't? And I'm attracted to you. But—"

"There's no need to explain." Steady now, she rose. "Really, there isn't. I don't expect anything from you, and I'm sorry if I made you uncomfortable. But I feel a lot better." And, oddly enough, she did. "When I go to bed with you, we'll understand each other."

"When you—"

"I think we both know that's going to happen," she said calmly. "We both want it to, and it's smarter to face that than to live with all this tension. Keenan's been wanting to spend the night with a friend of his. I'll arrange it." She laughed a little at Coop's expression. "It's a little hard to be spontaneous with a four-year-old around. I hope you don't mind planning out a night together."

"No, I mean, I don't— God, Zoe."

"If you'd rather not, or if you want some time to decide, that's all right."

He studied her face, felt that same greedy tug, and a flare of something entirely different. Entirely new. "No, I want you. Whenever."

"How about Monday night?"

"I've got a twilight doubleheader on Monday." He couldn't believe he was standing here planning out a wild night of love like a dentist's appointment.

"Ah…Wednesday?"

He nodded. "Wednesday's good for me. Do you want to go out somewhere?"

It was sweet, she thought, really sweet of him to ask. "It's not necessary." She laid a hand on his cheek. "I don't need flowers and candlelight. I'll come upstairs after Keenan's settled."

"Good. Fine. I…better get back to work."

"Do you still want to have Keenan tomorrow?"

"Yeah, no problem. Tell him to come on up." Coop backed toward the door as Zoe began folding laundry again. "I guess I'll see you."

She listened to him walk up the steps. He was certainly a mistake, she told herself. But she'd made others. Life got too mundane when you avoided all the wrong turns.

Chapter 7

"He shoots, he scores!" Coop made appropriate crowd noises as Keenan dunked the basket.

"I can do it again! I can, okay?" From his perch on Coop's shoulders, Keenan swung his sneakered feet.

"Okay, you've drawn the foul." Coop scooped the palm-sized ball up and passed it into Keenan's eager hands. "It's game point, kid, ten seconds to play. This free throw is all-or-nothing. Got it?"

"Got it!"

"A hush falls over the crowd as Fleming steps up to the line. He's played the game of his life tonight, but it all comes down to this one shot. He eyes the basket. You eyeing the basket?"

"Eyeing it," Keenan said, with his tongue caught between his teeth.

"He sets...and shoots." Coop winced as the little rubber ball circled the rim, then watched through squinted eyes as it tipped in and dropped through the net.

"And the crowd goes wild!" Coop danced around the sofa while Keenan hooted and clapped on his shoulders. When he dumped the boy on the cushions of the sofa, Keenan let go with one of the rolling belly laughs that always made Coop grin. "You're a natural."

"You shoot it, Coop! You!"

Obliging, Coop executed a quick turnaround jump shot. This wasn't such a bad way to spend a rainy afternoon, he decided. And it helped keep his mind off how he was going to spend the rainy night ahead.

It was Wednesday.

"Okay, time out. I've got to finish up my piece on the track meet."

"Are we going to go to the paper again? It's neat there."

"Not today. I'm going to fax it in when it's done. You watch some tube." Coop hit the remote, then handed it over.

"Can I get a drink?"

"Yeah, there's some of that juice your mom sent up for you. Stay out of trouble, right?"

"Right."

When Coop headed into his office, Keenan scrambled up from the couch. He liked it best when he got to stay with Coop after school. They always got to do something neat, and Coop never asked if he'd washed his hands or said too many cookies would spoil his appetite.

Best of all, he liked when Coop picked him up. It was different than when his mother did. He liked when she held him, nuzzled him after his bath or rocked him when he had a bad dream. But Coop smelled different, and felt different.

He knew why, Keenan thought as he wandered into the kitchen. It was because Coop was a daddy instead of a mom.

He liked to pretend Coop was his daddy, and figured that maybe if he didn't do anything bad, Coop wouldn't go away.

After a couple of tugs, Keenan had the refrigerator open. He was proud that Coop had hung the pictures he had drawn for him on the door. He peered inside, saw the jug of juice his mother had bought for him. And the green bottles Coop liked.

"B-E-E-R," Keenan said to himself. He remembered that he'd asked Coop if he could have a taste from the bottle, and that Coop had told him he couldn't until he was big. After Coop had let him sniff the beer, Keenan had been glad he wasn't big yet.

There was a new bottle in the fridge today, and Keenan knit his brow and tried to recognize the letters. *C-H-A-R-D-O-N*— There were too many letters to read, so he lost interest.

He took out the jug, gripping it manfully and setting it on the floor. Humming to himself, he dragged a chair over to get cups from the cabinet. One day he'd be as tall as Coop and wouldn't need to stand on a chair. He leaned forward on his toes.

The crash and the howl had Coop leaping up, rapping his knee hard against the desk. Papers scattered as he raced out of the office and into the kitchen.

Keenan was still howling. A chair was overturned, juice was glugging cheerfully onto the floor, and the refrigerator was wide open. Coop splashed through the puddle and scooped Keenan up.

"Are you hurt? What'd you do?" When his only answer was another sob, he stood Keenan on the kitchen table and searched for blood. He imagined gaping wounds, broken bones.

"I fell down." Keenan wriggled back into Coop's arms.

"Okay, it's okay. Did you hit your head?"

"Nuh-uh." With a sniffle, Keenan waited for the kisses he expected after a hurt. "I fell on my bottom." Keenan's lip poked out. "Kiss it."

"You want me to kiss your— Come on, kid, you're joking."

The lip trembled, another tear fell. "You gotta kiss where it hurts. You gotta, or it won't get better."

"Oh, man." Flummoxed, Coop dragged a hand through his hair. He was desperately relieved that no blood had been spilled, but if anyone, anyone, found out what he was about to do, he'd never live it down. He turned Keenan around and made a kissing noise in the air. "Does that do it?"

"Uh-huh." Keenan knuckled his eyes, then held out his arms. "Will you pick me up?"

"Yeah." He didn't feel as ridiculous as he'd expected when the boy's arms went around his neck. "Okay now?"

With his head resting on Coop's shoulder, he nodded. "I didn't mean to do it. I spilled all the juice."

"No big deal." Hardly realizing he did so, Coop turned his head to brush his lips over Keenan's hair. Something was shifting inside him, creaking open.

"You aren't mad at me? You won't go away?"

"No." What the hell was going on? Coop wondered as unexplored and unexpected emotions swirled inside him. "No, I'm not going anywhere."

"I love you," Keenan said, with the simple ease of a child.

Coop closed his eyes and wondered how a grown man was supposed to handle falling for a four-year-old boy.

Well, here she was, Zoe thought as she stood at the bottom of the steps leading to Coop's apartment. All she had to do was go upstairs, open the door and start an affair. Her stomach clenched.

Silly to be nervous, she told herself, and climbed the first step. She was a normal woman with normal needs. If her emotions were too close to the surface, she would deal with it. It was much more difficult to be hurt when you had no expectations.

She'd had expectations once, but she knew better now.

This was simply a physical attraction between two single, healthy people. She'd nearly backed down a step before she forced herself to move forward. All the practical details had been seen to. Her son was safely tucked away for the night at his sleepover. She'd arranged for birth control—that wasn't an oversight she would make again.

No regrets, she promised herself as she lifted a hand to knock. She knew how useless they were.

He answered so quickly, she nearly jumped. Then they stood and stared at each other.

She'd worn a dress, one of those thin, breezy sundresses designed to make a man give thanks for the end of winter. Her hair was loose, falling over thin raspberry-colored straps and bare, peach-toned shoulders. There were nerves in her eyes.

"Hi." He glanced down to the cordless phone she held. "Expecting a call?"

"What? Oh." She laughed, miserably self-conscious. "No, I just don't like to be out of touch when Keenan's not home."

"He's all settled at his pal's?"

"Yeah." She stepped inside, set the phone on the counter. "He was so excited, he—" She broke off when her sandal stuck to the floor.

Coop grimaced. "I guess I missed some of it. We had a spill."

"Oh?"

"The kid took a tumble, sheared off ten years of my life. No blood lost, though. Just a half gallon of orange juice." When she only smiled, he stepped to the refrigerator. Why in hell was he babbling? "Want some wine?"

"That would be nice." *Why, he's as nervous as I am,* she realized, *and I loved him for it.* "Keenan's having a wonderful time staying with you. I have to study the sports pages now just to keep up with what he's talking about."

"He catches on fast."

"So do I. Go ahead," she said as he handed her a glass of wine, "Ask me about stats. I know all about RBIs and ERAs." She took a sip, then gestured with her glass. "I think the Orioles would have taken the second game of that doubleheader the other night if they'd put in a relief pitcher in the second inning."

His lips twitched. "Do you?"

"Well, the starter had lost his stuff, obviously. The guy who was announcing—"

"The play-by-play man."

"Yes, he said so himself."

"So, you watched the game."

"I watch 'Sesame Street,' too. I like to keep up with Keenan's interests." She trailed off when Coop reached out to twine a lock of her hair around his finger.

"He's got a thing for dinosaurs, too."

"I know, I've checked a half dozen books out of the library. We've—" The fingers trailed over her shoulder. "We've been down to the natural history museum twice."

She set the glass aside and fell into his arms.

He kissed her as though he'd been starved for her taste. The impact was fast, deep, desperate. The little purring sounds that vibrated in her throat had his muscles turning into bundles of taut wire.

"I wasn't sure you'd come."

"Neither was I. I—"

"Can't think of anything but you," he said as he swept her off her feet. "I thought we'd take this slow."

"Let's not," she murmured, pressing her lips to his throat as he carried her into the bedroom.

She had a quick impression of Spartan neatness and simple masculine colors and lines before they tumbled onto the bed.

Neither of them was looking for patience. They rolled together, a tangle of limbs grasping, groping, glorying. The sheer physicality of it, flesh to flesh, mouth to mouth, had Zoe's head reeling. Oh, she wanted to be touched like this, to feel so desperately like a woman, with a man's hand streaking over her, with his lips savoring every thud of her pulse.

So she lost herself. No more nerves, no more fears. And if she loved, it only made the joy of mating more lovely.

She was every man's fantasy. Stunningly responsive, breathlessly aggressive. And so beautiful, he thought. Undraped, the exquisite body was so slim, so perfect, he couldn't believe it had ever carried a child. In the gilded light of dusk, her face was elegant, heart-stopping. Whenever he touched, wherever he touched, he could see the bold echo of her pleasure reflected in her eyes.

He watched those eyes glaze over, felt her body tense, heard her strangled cry of release. Swamped with the power of it, he drove her upward again until they were both panting for air, until she reared up from the bed and wrapped herself around him.

Damp skin slid over damp skin, hungry mouth sought hungry mouth. They rolled over the bed again, moaning, quivering. Then his hands gripped hers, and his mouth crushed her mouth. And he thrust inside her, hard and deep.

She felt the sensation as if it were a lance through her system, painful, glorious. For an instant, neither of them moved, they just stayed tensed and shuddering on the edge.

Then it was all movement, all speed, a wild race that ended with them both plunging deliriously over the finish line.

It wasn't exactly the way he'd imagined, Coop thought. They were sprawled across his bed, Zoe curled against him. The light was nearly gone, and the room was full of shadows.

He'd imagined they would progress to the bedroom by stages. They were both adults and had known that was the ultimate goal, but he'd thought they would move slowly.

Then she'd been standing there smiling, the nerves shining in her eyes... He'd never wanted anything or anyone more in his life.

Still, he thought she deserved more than a quick tussle, however rewarding. But the night was young.

He flexed his arm to bring her head a little closer, brushed his lips over her temple. "Okay?"

"Mmm... At the very least." Her body felt golden. She was surprised her skin didn't glow in the dark.

"I rushed you a little."

"No, perfect timing."

He began to trail a finger up and down her arm. He wanted her again. Good God, his system was already churning to life. A little control, Coop, he ordered himself. "You're going to stay?"

She opened her eyes, looking into his. "Yes."

"I'm going to go get the wine."

"That's good." She sighed as he left the bed. She'd forgotten how to deal with the after, she realized. Or with the before and during, for that matter, she thought with a wry smile. Though she thought she'd done pretty well so far.

She hadn't known how much had been bottled up inside her. Or just how much she'd needed to feel like a woman again. But then, she hadn't known she could love again.

She shifted, slipping under the tangled sheets, automatically lifting them to her breasts when Coop came back with the wine and glasses.

The sight of her in his bed shot to his loins, with a quick detour through the heart. He said nothing, pouring wine, offering her a fresh glass and settling beside her.

"Why haven't you been with anyone?" The moment the question was out, he wished for a rusty knife to hack off his tongue. "Sorry, none of my business."

"It's all right." *Because I haven't fallen in love with anyone before you,* she thought. But that wasn't what he wanted to hear, she knew. Nor was it really what he'd asked.

"You want to know about Keenan's father."

"None of my business," he repeated. "Sorry, it's the reporter in me."

"It was a long time ago—a lifetime ago. I don't mind telling you. I grew up in New York. I think I mentioned that my mother's an actress. I was the result of a second marriage. She's had five. So far."

"Five?"

Zoe chuckled into her wine, sipped. "Clarice falls in love and changes husbands the way some women change hairstyles. My father lasted about four years before they parted amicably. Clarice always has friendly divorces. I didn't see much of him, because he moved to Hollywood. He does commercials and voice-overs mostly. Anyway, I think she was on husband number four when I was in high school. He had some pull with the Towers Modeling Agency. They're pretty big."

"I've heard of them."

"Well, he got me in. I started doing some shoots. And I caught on."

"That's it," Coop said, interrupting her. "I knew I'd seen your face before."

She moved her shoulders. "Five, six years ago, it was hard to avoid it. I did twenty covers in one month, the year after I graduated school."

"Cover of *In Sports,* swimsuit edition."

She smiled. "You've got a good memory. That was six years ago."

He remembered the long, sand-dusted legs, the lush wet red excuse for a bathing suit, the laughing, seductive face. He gulped down wine. "It was a hell of a shot."

"And a long, grueling shoot. Anyway, I was making a lot of money, getting a lot of press, going to lots of parties. I met Roberto at one of them."

"Roberto." Coop grimaced at the sound of the name.

"Lorenzi. Tennis player. You might have heard of him."

"Lorenzi? Sure—took the French Open three years ago in straight sets, then blew Wimbledon in the semis. He's got a bad attitude and likes to race cars and chase women on the side. Hasn't been seeded above twenty-fifth in the last two years. Got some bad press this spring when he tipped back too many vinos and punched out a photographer." Coop started to drink, stopped. "Lorenzi? He's Keenan's father? But he's—"

"A womanizer?" Zoe supplied. "A creep, a rich, spoiled egotist? I know—now. What I saw then was a gorgeous, charming man who sent me roses and jetted me off to Monte Carlo for intimate dinners. I was dazzled. He told me he loved me, that he adored me, worshiped me, he couldn't live without me. I believed him, and we became lovers. I thought, since he was my first, he'd be my only. Anyway, I didn't realize he was already getting tired of me when I found out I was pregnant. When I told him, he was angry, then he was very calm, very reasonable. He assumed I'd want an abortion and agreed to pay all the expenses, even to make the arrangements."

"A real prince."

"It was a logical assumption," Zoe said calmly. "I had a career on fast forward, in a field that wouldn't wait while I put on weight and suffered from morning sickness. He, of course, had no intention of marrying me, and thought, rightly enough, that I knew the rules of the game. I did know them," she said quietly. "But something had changed when the doctor confirmed the pregnancy. After the disbelief, the panic, even the anger, I felt good. I felt right. I wanted the baby, so I quit my job, moved away from New York and read everything I could get my hands on about parenting."

"Just like that?"

"Well, there were some scenes, some dire predictions, and a lot of anger, but that's how it worked. Roberto and I parted less than amicably, but with the agreement that he would stay out of my life and I would stay out of his."

"What have you told Keenan?"

"It's tough." And it never failed to make her feel guilty. "So far I've just told him his father had to go away, that he wasn't going to come back. He's happy, so he doesn't ask a lot of questions."

"Are you? Happy?"

"Yes." She smiled and touched his cheek. "I am. All my life I wanted a home, a family, something solid and settled. I didn't even know it until Keenan. He changed my life."

"No urge to go back and smile for the camera?"

"Oh, no. Not even a twinge."

He cupped a hand behind her neck, studying her. "It's such a face," he murmured. Right now he liked the idea of having it all to himself.

Chapter 8

The concept of car pools obviously had been devised by someone with a foul and vicious sense of humor. Having lived most of his life in cities where public transportation or a quick jog would get a man from his home to his office, Coop had never experienced the adult version.

But he'd heard rumors.

Arguments, petty feuds, crowded conditions, spilled coffee.

After a week as designated driver, Coop had no doubt the kiddie version was worse. Infinitely worse.

"He's pinching me again, Mr. McKinnon. Brad's pinching me."

"Cut it out, Brad."

"Carly's looking at me. I told her to stop looking at me."

"Carly, don't look at Brad."

"I'm going to be sick. Mr. McKinnon, I'm going to be sick right now."

"No, you're not."

Though Matthew Finney made gagging noises that had the other kids screeching, Coop gritted his teeth and kept driving. Matt threatened to be sick twice a day unless he rode in the front seat. After five miserable days Coop had his number. But that did very little to soothe his nerves.

Keenan, who had waited all week for his turn in the front, swiveled in his seat to make monster faces at Matt. This incited a small riot of elbow jabs, howls, screaming giggles and shoves.

"Keenan, turn around!" Coop snapped. "You guys straighten up back there. Cut it out! If I have to stop this car…" He trailed off, shuddered. He'd sounded like his own mother. Now Coop was afraid *he* would be sick. "Okay, first stop. Matt, scram."

Fifteen minutes later, his backseat thankfully empty, Coop pulled into the drive and rested his throbbing head on the steering wheel. "I need a drink."

"We got lemonade," Keenan told him.

"Great." He reached over to unbuckle Keenan's seat belt. All he needed was a pint of vodka to go with it.

"Can we go swimming again soon?"

The idea of taking a herd of screaming kids back to the community pool anytime within the next century had a stone lodging in Coop's heart. "Ask your mother."

Coop started to look in the backseat and realized he couldn't face it. Earlier in the week he'd made that mistake, and discovered wads of chewing gum on the rug, cookie crumbs everywhere, and a mysterious green substance smeared on the seat.

In his weakened state, even a candy wrapper was likely to tip the balance.

"Yoo-hoo!" Mrs. Finkleman stripped off her flowered garden gloves and headed across the lawn in a flowing tent dress and electric-blue sandals. "How was your swim, little man?"

"We had races, and Brad dunked Carly and made her cry even though Coop told him not to, and I can hold my breath underwater for twelve seconds."

"My goodness." She laughed and ruffled Keenan's hair. "You'll be in the Olympics next." Her shrewd eyes took in Coop's haggard face. "You look a little frazzled, Coop. Keenan, why don't you run in and tell Mr. Finkleman you want a piece of that cherry cobbler he baked today?"

"Okay!" He tugged on Coop's hand. "Do you want some? Do you wanna come?"

"I'll pass. You go ahead."

Mrs. Finkleman chuckled as Keenan darted away and scrambled up the steps. "Little angel. We'll keep him entertained for a couple of hours—or he'll keep us entertained. You look like you could use a few minutes in a quiet room."

"Padded room," Coop muttered. "How does anyone survive kids?"

"It's easier if you go through the stages with them. Once you've walked the floor all night with a colicky baby, nothing much fazes you." She sighed. "Except science projects. Science projects always took me to the edge. And that first driving lesson." She shook her head at the memory. "That can bring you to your knees." She beamed and patted his arm. "But there's years yet to worry about that. And you've been doing a fine job.

Why, Harry and I were just saying how nice it is that
Zoe and Keenan have a man in their lives. Not that Zoe
hasn't been handling everything. Raising that sweet-
natured boy all alone, and working two jobs and tend-
ing the house. But it does my heart good to see you and
that little angel playing ball in the yard, or the way Zoe
lights up when you're around. You make a lovely little
family. Now, you go and take a nice nap. We'll keep an
eye on your boy."

"I'm not— He's not—" But even as Coop stam-
mered, she was drifting away.

Family? he thought as a ball of ice formed in his
stomach. They weren't a family. Oh, no, he promised
himself as he walked around the house to his steps. He
hadn't taken that on.

He liked the kid, sure. What wasn't to like? And he
was damn near nuts about the mother. But that didn't
make them a family. That didn't make things permanent. Maybe he'd volunteered to spend time with the
kid, taught him a few things about ball, pitched him a
few, but that didn't make him Daddy.

He headed straight for the refrigerator, popped the
top off a beer and took a long pull.

Sure, maybe he enjoyed having the kid around, and
Lord knows he enjoyed being with Zoe. He'd even
been sort of pleased when a woman at the pool mistook
Keenan for his and commented on what a handsome
son he had. But that didn't mean he was going to start
thinking about family health insurance or college funds.

He was single. He liked being single. It meant coming and going as he pleased, planning all-night poker
games, spending all day with the sports channel blaring.

He liked working in his own space—that was why he did the bulk of his writing at home, rather than at the paper. He didn't like people messing with his things or structuring his time or planning outings.

Family life—as he remembered from his childhood—was lousy with outings.

No way was he changing his nice comfortable existence to accommodate a family.

So he'd made a mistake, Coop decided, and stretched out on the couch with his beer. He'd given Zoe and the kid a little too much of his time, a little too much of his attention. It hadn't been anything he didn't want to give, but he could see now that the gesture could be misconstrued. Particularly since Zoe had once brought up the *L* word. Only once, he reminded himself, and he'd like to think that had just been a woman thing.

Still, if he didn't back off, they might start to depend on him. He shifted uncomfortably as the idea flitted through his mind that he might also come to depend on them.

It was time to reestablish himself as the tenant upstairs.

Keenan raced out of the house next door the minute his mother pulled her car in the drive.

"Hi, Mama, hi! I held my breath for twelve seconds underwater!"

Zoe caught him on the fly and swung him twice. "You must be hiding gills in there," she said, tickling his ribs. "Hi, Mrs. Finkleman."

"Hi yourself. We've had ourselves a fine hour. I sent Coop up for a nap when they got home. He looked like he'd had a rough day."

"Thanks." She kissed Keenan's waiting lips, then smacked her own. "Mmm… Cherries."

"Mr. Finkleman baked them, and they were good."

"I bet. Did you say thank you?"

"Uh-huh. Matt almost throwed up in Coop's car."

"Threw up," Zoe said as she carried Keenan inside.

"Uh-huh. 'Cause it was my turn to ride in the front. I had the best time, and Coop helped me to swim without my bubbles. He said I was a champ."

"That's just what you are." She collapsed with him on a chair. The idea of fixing dinner, changing into her uniform and serving drinks for six hours loomed heavily. "Give me a hug," she demanded, then soothed herself with some nuzzling. "Definitely a champion hugger. Why don't you come in the kitchen and tell me what else you did today while I fix dinner?"

A half hour later, as Zoe was draining pasta and Keenan was entertaining himself with crayons and paper on the kitchen floor, she heard the sound of Coop's feet on the stairs. Her heart sped up. The normal, healthy reaction made her smile. Imagine, she thought, believing herself immune to men.

She left the pasta draining in the sink and went to the back door just as he came to the foot of the steps.

"Hi."

"How's it going?" Coop jingled the keys in his pocket. Did she look all lit up? he wondered. She was smiling, and despite the shadows of fatigue under them, her eyes did have the prettiest lights in them.

"I was just going to call upstairs. I thought you'd like some dinner after a hard day at the pool." She opened the screen door and leaned out to kiss him. The smile dimmed a bit when he eased back. "It's just chicken and pasta."

It smelled nearly as good as she did. He glanced inside—the homey scene, cluttered counters, fresh flowers, steam rising from a pan on the stove, the child sprawled on the floor, the pretty woman offering him food and kisses.

A definite trap.

"Thanks, but I'm on my way out."

"Oh. I thought you had a couple hours before game time." She laughed at his arched brow. "I guess I've been paying more attention to the sports scene. Baltimore versus Toronto, game one of three."

"Yeah." When she starts to take an interest in *your* interests, she's really shutting the cage door. "I've got some stuff to do."

"Can I go with you?" Keenan dashed to the door to tug on Coop's slacks. "Can I go to the game? I like watching them with you best."

Coop could almost hear the locks clicking into place. "I've got too much to do," he said, with an edge to his voice that had Keenan's lips quivering. "Look, it's not just a game, it's my job."

"You said I was good luck."

"Keenan." Zoé put her hand on her son's shoulder to draw him back, but her eyes stayed on Coop's. "Did you forget Beth was coming over to stay with you tonight? She'll be here soon, and you're going to watch a tape of your favorite movie."

"But I wanna—"

"Now go wash your hands for dinner."

"But—"

"Go on now."

The way Keenan's face crumpled would have softened an ogre's heart. Dragging his feet, he headed out
of the kitchen.

"I can't take him with me everywhere...." Coop
began defensively.

"Of course not. He's just overtired. I couldn't have let
him go, in any case." She hesitated, wishing she could
ignore her instincts. "Is everything all right?"

"Everything's fine." He didn't know why he shouted
it. He didn't know why he felt like something slimy
stuck to the bottom of a shoe. "I have a life, you know.
I don't need kids climbing up my back or you fixing me
dinner. And I don't have to explain myself."

Her eyes turned very cool, her face very composed.
"You certainly don't. I appreciate you helping me out
the past couple of weeks. Let me know if I can return
the favor."

"Look, Zoe—"

"I've got to get dinner on the table, or I'll be late
for work." She let the screen door slam between them.
"Enjoy the game."

She knew exactly how long he continued to stand
there while she worked at the stove. Knew exactly when
he turned and walked away.

It wasn't unexpected, she reminded herself. This
backing away was typical, even understandable. Perhaps it had taken Coop a few weeks to completely com-
prehend that she didn't come as a single. She was part
of a pair, a ready-made family, with its share of responsibilities and problems and routines.

And he was opting out.

He might not even know it yet, she thought, but he
was in the first stages of a full retreat.

Her eyes blurred, her chest heaved. Resolutely she choked the tears back. She would indulge herself with a nice long cry later, she promised. But for now she had a little boy to soothe.

When he came back in, she crouched down until they were eye-to-eye.

"You had a good time with Coop today, didn't you?"

Keenan sniffled, nodded.

"And he's taken you a lot of places. You've had fun, and done a lot of new things."

"I know."

"You should be grateful for that, baby, instead of pouting because you can't have more."

She straightened again and hoped she could take her own advice.

Chapter 9

"You're spending a lot of time around here." Ben edged a hip onto the corner of Coop's desk. All around Coop's cubicle phones rang, keyboards clattered.

"So?" Without taking his eyes from the computer screen, Coop hammered out the draft of his weekly column.

"I just figured you had it made in that apartment of yours. I mean, great location." He thought of Zoe. "Great view. You didn't spend as much time in here when you lived downtown."

"I needed a change of scene."

"Yeah." Ben snorted and picked up a baseball from Coop's desk. "Trouble in paradise?"

"I don't know what you're talking about. And I've got a column to write."

"Pretty obvious the last few weeks that you've been stuck on the landlady." He tossed the ball from one hand to the other. "I mean, when a man hauls a kid around, buys little baseball jerseys, it follows that he's hooking a line into Mom."

Coop's eyes flashed up. "I like the kid, okay? I don't have to use a four-year-old to get a woman. The kid's cool."

"Hey, I got nothing against rug rats. Might even have a few of my own one day. The thing is, when a woman's got one, a man has to play Daddy if he wants the inside track."

"Who says I have to play at anything to get a woman?"

"Not me. But it was you who couldn't shoot hoop last week because you were taking the family to the aquarium." Ben winked, set the ball down. "Still, I bet you scored better than I did." Ben jerked back as Coop lunged for his throat.

"It's not like that," Coop said between his teeth.

"Hey, hey. Just yanking your chain. I wouldn't have made any cracks if I'd known you were serious about her."

Coop's grip loosened. "I didn't say I was serious. I said it wasn't like that."

"Whatever you say."

Disgusted with himself, Coop dropped back in his chair. He and Ben had been riding each other about women for better than five years. No reason to overreact, he thought. Or to make a fool of himself. "Sorry. I've got a lot on my mind."

"Forget it. What you need's a distraction. You coming to the poker game tonight?"

"Yeah."

"Good. Losing money should put you back on track."

Something had to, Coop thought as he sat back alone in his cubicle to stare at his screen. For the past three days he'd slept little, eaten less, and gone around in a constant state of flux.

Because he was avoiding the issue, he decided. Opting to bunt, when he should be swinging away. The only solution to getting his life back in order was to face the problem head-on.

He flicked off his terminal.

The beautiful thing about an afternoon off, Zoe thought, was the solitude. No customers to talk to, no orders to fill. It meant she didn't have to be salesclerk, or waitress, or Mom, or anything but Zoe.

Sitting on the back stoop, she struggled to understand the assembly instructions for the new barbecue grill she'd bought. She was going to surprise Keenan with hamburgers.

She liked the quiet—her kind of quiet, which meant there was music throbbing from the kitchen radio. She liked the loneliness—her kind of loneliness, which meant Keenan would dash toward her shortly with open arms and chattering voice.

She knew the upstairs apartment was empty, and she tried not to think about that. Tried not to think about the fact that Coop had been away more than he'd been home in the last few days.

Foolish of her to have thought he was different. He'd wanted her, he'd had her, and now he'd lost interest. Well, she had wanted him, so they were even there. If her heart was suffering it would pass. It had passed before. She and Keenan could get along fine on their own. Just like always.

Her screwdriver slipped, scraped her knuckles, had her swearing.

"What the hell are you doing?"

Eyes hot, she looked up at Coop. "Baking a cake. What does it look like I'm doing?"

"You can't put something together if you're going to spread parts all over the damn place." Automatically he bent down to organize. She rapped his hand away with the rubber grip of the screwdriver.

"I don't need you to put things together for me. I'm not some poor helpless female who needs a man to pick up the slack. I managed just fine before you came along."

Stung, he rammed his hands in his pockets. "Fine. Do it yourself."

"I am doing it myself. I like doing it myself."

"Terrific. And when the thing topples over, you won't have anyone else to blame."

"That's right." She blew her hair out of her eyes. "I accept when something's my fault." She picked up a wrench and locked a bolt in place. "Do you plan to hover over me all afternoon?"

"I want to talk to you."

"So talk."

He had it well planned. He was a writer, after all. "I realize the way I've been hanging around with you and the kid—"

"His name is Keenan," Zoe said between her teeth.

"I know what his name is. The way I've been hanging around the last few weeks might give the wrong impression."

"Oh, really?" She looked up again, tapping the wrench against her palm.

"He's a great kid, he kind of grows on you. I've gotten a kick out of spending time with him."

Though she hated herself for it, Zoe softened. She understood that he was genuinely fond of Keenan. That only made it all the more difficult. "He likes spending time with you. It's been good for him."

"Well, yeah, on the one hand. On the other, I started thinking that he—that you—that both of you might get the wrong idea. I mean, tossing a ball around or taking him to a game, that's cool. I just don't want him thinking it's like—permanent."

"I see." She was calm now, frigidly so. It would help keep the hurt in check. "You're afraid he might begin to see you as a father figure."

"Well, yeah. Kind of."

"That's natural enough. But then, he spends a lot of time with Mr. Finkleman, too, and with Billy Bowers down the street."

"Finkleman's old enough to be his grandfather, and the Bowers kid is eighteen." Coop backed off, realizing there was a touch of jealousy in the defense. "And they don't have the same sort of thing going with you."

She arched both brows. "Thing?"

"Relationship," he said tightly. "Whatever the hell you want to call it. Damn it, we only slept together once."

"I'm aware of that." Carefully she set the wrench aside. It would give her only momentary pleasure to heave it at his head.

"That came out wrong," he said, furious with himself. "It sounded like it didn't mean anything. It did, Zoe." A great deal, he was afraid. A very great deal. "It's just that…"

"Now you're terrified that Keenan and I will trap you into a family. That you'll wake up one morning and be Daddy, with a wife and a mortgage and a small boy who needs attention."

"Yes. No. Something like that." He was burying himself, he realized, and he suddenly didn't know why. "I just want to make myself clear."

"Oh, I think you have. Perfectly." She rubbed her hands on her knees as she studied him. "You needn't worry, Coop. I advertised for a tenant, not a father for my child, or a husband for myself. I slept with you because I wanted to, not because I thought I could lure you to the altar."

"I didn't mean it like that." Frustrated, he dragged a hand through his hair. However well he'd planned this little scene, it was going all wrong. "I wanted you. I still do. But I know how badly you were let down before. I don't want to hurt you, Zoe. Or the kid. I just don't want you thinking I'd slide into the gap."

The anger came back, one swift wave of it that reddened her vision. She was on her feet before either of them realized she'd moved. "Keenan and I don't have a gap. We're a family, as real and as complete and as full a family as any could be." She jabbed the wrench at his chest. "Just because Daddy doesn't make three doesn't mean we're less of a unit."

"I didn't mean—"

"I'll tell you what you mean. You see a woman and a small boy and you think they're just pining away for some big strong man to come along and fulfill them. Well, that's bull. If I needed a man, I'd have one. And if I thought Keenan needed a father to make him happy, I'd find him one. And," she continued, advancing and giving him another jab, "if you think you're at the head of some fictional list, you're wrong. Maybe I'm in love with you, but that's not enough. It's not just me, and it's not just you. Keenan comes first. When and if I want a father for Keenan, he'll be someone with compassion and patience, someone willing to adjust his life to make room for my son. So relax, Cooper. You're in the clear."

"I didn't come here to fight with you."

"Good, because I'm finished."

He grabbed her arm before she could turn away. "I haven't. I'm trying to be straight with you, Zoe. I care about you, okay? About both of you. I just don't want it to get out of hand."

"Out of whose hands?" she retorted. "Yours? Then that's no problem, is it? Because you know how to hold on to everything inside, really tight. Just keep holding on to it, Coop. Don't worry about me or about Keenan. We'll be fine." She jerked her arm free and sat again. Picking up the instruction sheet, she gave it her full attention.

Now why, he wondered, did he feel as though he'd just been rejected? Shaking his head, Coop took a step in retreat. "As long as we're clear."

"We are."

"I've, ah, got a little time, if you want me to help you put that grill together."

"No thanks. I can do it." She slanted him a look. "I'm going to grill burgers later. You're welcome to join us. Unless you're afraid it will lead to a commitment."

She shoots, he thought wryly, she scores. "Thanks anyway. I've got plans. Maybe I could take a rain check."

"Fine. You know where to find us."

* * *

He got drunk. Not sloppily, but thoroughly. When Coop poured himself out of the cab and staggered toward the house, he already knew he'd hate himself in the morning. But it was tonight he had to deal with.

He leaned heavily against Zoe's front door and waited for the porch to settle down under his feet. She might think they'd finished, he told himself blearily, but she was wrong. Dead wrong.

He'd thought of a dozen things he had to say to her.

There was no time like the present.

Lifting a fist, he pounded on the door. "Come on, Zoe." He pounded again. "I know you're in there." He saw a light flick on inside and kept on pounding. "Come on, come on. Open up."

"Coop?" From the other side of the door, Zoe belted her hastily donned robe. She'd been home from the lounge for barely twenty minutes, and in bed for less than five. "It's after two o'clock in the morning. What do you want?"

"I want to talk to you. Let me in."

"We'll talk in the morning."

"You just said it was morning."

When he pounded again, she flicked off the locks. "Stop that—you'll wake Keenan." Furious, she yanked open the door and had the surprise of a hundred-and-seventy-pound male tumbling against her. "Are you hurt? What happened?" The alarm signals that had screamed on shifted when she caught the scent of beer. "You're drunk."

"Mostly." He started to straighten, then lost himself in the smell of her. "God, you feel good. What d'you wash this in?" He nuzzled her hair. "Smells like moonbeams."

"Really drunk," she said with a sigh. "Sit down. I'll get you some coffee."

"Don't want coffee. Doesn't sober you up, only wakes you up. And I'm awake, and I have something to say to you." He drew away then, and discovered he wasn't as steady as he'd hoped. "But I'll sit down." He did, heavily. "Hate getting drunk. Haven't done it like this since I played minor league. Did I tell you I played minor league ball? Triple A."

"No." Baffled, she stood her ground and watched him.

"Right out of high school. Two years. Thought I'd make it to the show. The majors. But I didn't, so I went to college, and now I write about people who did."

"I'm sorry."

"No." He waved that away. "I like writing. Always did. Like watching the games and seeing all the little dramas. If I'd've played, I'd be nearly washed up now. I'm almost thirty-three. Old man for the game." He focused on her, smiled. "You're the most beautiful woman I've ever seen in my life. You know, the kid looks just like you. Look at him, see you. It's spooky. I see you all the time. Minding my own business, and pop! There's your face in my head. What d'ya make of that?"

"I don't know." She wanted to be angry with him, really she did. But he was so foolishly drunk. "Why don't I take you upstairs, Coop? Put you to bed."

"I want you in my bed, Zoe. I want to make love with you. I want to touch you again."

She wanted that, too. Very much. But new lines had been drawn. "You said you wanted to talk to me."

"Do you know what your skin feels like? I can't describe it, it's all soft and smooth and warm. I started thinking about your skin when I was playing poker and getting drunk tonight. I won, too. Took a big pot with a pair of sixes. Pulled in over two hundred and fifty dollars."

"Congratulations."

"But I kept thinking about you. You have this little dimple right here." He nearly poked himself in the eye, then dragged a finger down his cheek to the corner of his mouth. "I kept thinking about that little dimple, and your skin, and those big eyes and killer legs. And I kept thinking how I like to watch you with the kid, like I do sometimes from upstairs, when you don't know. Didn't know that, did you?"

"No," she said quietly. "I didn't."

"Well, see…" He gestured wildly. "You've got this way of running your hand over his hair. It gets to me." He shook his head. "It really gets to me. Keenan loves me, you know. He told me he did. So did you."

"I know."

"And I meant everything I said this afternoon."

"I know." Sighing, she walked over to undo his shoelaces.

"Every word, Zoe. I've got my life set, just like I want it."

"Okay." She pried off his shoes, hefted his legs onto the couch.

"So you can stop popping into my head, 'cause it's not changing anything."

"I'll keep that in mind."

He was asleep before she bent over and kissed his cheek.

Chapter 10

As hangovers went, Coop knew, this would be a champ. He didn't have to open his eyes, he didn't have to move, not when his head was already beating like the Army drum corps.

He wasn't sure how he'd managed to get home and into bed, but the blur of the evening wasn't comforting. Still, he thought it best to wait to tax his brain.

Cautious, close to fearful, he opened his eyes. The little face directly above him had him jerking back, then moaning at the pain.

"Good morning," Keenan said cheerfully. "Did you sleep over?"

"I don't know." Coop lifted a hand to his head. "Where's your mother?"

"She's making my lunch. She said I could come in and look at you if I didn't wake you up. I didn't wake you up, did I? I was really quiet."

"No." Coop closed his eyes again and prayed for oblivion.

"Are you sick? Do you have a tempature?" Keenan laid a small, light hand on Coop's aching forehead. "Mama can make it better. She always makes it better." Very gently, Keenan replaced his hand with a kiss. "Does that help?"

Oh, hell, Coop thought. Even a hangover didn't have a chance against this kid. "Yeah, thanks. What time is it?"

"The big hand's on the ten and the little hand's on the eight. You can sleep in my bed until you're better, and play with my toys."

"Thanks." Coop made the supreme effort and sat up. When his head rolled, he did his best to catch it in his hands. "Keenan, be a pal and ask your mom for some aspirin."

"Okay." He raced off, and the sound of his sneakers pounding the floor had Coop shuddering.

"Headache?" Zoe asked a moment later.

Coop lifted his head. She was still in her robe. The robe he remembered from the night before. He was beginning to remember quite a bit from the night before. "If you're going to yell at me, could you do it later?"

In answer, she held out aspirin and a glass filled with reddish liquid.

"What is it?"

"A remedy from Joe the bartender. He guarantees it'll take the edge off."

"Thanks."

There was a blast of a horn from outside that cut through Coop's skull like a dulled knife. While he

was dealing with the shock of that, Keenan came racing back.

"Bye, Mama, bye!" He gave her a smacking kiss,
then turned to hug Coop. "Bye."

As the door slammed behind him, Coop gulped
down Joe's remedy.

"Do you want coffee?" Zoe ran her tongue around
her teeth and tried not to smile. "Some breakfast?"

"You're not going to yell at me?"

"For barging in here, drunk, in the middle of the
night? And for passing out on my sofa?" She paused
just long enough to make her point. "No, I'm not going
to yell at you. I figure you're suffering enough."

"I am, I promise you." He got up to follow her into
the kitchen. "Not just physically. I feel like a total jerk."

"You *were* a total jerk." She poured a mug of coffee,
set it on the table for him. "My mother's third husband
had a fondness for bourbon. He swore eggs the morning
after were the cure. How do you want them?"

"Scrambled would be good." He sat gingerly at the
table. "I'm sorry, Zoe."

She kept her back to him. "For?"

"For being a jackass yesterday afternoon, and a bigger jackass last night."

"Oh, that." With the bacon frying, she chose a small
bowl to scramble eggs in. "I don't imagine it's the first
or the last time you'll be one."

"You didn't…" He shifted miserably. "Ah, you didn't
tell Keenan I was…"

"Drunk and disorderly?" A half smile on her face,
she glanced over her shoulder. "I told him you weren't
feeling well and went to sleep on the couch. Which was
close enough."

"Thanks. I wouldn't want him to think…you know. I don't make a habit out of it."

"So you said last night." She turned the bacon, whipped the eggs.

He watched her, gradually getting past the astonishment that she wasn't going to rub his nose in the mess he'd made of things. Remembering the afternoon before, when she'd stood up to him with all that pride and fury shining in her eyes. And the other night, when he'd fallen asleep on her couch—the way she'd looked when she slipped the boy from his arms into hers and carried him into bed.

A dozen other pictures, captured in so short a time, flitted through his head, until they were whittled down to one. This one. Zoe standing at the stove, with the morning sun streaming over her tousled hair, her robe flowing down, breakfast smells warming the room.

How could he have thought he didn't want this? Just this. And what did he do now that he knew the truth?

"Food should help." She set the plate in front of him. "I've got to get ready for work."

"Can you— Have you got a minute?"

"I suppose." She poured herself another cup of coffee. "I don't have to be in until ten."

He began to eat while thoughts scrambled in his brain. "This is good. Thanks."

"You're welcome." She leaned back against the counter. "Did you want something else?"

"Yeah." He ate more, hoping eggs equaled courage. Then he put his fork down. It was the ninth inning, he thought, and there were already two outs. "You. I want you."

She smiled a little. "Coop, I doubt you're in any shape for that, and I really have to go to work, so—"

"No, I don't mean that. I mean I do, but not—" He broke off, took a long, deep breath. "I want you to marry me."

"I beg your pardon?"

"I think you should marry me. It's a good idea." Somewhere in the back of his mind, he realized, he'd been working on this all along. He had it figured. "You can quit your night job and go back to school if you want. Or open that flower shop. Whatever. I think that's what we should do."

"Really." Because her hand was unsteady, she set her coffee down. "Well that's very generous of you, Coop, but I don't have to get married to do any of those things. So thanks just the same."

He stared. "No? You're saying no? But you love me. You said it. Twice you said it."

"We can make it three," she said evenly. "Yes, I love you. No, I won't marry you. Now I really have to get ready for work."

"Just a damn minute." Hangover forgotten, he pushed back from the table and rose. "What kind of game is this? You love me, your kid's crazy about me, we're terrific in bed, I even know how to drive a damn car pool, but you won't marry me."

"You're such an idiot. You're such a fool. Do you think because I didn't put up a struggle before I fell into your bed that you can have everything your own way? When you want it, how you want it? Well, you're wrong. And you *are* a jackass."

He winced as she stormed from the room. Strike one, he thought. And he hadn't even seen the pitch.

But the game wasn't over, he thought grimly, until the fat lady sang.

* * *

Zoe was still steaming when she came home from work. Of all the arrogant, interfering, self-absorbed idiots she'd ever known, J. Cooper McKinnon took the gold medal. Imagine him telling her that marrying him was a good idea, then ticking off all the advantages she'd gain.

Oh, he thought he was a prize.

One day he's telling her to get any ideas of sneaking him into a relationship out of her head. As if she'd been baiting traps for him. The next he's taking pity on her and offering her a big male helping hand.

She should have bitten it off.

Not once, not once had he said what she would bring to him, what he felt for her, what he wanted. Not once had he brought up the fact that he could or would accept another man's child as his own.

She jerked open the front door, slammed it. He could take his half-baked proposal and sit on it.

"Mama! Hey, Mama!" Keenan zipped into the living room and grabbed her hand. "Come on, come on. We've got a surprise."

"What surprise? What are you doing home, Keenan? You're supposed to be at the Finklemans'."

"Coop's here." He tugged manfully on her hand. "We have a surprise. And we have a secret. And you have to come *now!*"

"All right, I'm coming." She braced herself and let Keenan drag her into the kitchen.

There were flowers, banks of them, vases and baskets overflowing on the counters, on the floor, on the windowsills. There was music, some soft, dreamy classical sonata, on the radio. The table was set, crystal she'd never seen before glinting in the sunlight, a bottle of champagne chilling in a silver bucket. And Coop was standing there, in a neatly pressed shirt and slacks.

"It's a surprise," Keenan announced gleefully. "We made everything look nice so you'd like it. And Mrs. Finkleman said we could use the glasses and the plates. And Mr. Finkleman made his special chicken 'cause it's resistible."

"Irresistible," Coop said, his eyes on Zoe. "You, ah, said you didn't need flowers and candlelight, but I've never taken you out on a date. I thought this was the next-best thing."

"Do you like it, Mama? Do you?"

"Yes, it's very nice." She bent down to kiss Keenan. "Thank you."

"I get to go to the Finklemans' so you can have romance."

"Ah, come on, kid." Coop scooped Keenan up. "Let's get you started. You were supposed to keep quiet about it," he muttered when he carried the boy outside.

"What's romance?"

"I'll tell you later."

Satisfied with that, Keenan draped his arm around Coop's neck. "Are you gonna tell Mama the secret about us all getting married?"

"That's the plan."

"And you'll live with us and you can be my Daddy and that'll be okay?"

"That'll be great. It'll be perfect." He stopped by the fence to press a kiss to Keenan's mouth. "I love you, Keenan."

"Okay." He squeezed his arms hard around Coop's neck. "Bye."

"Bye."

"Yoo-hoo!" Mrs. Finkleman stood at the back door. She sent Coop a wink and an exaggerated thumbs-up sign before whisking Keenan inside.

She was standing pretty much where Coop had left her when he came back. He wasn't sure whether or not that was a good sign.

"So, ready for some champagne?"

"Coop, this is very nice of you, but—"

"Like the flowers?" Nervous as a cat, he popped the cork.

"Yes, they're wonderful, but—"

"I couldn't get them where you work, or I'd have spoiled the surprise. Keenan really gave me a hand setting things up." He handed her the glass, and when she was distracted, he leaned in for a slow, warm kiss. "Hi."

"Coop." She had to wait for her heart to finish its lazy somersault. "I know you must have gone to a lot of trouble—"

"I should have gone to it before. I didn't know I wanted to."

"Oh, Lord." She turned away and struggled to get her emotions under control. "I've given you the wrong impression this time. I don't need the trappings. I don't have to have romantic evenings and—" she waved toward the tapers on the table, waiting to be lit "—candlelight."

"Sure you do. So do I, when they're with you."

"You're trying to charm me," she said unsteadily. "That's new."

"You know what I am. The way this house is set up, we've practically been living together for the past month or so. People get to know each other quicker that way

than just by socializing. So you know what I am, and
you fell for me anyway."

She took a drink. "You're awfully smug about it.
I told you my feelings are my responsibility, and that
holds true. A romantic dinner doesn't change it."

It looked like strike two, but Coop knew that if he
was going to go down, he'd go down swinging. "So I
want to give you a nice evening. Is something wrong
with that? I want to do better than propose over scrambled eggs when I've got a hangover." His voice had
risen, and he bit down on it. "Damn it, this is my first
time, have a little tolerance. No, don't say anything, let
me finish this. You don't need me." He took another
long breath. "Not for taking care of things, for you or
the kid, I mean, for mowing the grass or putting stupid
barbecue grills together. What about what I need, Zoe?"

She blinked at him. "Well, that's just it. Don't you
see? You made it clear that you don't need or want ties.
I come with ties, Coop."

"I made it clear," he muttered. "I didn't make anything clear, because I didn't know. Didn't want to know.
I was scared. There. You feel better knowing that?" He
glared at her. "I was scared, because I need you. Because I need to see your face and hear your voice and
smell your hair. I just need you to be there. And I need
to help you mow the grass and put the grill together. I
need you to need me back."

"Oh." She shut her eyes. "I like hearing that."

"Then tell me you will." He took her arms until she
opened her eyes again. "It's my last swing, Zoe. Marry
me."

"I—" Yes. She wanted to say yes. "It's not just me,
Coop."

"You think I don't want the kid? God, open your eyes. I'm crazy about him. I fell for him before I fell for you. I want to marry both of you, then maybe have another kid or two so I can start out on the ground floor. We already worked that out."

"You— Who did what?"

He swore, stepped back, shrugged. "I kind of ran it by the kid. I figured I should smooth the way a little, and find out where he stood." When she just stared, he jammed his hands in his pockets. "It didn't seem fair not to bring him into it, since he'd be mine."

"Yours," she murmured, staring blindly into her wine.

"Since you two are a team, it would be sort of like an expansion. Anyway, he's for it. So it's two against one."

"I see."

"Maybe I don't know a lot about the daddy stuff, but I love him. That's a good start."

She looked at him again, looked into his eyes. Her heart opened, flooded. "It's a good one, all right."

"I love you." His hands relaxed in his pockets. "That's the first time I've said that to any woman— except my mother. I love you, Zoe. So why don't you marry me and give me and the kid a break?"

"It looks like I'm outvoted." She lifted a hand to his cheek.

"Is that a yes?"

"That's definitely a yes." She laughed as he swung her into his arms. "Daddy."

"I like the sound of that." He crushed his lips down on hers. "I like it a lot."

* * * * *

For Dan, with thanks for the idea
and the tons of research material.
And for Jason, for keeping me in tune
with the ten-year-old mind.

Chapter 1

Zark drew a painful breath, knowing it could be his last. The ship was nearly out of oxygen, and he was nearly out of time. A life span could pass in front of the eyes in a matter of seconds. He was grateful that he was alone so no one else could witness his joys and mistakes.

Leilah, it was always Leilah. With each ragged breath he could see her, the clear blue eyes and golden hair of his one and only beloved. As the warning siren inside the cockpit wailed, he could hear Leilah's laughter. Tender, sweet. Then mocking.

"By the red sun, how happy we were together!" The words shuddered out between gasps as he dragged himself over the floor toward the command console. "Lovers, partners, friends."

The pain in his lungs grew worse. It seared through

him like dozens of hot knives tipped with poison from the pits of Argenham. He couldn't waste air on useless words. But his thoughts…his thoughts even now were on Leilah.

That she, the only woman he had ever loved, should be the cause of his ultimate destruction! His destruction, and the world's as they knew it. What fiendish twist of fate had caused the freak accident that had turned her from a devoted scientist to a force of evil and hate?

She was his enemy now, the woman who had once been his wife. Who was still his wife, Zark told himself as he painfully pulled himself up to the console. If he lived, and stopped her latest scheme to obliterate civilization on Perth, he would have to go after her. He would have to destroy her. If he had the strength.

Commander Zark, Defender of the Universe, Leader of Perth, hero and husband, pressed a trembling finger to the button.

CONTINUED IN THE NEXT EXCITING ISSUE!

"Damn!" Radley Wallace mumbled the oath, then looked around quickly to be sure his mother hadn't heard. He'd started to swear, mostly in whispers, about six months ago, and wasn't anxious for her to find out. She'd get that look on her face.

But she was busy going through the first boxes the movers had delivered. He was supposed to be putting his books away, but had decided it was time to take a break. He liked breaks best when they included Universal Comics and Commander Zark. His mother liked him to read real books, but they didn't have many pictures. As far as Radley was concerned, Zark had it all over Long John Silver or Huck Finn.

Rolling over on his back, Radley stared at the freshly painted ceiling of his new room. The new apartment was okay. Mostly he liked the view of the park, and having an elevator was cool. But he wasn't looking forward to starting in a new school on Monday.

Mom had told him it would be fine, that he would make new friends and still be able to visit with some of the old ones. She was real good about it, stroking his hair and smiling in that way that made him feel everything was really okay. But she wouldn't be there when all the kids gave him the once-over. He wasn't going to wear that new sweater, either, even if Mom said the color matched his eyes. He wanted to wear one of his old sweatshirts so at least something would be familiar. He figured she'd understand, because Mom always did.

She still looked sad sometimes, though. Radley squirmed up to the pillow with the comic clutched in his hand. He wished she wouldn't feel bad because his father had gone away. It had been a long time now, and he had to think hard to bring a picture of his father to his mind. He never visited, and only phoned a couple of times a year. That was okay. Radley wished he could tell his mother it was okay, but he was afraid she'd get upset and start crying.

He didn't really need a dad when he had her. He'd told her that once, and she'd hugged him so hard he hadn't been able to breathe. Then he'd heard her crying in her room that night. So he hadn't told her that again.

Big people were funny, Radley thought with the wisdom of his almost ten years. But his mom was the best. She hardly ever yelled at him, and was always sorry when she did. And she was pretty. Radley smiled as he began to sleep. He guessed his mom was just about as pretty as Princess Leilah. Even though her hair was brown instead of golden and her eyes were gray instead of cobalt blue.

She'd promised they could have pizza for dinner, too, to celebrate their new apartment. He liked pizza best, next to Commander Zark.

He drifted off to sleep so he, with the help of Zark, could save the universe.

When Hester looked in a short time later, she saw her son, her universe, dreaming with an issue of Universal Comics in his hand. Most of his books, some of which he paged through from time to time, were still in the packing boxes. Another time she would have given him a mild lecture on responsibility when he woke, but she didn't have the heart for it now. He was taking the move so well. Another upheaval in his life.

"This one's going to be good for you, sweetie." Forgetting the mountain of her own unpacking, she sat on the edge of the bed to watch him.

He looked so much like his father. The dark blond hair, the dark eyes and sturdy chin. It was a rare thing now for her to look at her son and think of the man who had been her husband. But today was different. Today was another beginning for them, and beginnings made her think of endings.

Over six years now, she thought, a bit amazed at the passage of time. Radley had been just a toddler when Allan had walked out on them, tired of bills, tired of family, tired of her in particular. That pain had passed, though it had been a long, slow process. But she had never forgiven, and would never forgive, the man for leaving his son without a second glance.

Sometimes she worried that it seemed to mean so little to Radley. Selfishly she was relieved that he had never formed a strong, enduring bond with the man who would leave them behind, yet she often wondered, late at night when everything was quiet, if her little boy held something inside.

When she looked at him, it didn't seem possible. Hester stroked his hair now and turned to look at his view of Central Park. Radley was outgoing, happy and good-natured. She'd worked hard to help him be those things. She never spoke ill of his father, though there had been times, especially in the early years, when the bitterness and anger had simmered very close to the surface. She'd tried to be both mother and father, and most of the time thought she'd succeeded.

She'd read books on baseball so she would know how to coach him. She'd raced beside him, clinging to the back of the seat of his first two-wheeler. When it had been time to let go, she'd forced back the urge to hang on and had cheered as he'd made his wobbly way down the bike path.

She even knew about Commander Zark. With a smile, Hester eased the wrinkled comic book from his fist. Poor, heroic Zark and his misguided wife Leilah. Yes, Hester knew all about Perth's politics and tribulations. Trying to wean Radley from Zark to Dickens or Twain wasn't easy, but neither was raising a child on your own.

"There's time enough," she murmured as she stretched out beside her son. Time enough for real books and for real life. "Oh, Rad, I hope I've done the right thing." She closed her eyes, wishing, as she'd learned to wish rarely, that she had someone to talk to, someone who could advise her or make decisions, right or wrong.

Then, with her arm hooked around her son's waist, she, too, slept.

The room was dim with dusk when she awoke, groggy and disoriented. The first thing Hester realized was that Radley was no longer curled beside her. Grogginess disappeared in a quick flash of panic she knew was foolish. Radley could be trusted not to leave the apartment without permission. He wasn't a blindly obedient child, but her top ten rules were respected. Rising, she went to find him.

"Hi, Mom." He was in the kitchen, where her homing instinct had taken her first. He held a dripping peanut butter and jelly sandwich in his hands.

"I thought you wanted pizza," she said, noting the good-sized glop of jelly on the counter and the yet-to-be-resealed loaf of bread.

"I do." He took a healthy bite, then grinned. "But I needed something now."

"Don't talk with your mouth full, Rad," she said automatically, even as she bent to kiss him. "You could have woken me if you were hungry."

"That's okay, but I couldn't find the glasses."

She glanced around, seeing that he'd emptied two boxes in his quest. Hester reminded herself that she should have made the kitchen arrangements her first priority. "Well, we can take care of that."

"It was snowing when I woke up."

"Was it?" Hester pushed the hair out of her eyes and straightened to see for herself. "Still is."

"Maybe it'll snow ten feet and there won't be any

school on Monday." Radley climbed onto a stool to sit at the kitchen counter.

Along with no first day on the new job, Hester thought, indulging in some wishful thinking of her own for a moment. No new pressures, new responsibilities. "I don't think there's much chance of that." As she washed out glasses, she looked over her shoulder. "Are you really worried about it, Rad?"

"Sort of." He shrugged his shoulders. Monday was still a day away. A lot could happen. Earthquakes, blizzards, an attack from outer space. He concentrated on the last.

He, Captain Radley Wallace of Earth's Special Forces, would protect and shield, would fight to the death, would—

"I could go in with you if you'd like."

"Aw, Mom, the kids would make fun of me." He bit into his sandwich. Grape jelly oozed out the sides. "It won't be so bad. At least that dumb Angela Wiseberry won't be at this school."

She didn't have the heart to tell him there was a dumb Angela Wiseberry at every school. "Tell you what. We'll both go to our new jobs Monday, then convene back here at 1600 for a full report."

His face brightened instantly. There was nothing Radley liked better than a military operation. "Aye, aye, sir."

"Good. Now I'll order the pizza, and while we're waiting we'll put the rest of the dishes away."

"Let the prisoners do it."

"Escaped. All of them."

"Heads will roll," Radley mumbled as he stuffed the last of the sandwich into his mouth.

* * *

Mitchell Dempsey II sat at his drawing board without an idea in his head. He sipped cold coffee, hoping it would stimulate his imagination, but his mind remained as blank as the paper in front of him. Blocks happened, he knew, but they rarely happened to him. And not on deadline. Of course, he was going about it backward. Mitch cracked another peanut, then tossed the shell in the direction of the bowl. It hit the side and fell on the floor to join several others. Normally the story line would have come first, then the illustrations. Since he'd been having no luck that way, Mitch had switched in the hope that the change in routine would jog something loose.

It wasn't working, and neither was he.

Closing his eyes, Mitch tried for an out-of-body experience. The old Slim Whitman song on the radio cruised on, but he didn't hear it. He was traveling light-years away; a century was passing. The second millennium, he thought with a smile. He'd been born too soon. Though he didn't think he could blame his parents for having him a hundred years too early.

Nothing came. No solutions, no inspiration. Mitch opened his eyes again and stared at the blank white paper. With an editor like Rich Skinner, he couldn't afford to claim artistic temperament. Famine or plague would barely get you by. Disgusted, Mitch reached for another peanut.

What he needed was a change of scene, a distraction. His life was becoming too settled, too ordinary and, despite the temporary block, too easy. He needed challenge. Pitching the shells, he rose to pace.

He had a long, limber body made solid by the hours

he spent each week with weights. As a boy he'd been preposterously skinny, though he'd always eaten like a horse. He hadn't minded the teasing too much until he'd discovered girls. Then, with the quiet determination he'd been born with, Mitch had changed what could be changed. It had taken him a couple of years and a lot of sweat to build himself, but he had. He still didn't take his body for granted, and exercised it as regularly as he did his mind.

His office was littered with books, all read and reread. He was tempted to pull one out now and bury himself in it. But he was on deadline. The big brown mutt on the floor rolled over on his stomach and watched.

Mitch had named him Taz, after the Tasmanian Devil from the old Warner Brothers cartoons, but Taz was hardly a whirlwind of energy. He yawned now and rubbed his back lazily on the rug. He liked Mitch. Mitch never expected him to do anything that he didn't care to, and hardly ever complained about dog hair on the furniture or an occasional forage into the trash. Mitch had a nice voice, too, low and patient. Taz liked it best when Mitch sat on the floor with him and stroked his heavy brown fur, talking out one of his ideas. Taz could look up into the lean face as if he understood every word.

Taz liked Mitch's face, too. It was kind and strong, and the mouth rarely firmed into a disapproving line. His eyes were pale and dreamy. Mitch's wide, strong hands knew the right places to scratch. Taz was a very contented dog. He yawned and went back to sleep.

When the knock came to the door, the dog stirred enough to thump his tail and make a series of low noises in his throat.

"No, I'm not expecting anyone. You?" Mitch responded. "I'll go see." He stepped on peanut shells in his bare feet and swore, but didn't bother to stoop and pick them up. There was a pile of newspapers to be skirted around, and a bag of clothes that hadn't made it to the laundry. Taz had left one of his bones on the Aubusson. Mitch simply kicked it into a corner before he opened the door.

"Pizza delivery."

A scrawny kid of about eighteen was holding a box that smelled like heaven. Mitch took one long, avaricious sniff. "I didn't order any."

"This 406?"

"Yeah, but I didn't order any pizza." He sniffed again. "Wish I had."

"Wallace?"

"Dempsey."

"Shoot."

Wallace, Mitch thought as the kid shifted from foot to foot. Wallace was taking over the Henley apartment, 604. He rubbed a hand over his chin and considered. If Wallace was that leggy brunette he'd seen hauling in boxes that morning, it might be worth investigating.

"I know the Wallaces," he said, and pulled crumpled bills out of his pocket. "I'll take it on up to them."

"I don't know, I shouldn't—"

"Worry about a thing," Mitch finished, and added another bill. Pizza and the new neighbor might be just the distraction he needed.

The boy counted his tip. "Okay, thanks." For all he knew, the Wallaces wouldn't be half as generous.

With the box balanced in his hand, Mitch started out. Then he remembered his keys. He took a moment to search through his worn jeans before he remembered he'd tossed them at the gateleg table when he'd come in the night before. He found them under it, stuck them in one pocket, found the hole in it and stuck them in the other. He hoped the pizza had some pepperoni.

"That should be the pizza," Hester announced, but caught Radley before he could dash to the door. "Let me open it. Remember the rules?"

"Don't open the door unless you know who it is," Radley recited, rolling his eyes behind his mother's back.

Hester put a hand on the knob, but checked the peephole. She frowned a little at the face. She'd have sworn the man was looking straight back at her with amused and very clear blue eyes. His hair was dark and shaggy, as if it hadn't seen a barber or a comb in a little too long. But the face was fascinating, lean and bony and unshaven.

"Mom, are you going to open it?"

"What?" Hester stepped back when she realized she'd been staring at the delivery boy for a good deal longer than necessary.

"I'm starving," Radley reminded her.

"Sorry." Hester opened the door and discovered the fascinating face went with a long, athletic body. And bare feet.

"Did you order pizza?"

"Yes." But it was snowing outside. What was he doing barefoot?

"Good." Before Hester realized his intention, Mitch strolled inside.

"I'll take that," Hester said quickly. "Take this into the kitchen, Radley." She shielded her son with her body and wondered if she'd need a weapon.

"Nice place." Mitch looked casually around at crates and open boxes.

"I'll get your money."

"It's on the house." Mitch smiled at her. Hester wondered if the self-defense course she'd taken two years before would come back to her.

"Radley, take that into the kitchen while I pay the delivery man."

"Neighbor," Mitch corrected. "I'm in 406—you know, two floors down. The pizza got delivered to my place by mistake."

"I see." But for some reason it didn't make her any less nervous. "I'm sorry for the trouble." Hester reached for her purse.

"I took care of it." He wasn't sure whether she looked more likely to lunge or to flee, but he'd been right about her being worth investigating. She was a tall one, he thought, model height, with that same kind of understated body. Her rich, warm brown hair was pulled back from a diamond-shaped face dominated by big gray eyes and a mouth just one size too large.

"Why don't you consider the pizza my version of the welcoming committee?"

"That's really very kind, but I couldn't—"

"Refuse such a neighborly offer?"

Because she was a bit too cool and reserved for his taste, Mitch looked past her to the boy. "Hi, I'm Mitch." This time his smile was answered.

"I'm Rad. We just moved in."

"So I see. From out of town?"

"Uh-uh. We just changed apartments because Mom got a new job and the other was too small. I can see the park from my window."

"Me, too."

"Excuse me, Mr.—?"

"It's Mitch," he repeated with a glance at Hester.

"Yes, well, it's very kind of you to bring this up." As well as being very odd, she thought. "But I don't want to impose on your time."

"You can have a piece," Radley invited. "We never finish it all."

"Rad, I'm sure Mr.—Mitch has things to do."

"Not a thing." He knew his manners, had been taught them painstakingly. Another time, he might even have put them to use and bowed out, but something about the woman's reserve and the child's warmth made him obstinate. "Got a beer?"

"No, I'm sorry, I—"

"We've got soda," Radley piped up. "Mom lets me have one sometimes." There was nothing Radley liked more than company. He gave Mitch a totally ingenuous smile. "Want to see the kitchen?"

"Love to." With something close to a smirk for Hester, Mitch followed the boy.

She stood in the center of the room for a moment, hands on her hips, unsure whether to be exasperated or furious. The last thing she wanted after a day of lugging boxes was company. Especially a stranger's. The only thing to do now was to give him a piece of the damn pizza and blot out her obligation to him.

"We've got a garbage disposal. It makes great noises."

"I bet." Obligingly Mitch leaned over the sink while Radley flipped the switch.

"Rad, don't run that with nothing in it. As you can

see, we're a bit disorganized yet." Hester went to the freshly lined cupboard for plates.

"I've been here for five years, and I'm still disorganized."

"We're going to get a kitten." Radley climbed up on a stool, then reached for the napkins his mother had already put in one of her little wicker baskets. "The other place wouldn't allow pets, but we can have one here, can't we, Mom?"

"As soon as we're settled, Rad. Diet or regular?" she asked Mitch.

"Regular's fine. Looks like you've gotten a lot accomplished in one day." The kitchen was neat as a pin. A thriving asparagus fern hung in a macramé holder in the single window. She had less space than he did, which he thought was too bad. She would probably make better use of the kitchen than he. He took another glance around before settling at the counter. Stuck to the refrigerator was a large crayon drawing of a spaceship. "You do that?" Mitch asked Rad.

"Yeah." He picked up the pizza his mother had set on his plate and bit in eagerly—peanut butter and jelly long since forgotten.

"It's good."

"It's supposed to be the Second Millennium, that's Commander Zark's ship."

"I know." Mitch took a healthy bite of his own slice. "You did a good job."

As he plowed through his pizza, Radley took it for granted that Mitch would recognize Zark's name and mode of transportation. As far as he was concerned, everybody did. "I've been trying to do the Defiance,

Leilah's ship, but it's harder. Anyway, I think Commander Zark might blow it up in the next issue."

"Think so?" Mitch gave Hester an easy smile as she joined them at the counter.

"I don't know, he's in a pretty tough spot right now."

"He'll get out okay."

"Do you read comic books?" Hester asked. It wasn't until she sat down that she noticed how large his hands were. He might have been dressed with disregard, but his hands were clean and had the look of easy competence.

"All the time."

"I've got the biggest collection of all my friends. Mom got me the very first issue with Commander Zark in it for Christmas. It's ten years old. He was only a captain then. Want to see?"

The boy was a gem, Mitch thought, sweet, bright and unaffected. He'd have to reserve judgment on the mother. "Yeah, I'd like that."

Before Hester could tell him to finish his dinner, Radley was off and running. She sat in silence a moment, wondering what sort of man actually read comic books. Oh, she paged through them from time to time to keep a handle on what her son was consuming, but to actually read them? An adult?

"Terrific kid."

"Yes, he is. It's nice of you to…listen to him talk about his comics."

"Comics are my life," Mitch said, straight-faced.

Her reserve broke down long enough for her to stare at him. Clearing her throat, Hester went back to her meal. "I see."

Mitch put his tongue in his cheek. She was some

piece of work, all right, he decided. First meeting or not, he saw no reason to resist egging her on. "I take it you don't."

"Don't what?"

"Read comic books."

"No, I, ah, don't have a lot of time for light reading." She rolled her eyes, unaware that that was where Radley had picked up the habit. "Would you like another piece?"

"Yeah." He helped himself before she could serve him. "You ought to take some time, you know. Comics can be very educational. What's the new job?"

"Oh, I'm in banking. I'm the loan officer for National Trust."

Mitch gave an appreciative whistle. "Big job for someone your age."

Hester stiffened automatically. "I've been in banking since I was sixteen."

Touchy, too, he mused as he licked sauce from his thumb. "That was supposed to be a compliment. I have a feeling you don't take them well." Tough lady, he decided, then thought perhaps she'd had to be. There was no ring on her finger, not even the faintest white mark to show there had been one recently. "I've done some business with banks myself. You know, deposits, withdrawals, returned checks."

She shifted uncomfortably, wondering what was taking Radley so long. There was something unnerving about being alone with this man. Though she had always felt comfortable with eye contact, she was having a difficult time with Mitch. He never looked away for very long.

"I didn't mean to be abrupt."

"No, I don't suppose you did. If I wanted a loan at National Trust, who would I ask for?"

"Mrs. Wallace."

Definitely a tough one. "Mrs. is your first name?"

"Hester," she said, not understanding why she resented giving him that much.

"Hester, then." Mitch offered a hand. "Nice to meet you."

Her lips curved a bit. It was a cautious smile, Mitch thought, but better than none at all. "I'm sorry if I've been rude, but it's been a long day. A long week, really."

"I hate moving." He waited until she'd unbent enough to put her hand in his. Hers was cool and as slender as the rest of her. "Got anyone to help you?"

"No." She removed her hand, because his was as overwhelming as it looked. "We're doing fine."

"I can see that." *No Help Wanted.* The sign was up and posted in big letters. He'd known a few women like her, so fiercely independent, so suspicious of men in general that they had not only a defensive shield but an arsenal of poisonous darts behind it. A sensible man gave them a wide berth. Too bad, because she was a looker, and the kid was definitely a kick.

"I forgot where I'd packed it." Radley came back in, flushed with the effort. "It's a classic, the dealer even told Mom."

He'd also charged her an arm and a leg for it, Hester thought. But it had meant more to Radley than any of his other presents.

"Mint condition, too." Mitch turned the first page with the care of a jeweler cutting a diamond.

"I always make sure my hands are clean before I read it."

"Good idea." It was amazing that after all this time the pride would still be there. An enormous feeling it was, too, a huge burst of satisfaction.

It was there on the first page. Story and drawings by Mitch Dempsey. Commander Zark was his baby, and in ten years they'd become very close friends.

"It's a great story. It really explains why Commander Zark devoted his life to defending the universe against evil and corruption."

"Because his family had been wiped out by the evil Red Arrow in his search for power."

"Yeah." Radley's face lit up. "But he got even with Red Arrow."

"In issue 73."

Hester put her chin in her hand and stared at the two of them. The man was serious, she realized, not just humoring the child. He was as obsessed by comic books as her nine-year-old son.

Strange, he looked fairly normal; he even spoke well. In fact, sitting next to him had been uncomfortable largely because he was so blatantly masculine, with that tough body, angular face and large hands. Hester shook off her thoughts quickly. She certainly didn't want to lean in that direction toward a neighbor, particularly not one whose mental level seemed to have gotten stuck in adolescence.

Mitch turned a couple of pages. His drawing had improved over a decade. It helped to remind himself of that. But he'd managed to maintain the same purity, the same straightforward images that had come to him ten years ago when he'd been struggling unhappily in commercial art.

"Is he your favorite?" Mitch pointed a blunt fingertip toward a drawing of Zark.

"Oh, sure. I like Three Faces, and the Black Diamond's pretty neat, but Commander Zark's my favorite."

"Mine, too." Mitch ruffled the boy's hair. He hadn't realized when he'd delivered a pizza that he would find the inspiration he'd been struggling for all afternoon.

"You can read this sometime. I'd lend it to you, but—"

"I understand." He closed the book carefully and handed it back. "You can't lend out a collector's item."

"I'd better put it away."

"Before you know it, you and Rad will be trading issues." Hester stood up to clear the plates.

"That amuses the hell out of you, doesn't it?"

His tone had her glancing over quickly. There wasn't precisely an edge to it, and his eyes were still clear and mild, but…something warned her to take care.

"I didn't mean to insult you. I just find it unusual for a grown man to read comic books as a habit." She stacked the plates in the dishwasher. "I've always thought it was something boys grew out of at a certain age, but I suppose one could consider it, what, a hobby?"

His brow lifted. She was facing him again, that half smile on her lips. Obviously she was trying to make amends. He didn't think she should get off quite that easily. "Comic books are anything but a hobby with me, Mrs. Hester Wallace. I not only read them, I write them."

"Holy cow, really?" Radley stood staring at Mitch as though he'd just been crowned king. "Do you really? Honest? Oh, boy, are you Mitch Dempsey? The real Mitch Dempsey?"

"In the flesh." He tugged on Radley's ear while Hester looked at him as though he'd stepped in from another planet.

"Oh, boy, Mitch Dempsey right here! Mom, this is Commander Zark. None of the kids are going to believe it. Do you believe it, Mom, Commander Zark right here in our kitchen!"

"No," Hester murmured as she continued to stare. "I can't believe it."

Chapter 2

Hester wished she could afford to be a coward. It would be so easy to go back home, pull the covers over her head and hide out until Radley came home from school. No one who saw her would suspect that her stomach was in knots or that her palms were sweaty despite the frigid wind that whipped down the stairs as she emerged from the subway with a crowd of Manhattan's workforce.

If anyone had bothered to look, they would have seen a composed, slightly preoccupied woman in a long red wool coat and white scarf. Fortunately for Hester, the wind tunnel created by the skyscrapers whipped color into cheeks that would have been deadly pale. She had to concentrate on not chewing off her lipstick as she walked the half block to National Trust. And to her first day on the job.

It would only take her ten minutes to get back home, lock herself in and phone the office with some excuse. She was sick, there'd been a death in the family—preferably hers. She'd been robbed.

Hester clutched her briefcase tighter and kept walking. Big talk, she berated herself. She'd walked Radley to school that morning spouting off cheerful nonsense about how exciting new beginnings were, how much fun it was to start something new. Baloney, she thought, and hoped the little guy wasn't half as scared as she was.

She'd earned the position, Hester reminded herself. She was qualified and competent, with twelve years of experience under her belt. And she was scared right out of her shoes. Taking a deep breath, she walked into National Trust.

Laurence Rosen, the bank manager, checked his watch, gave a nod of approval and strode over to greet her. His dark blue suit was trim and conservative. A woman could have powdered her nose in the reflection from his shiny black shoes. "Right on time, Mrs. Wallace, an excellent beginning. I pride myself on having a staff that makes optimum use of time." He gestured toward the back of the bank, and her office.

"I'm looking forward to getting started, Mr. Rosen," she said, and felt a wave of relief that it was true. She'd always liked the feel of a bank before the doors opened to the public. The cathedral-like quiet, the pregame anticipation.

"Good, good, we'll do our best to keep you busy." He noted with a slight frown that two secretaries were not yet at their desks. In a habitual gesture, he passed a hand over his hair. "Your assistant will be in momentarily. Once you're settled, Mrs. Wallace, I'll expect you to keep close tabs on her comings and goings. Your efficiency depends largely on hers."

"Of course."

Her office was small and dull. She tried not to wish for something airier—or to notice that Rosen was as stuffy as they came. The increase this job would bring to her income would make things better for Radley. That, as always, was the bottom line. She'd make it work, Hester told herself as she took off her coat. She'd make it work well.

Rosen obviously approved of her trim black suit and understated jewelry. There was no room for flashy clothes or behavior in banking. "I trust you looked over the files I gave you."

"I familiarized myself with them over the weekend." She moved behind the desk, knowing it would establish her position. "I believe I understand National Trust's policy and procedure."

"Excellent, excellent. I'll leave you to get organized then. Your first appointment's at—" he turned pages over on her desk calendar "—9:15. If you have any problems, contact me. I'm always around somewhere."

She would have bet on it. "I'm sure everything will be fine, Mr. Rosen. Thank you."

With a final nod, Rosen strode out. The door closed behind him with a quiet click. Alone, Hester let herself slide bonelessly into her chair. She'd gotten past the first hurdle, she told herself. Rosen thought she was competent and suitable. Now all she had to do was be those things. She would be, because too much was riding on it. Not the least of those things was her pride. She hated making a fool of herself. She'd certainly done a good job of that the night before with the new neighbor.

Even hours later, remembering it, her cheeks warmed. She hadn't meant to insult the man's—even now she couldn't bring herself to call it a profession—his work, then, Hester decided. She certainly hadn't meant to make any personal observations. The problem had been that she hadn't been as much on her guard as usual. The man had thrown her off by inviting himself in and joining them for dinner and charming Radley, all in a matter of minutes. She wasn't used to people popping into her life. And she didn't like it.

Radley loved it. Hester picked up a sharpened pencil with the bank's logo on the side. He'd practically glowed with excitement, and hadn't been able to speak of anything else even after Mitch Dempsey had left.

She could be grateful for one thing. The visit had taken Radley's mind off the new school. Radley had always made friends easily, and if this Mitch was willing to give her son some pleasure, she shouldn't criticize. In any case, the man seemed harmless enough. Hester refused to admit to the uncomfortable thrill she'd experienced when his hand had closed over hers. What possible trouble could come from a man who wrote comic books for a living? She caught herself chewing at her lipstick at the question.

The knock on the door was brief and cheerful. Before she could call out, it was pushed open.

"Good morning, Mrs. Wallace. I'm Kay Lorimar, your assistant. Remember, we met for a few minutes a couple of weeks ago."

"Yes, good morning, Kay." Her assistant was everything Hester had always wanted to be herself: petite, well-rounded, blond, with small delicate features. She folded her hands on the fresh blotter and tried to look authoritative.

"Sorry I'm late." Kay smiled and didn't look the least bit sorry. "Everything takes longer than you think it does on Monday. Even if I pretend it's Tuesday it doesn't seem to help. I don't know why. Would you like some coffee?"

"No, thank you, I've an appointment in a few minutes."

"Just ring if you change your mind." Kay paused at the door. "This place could sure use some cheering up, it's dark as a dungeon. Mr. Blowfield, that's who you're replacing, he liked things dull—matched him, you know." Her smile was ingenuous, but Hester hesitated to answer it. It would hardly do for her to get a reputation as a gossip the first day on the job. "Anyway, if you decide to do any redecorating, let me know. My roommate's into interior design. He's a real artist."

"Thank you." How was she supposed to run an office with a pert little cheerleader in tow? Hester wondered. One day at a time. "Just send Mr. and Mrs. Browning in when they arrive, Kay."

"Yes, ma'am." She sure was more pleasant to look at than old Blowfield, Kay thought. But it looked as if she had the same soul. "Loan application forms are in the bottom left drawer of the desk, arranged according to type. Legal pads in the right. Bank stationery, top right. The list of current interest rates are in the middle drawer. The Brownings are looking for a loan to remodel their loft as they're expecting a child. He's in electronics, she works part-time at Bloomingdale's. They've been advised what papers to bring with them. I can make copies while they're here."

Hester lifted her brow. "Thank you, Kay," she said, not certain whether to be amused or impressed.

When the door closed again, Hester sat back and smiled. The office might be dull, but if the morning was any indication, nothing else at National Trust was going to be.

Mitch liked having a window that faced the front of the building. That way, whenever he took a break, he could watch the comings and goings. After five years, he figured he knew every tenant by sight and half of them by name. When things were slow or, better, when he was ahead of the game, he whiled away time by sketching the more interesting of them. If his time stretched further, he made a story line to go with the faces.

He considered it the best of practice because it amused him. Occasionally there was a face interesting enough to warrant special attention. Sometimes it was a cabdriver or a delivery boy. Mitch had learned to look close and quick, then sketch from lingering impressions. Years before, he had sketched faces for a living, if a pitiful one. Now he sketched them for entertainment and was a great deal more satisfied.

He spotted Hester and her son when they were still half a block away. The red coat she wore stood out like a beacon. It certainly made a statement, Mitch mused as he picked up his pencil. He wondered if the coolly distant Mrs. Wallace realized what signals she was sending out. He doubted it.

He didn't need to see her face to draw it. Already there were a half a dozen rough sketches of her tossed on the table in his workroom. Interesting features, he told himself as his pencil began to fly across the pad. Any artist would be compelled to capture them.

The boy was walking along beside her, his face all but obscured by a woolen scarf and hat. Even from this distance, Mitch could see the boy was chattering earnestly. His head was angled up toward his mother. Every now and again she would glance down as if to comment; then the boy would take over again. A few steps away from the building, she stopped. Mitch saw the wind catch at her hair as she tossed her head back and laughed. His fingers went limp on the pencil as he leaned closer to the window. He wanted to be nearer, near enough to hear the laugh, to see if her eyes lit up with it. He imagined they did, but how? Would that subtle, calm gray go silvery or smoky?

She continued to walk, and in seconds was in the building and out of sight.

Mitch stared down at his sketch pad. He had no more than a few lines and contours. He couldn't finish it, he thought as he set the pencil down. He could only see her laughing now, and to capture that on paper he'd need a closer look.

Picking up his keys, he jangled them in his hand. He'd given her the better part of a week. The aloof Mrs. Wallace might consider another neighborly visit out of line, but he didn't. Besides, he liked the kid. Mitch would have gone upstairs to see him before, but he'd been busy fleshing out his story. He owed the kid for that, too, Mitch considered. The little weekend visit had not only crumbled the block, but had given Mitch enough fuel for three issues. Yeah, he owed the kid.

He pushed the keys into his pocket and walked into his workroom. Taz was there, a bone clamped between his paws as he snoozed. "Don't get up," Mitch said mildly. "I'm going out for a while." As he spoke, he ruffled through papers. Taz opened his eyes to half-mast and grumbled. "I don't know how long I'll be." After wracking through his excuse for a filing system, Mitch found the sketch. Commander Zark in full military regalia, sober-faced, sad-eyed, his gleaming ship at his back. Beneath it was the caption: THE MISSION: Capture Princess Leilah—or DESTROY her!!

Mitch wished briefly that he had the time to ink and color it, but figured the kid would like it as is. With a careless stroke he signed it, then rolled it into a tube.

"Don't wait dinner for me," he instructed Taz.

"I'll get it!" Radley danced to the door. It was Friday, and school was light-years away.

"Ask who it is."

Radley put his hand on the knob and shook his head. He'd been going to ask. Probably. "Who is it?"

"It's Mitch."

"It's Mitch!" Radley shouted, delighted. In the bedroom, Hester scowled and pulled the sweatshirt over her head.

"Hi." Breathless with excitement, Radley opened the door to his latest hero.

"Hi, Rad, how's it going?"

"Fine. I don't have any homework all weekend." He reached out a hand to draw Mitch inside. "I wanted to come down and see you, but Mom said no 'cause you'd be working or something."

"Or something," Mitch muttered. "Look, it's okay with me if you come over. Anytime."

"Really?"

"Really." The kid was irresistible, Mitch thought as he ruffled the boy's hair. Too bad his mother wasn't as friendly. "I thought you might like this." Mitch handed him the rolled sketch.

"Oh, wow." Awestruck, reverent, Radley stared at the drawing. "Jeez, Commander Zark and the Second Millennium. Can I have it, really? To keep?"

"Yeah."

"I gotta show Mom." Radley turned and dashed toward the bedroom as Hester came out. "Look what Mitch gave me. Isn't it great? He said I could keep it and everything."

"It's terrific." She put a hand on Radley's shoulder as she studied the sketch. The man was certainly talented, Hester decided. Even if he had chosen such an odd way to show it. Her hand remained on Radley's shoulder as she looked over at Mitch. "That was very nice of you."

He liked the way she looked in the pastel sweats, casual, approachable, if not completely relaxed. Her hair was down, too, with the ends just sweeping short of her shoulders. Parted softly on the side and unpinned, it gave her a completely different look.

"I wanted to thank Rad." Mitch forced himself to look away from her face, then smiled at the boy. "You helped me through a block last weekend."

"I did?" Radley's eyes widened. "Honest?"

"Honest. I was stuck, spinning wheels. After I talked to you that night, I went down and everything fell into place. I appreciate it."

"Wow, you're welcome. You could stay for dinner again. We're just having Chinese chicken, and maybe I could help you some more. It's okay, isn't it, Mom? Isn't it?"

Trapped again. And again she caught the gleam of amusement in Mitch's eyes. "Of course."

"Great. I want to go hang this up right away. Can I call Josh, too, and tell him about it? He won't believe it."

"Sure." She barely had time to run a hand over his hair before he was off and running.

"Thanks, Mitch." Radley paused at the turn of the hallway. "Thanks a lot."

Hester found the deep side pockets in her sweats and slipped her hands inside. There was absolutely no reason for the man to make her nervous. So why did he? "That was really very kind of you."

"Maybe, but I haven't done anything that's made me feel that good in a long time." He wasn't completely at ease himself, Mitch discovered, and he tucked his thumbs into the back pockets of his jeans. "You work fast," he commented as he glanced around the living room.

The boxes were gone. Bright, vivid prints hung on the walls and a vase of flowers, fresh as morning, sat near the window, where sheer curtains filtered the light. Pillows were plumped, furniture gleamed. The only signs of confusion were a miniature car wreck and a few plastic men scattered on the carpet. He was glad to see them. It meant she wasn't the type who expected the boy to play only in his room.

"Dali?" He walked over to a lithograph hung over the sofa.

She caught her bottom lip between her teeth as Mitch studied one of her rare extravagances. "I bought that in a little shop on Fifth that's always going out of business."

"Yeah, I know the one. It didn't take you long to put things together here."

"I wanted everything back to normal as soon as possible. The move wasn't easy for Radley."

"And you?" He turned then, catching her off guard with the sudden sharp look.

"Me? I—ah…"

"You know," he began as he crossed over to her, attracted by her simple bafflement. "You're a lot more articulate when you talk about Rad than you are when you talk about Hester."

She stepped back quickly, aware that he would have touched her and totally unsure what her reaction might have been. "I should start dinner."

"Want some help?"

"With what?"

This time she didn't move quickly enough. He cupped her chin in his hand and smiled. "With dinner."

It had been a long time since a man had touched her that way. He had a strong hand with gentle fingers. That had to be the reason her heart leaped up to her throat and pounded there. "Can you cook?"

What incredible eyes she had. So clear, so pale a gray they were almost translucent. For the first time in years he felt the urge to paint, just to see if he could bring those eyes to life on canvas. "I make a hell of a peanut butter sandwich."

She lifted a hand to his wrist, to move his away, she thought. But her fingers lay there lightly a moment, experimenting. "How are you at chopping vegetables?"

"I think I can handle it."

"All right, then." She backed up, amazed that she had allowed the contact to go for so long. "I still don't have any beer, but I do have some wine this time."

"Fine." What the hell were they talking about? Why

were they talking at all, when she had a mouth that was made to fit on a man's? A little baffled by his own train of thought, he followed her into the kitchen.

"It's really a simple meal," she began. "But when it's all mixed up, Radley hardly notices he's eating something nutritious. A Twinkie's the true way to his heart."

"My kind of kid."

She smiled a little, more relaxed now that she had her hands full. She set celery and mushrooms on the chopping block. "The trick's in moderation." Hester took the chicken out, then remembered the wine. "I'm willing to concede to Rad's sweet tooth in small doses. He's willing to accept broccoli on the same terms."

"Sounds like a wise arrangement." She opened the wine. Inexpensive, he thought with a glance at the label, but palatable. She filled two glasses, then handed him one. It was silly, but her hands were damp again. It had been some time since she'd shared a bottle of wine or fixed a simple dinner with a man. "To neighbors," he said, and thought she relaxed fractionally as he touched his glass to hers.

"Why don't you sit down while I bone the chicken? Then you can deal with the vegetables."

He didn't sit, but did lean back against the counter. He wasn't willing to give her the distance he was sure she wanted. Not when she smelled so good. She handled the knife like an expert, he noted as he sipped his wine. Impressive. Most of the career women he knew were more experienced in takeouts. "So, how's the new job?"

Hester moved her shoulders. "It's working out well. The manager's a stickler for efficiency, and that trickles down. Rad and I have been having conferences all week so we can compare notes."

Was that what they'd been talking about when they'd walked home today? he wondered. Was that why she'd laughed? "How's Radley taking the new school?"

"Amazingly well." Her lips softened and curved again. He was tempted to touch a fingertip to them to feel the movement. "Whatever happens in Rad's life, he rolls with. He's incredible."

There was a shadow there, a slight one, but he could see it in her eyes. "Divorce is tough," he said, and watched Hester freeze up.

"Yes." She put the boned and cubed chicken in a bowl. "You can chop this while I start the rice."

"Sure." No trespassing, he thought, and let it drop. For now. He'd gone with the law of averages when he'd mentioned divorce, and realized he'd been on the mark. But the mark was still raw. Unless he missed his guess, the divorce had been a lot tougher on her than on Radley. He was also sure that if he wanted to draw her out, it would have to be through the boy. "Rad mentioned that he wanted to come down and visit, but you'd put him off."

Hester handed Mitch an onion before she put a pan on the stove. "I didn't want him disturbing your work."

"We both know what you think of my work."

"I had no intention of offending you the other night," she said stiffly. "It was only that—"

"You can't conceive of a grown man making a living writing comic books."

Hester remained silent as she measured out water. "It's none of my business how you make your living."

"That's right." Mitch took a long sip of wine before he attacked the celery. "In any case, I want you to know that Rad can come see me whenever he likes."

"That's very nice of you, but—"

"No buts, Hester. I like him. And since I'm in the position of calling my own hours, he won't bother me. What do I do with the mushrooms?"

"Slice." She put the lid on the rice before crossing over to show him. "Not too thin. Just make sure…" Her words trailed off when he closed his hand over hers on the knife.

"Like this?" The move was easy. He didn't even have to think about it, but simply shifted until she was trapped between his arms, her back pressed against him. Giving in to the urge, he bent down so that his mouth was close to her ear.

"Yes, that's fine." She stared down at their joined hands and tried to keep her voice even. "It really doesn't matter."

"We aim to please."

"I have to put on the chicken." She turned and found herself in deeper water. It was a mistake to look up at him, to see that slight smile on his lips and that calm, confident look in his eyes. Instinctively she lifted a hand to his chest. Even that was a mistake. She could feel the slow, steady beat of his heart. She couldn't back up, because there was no place to go, and stepping forward was tempting, dangerously so. "Mitch, you're in my way."

He'd seen it. Though it had been free briefly and suppressed quickly, he'd seen the passion come into her eyes. So she could feel and want and wonder. Maybe it was best if they both wondered a little while longer. "I think you're going to find that happening a lot." But he shifted aside and let her pass. "You smell good, Hester, damn good."

That quiet statement did nothing to ease her pulse rate. Humoring Radley or not, she vowed this would be the last time she entertained Mitch Dempsey. Hester turned on the gas under the wok and added peanut oil. "I take it you do your work at home, then. No office?"

He'd let her have it her way for the time being. The minute she'd turned in his arms and looked up at him, he'd known he'd have it his way—have her his way— before too long. "I only have to go a couple of times a week. Some of the writers or artists prefer working in the office. I do better work at home. After I have the story and the sketches, I take them in for editing and inking."

"I see. So you don't do the inking yourself?" she asked, though she'd have been hard-pressed to define what inking was. She'd have to ask Radley.

"Not anymore. We have some real experts in that, and it gives me more time to work on the story. Believe it or not, we shoot for quality, the kind of vocabulary that challenges a kid and a story that entertains."

After adding chicken to the hot oil, Hester took a deep breath. "I really do apologize for anything I said that offended you. I'm sure your work's very important to you, and I know Radley certainly appreciates it."

"Well said, Mrs. Wallace." He slid the vegetable-laden chopping block toward her.

"Josh doesn't believe it." Radley bounced into the room, delighted with himself. "He wants to come over tomorrow and see. Can he? His mom says okay if it's okay with you? Okay, Mom?"

Hester turned from the chicken long enough to give Radley a hug. "Okay, Rad, but it has to be after noon. We have some shopping to do in the morning."

"Thanks. Just wait till he sees. He's gonna go crazy. I'll tell him."

"Dinner's nearly ready. Hurry up and wash your hands."

Radley rolled his eyes at Mitch as he raced from the room again.

"You're a big hit," Hester commented.

"He's nuts about you."

"The feeling's mutual."

"So I noticed." Mitch topped off his wine. "You know, I was curious. I always thought bankers kept bankers' hours. You and Rad don't get home until five or so." When she turned her head to look at him, he merely smiled. "Some of my windows face the front. I like to watch people going in and out."

It gave her an odd and not entirely comfortable feeling to know he'd watched her walk home. Hester dumped the vegetables in and stirred. "I get off at four, but then I have to pick Rad up from the sitter." She glanced over her shoulder again. "He hates it when I call her a sitter. Anyway, she's over by our old place, so it takes awhile. I have to start looking for someone closer."

"A lot of kids his age and younger come home on their own."

Her eyes did go smoky, he noted. All she needed was a touch of anger. Or passion. "Radley isn't going to be a latchkey child. He isn't coming home to an empty house because I have to work."

Mitch set her glass by her elbow. "Coming home to empty can be depressing," he murmured, remembering his own experiences. "He's lucky to have you."

"I'm luckier to have him." Her tone softened. "If you'd get out the plates, I'll dish this up."

Mitch remembered where she kept her plates, white ones with little violet sprigs along the edges. It was odd to realize they pleased him when he'd become so accustomed to disposable plastic. He took them out, then set them beside her. Most things were best done on impulse, he'd always thought. He went with the feeling now.

"I guess it would be a lot easier on Rad if he could come back here after school."

"Oh, yes. I hate having to drag him across town, though he's awfully good about it. It's just so hard to find someone you can trust, and who Radley really likes."

"How about me?"

Hester reached to turn off the gas, but stopped to stare at him. Vegetables and chicken popped in hot oil. "I'm sorry?"

"Rad could stay with me in the afternoons." Again Mitch put a hand over hers, this time to turn off the heat. "He'd only be a couple floors away from his own place."

"With you? No, I couldn't."

"Why not?" The more he thought of it, the more Mitch liked the idea. He and Taz could use the company in the afternoons, and as a bonus he'd be seeing a lot more of the very interesting Mrs. Wallace. "You want references? No criminal record, Hester. Well, there was the case of my motorcycle and the prize roses, but I was only eighteen."

"I didn't mean that—exactly." When he grinned, she began to fuss with the rice. "I mean I couldn't impose that way. I'm sure you're busy."

"Come on, you don't think I do anything all day but doodle. Let's be honest."

"We've already agreed it isn't any of my business," she began.

"Exactly. The point is I'm home in the afternoons, I'm available and I'm willing. Besides, I may even be able to use Rad as a consultant. He's good, you know." Mitch indicated the drawing on the refrigerator. "The kid could use some art lessons."

"I know. I was hoping I'd be able to swing it this summer, but I don't—"

"Want to look a gift horse in the mouth," Mitch finished. "Look, the kid likes me, I like him. And I'll swear to no more than one Twinkie an afternoon."

She laughed then, as he'd seen her laugh a few hours before from his window. It wasn't easy to hold himself back, but something told him if he made a move now, the door would slam in his face and the bolt would slide shut. "I don't know, Mitch. I do appreciate the offer, God knows it would make things easier, but I'm not sure you understand what you're asking for."

"I hasten to point out that I was once a small boy." He wanted to do it, he discovered. It was more than a gesture or impulse; he really wanted to have the kid around. "Look, why don't we put this to a vote and ask Rad?"

"Ask me what?" Radley had run some water over his hands after he'd finished talking to Josh, and figured his mother was too busy to give them a close look.

Mitch picked up his wine, then lifted a brow. My ball, Hester thought. She could have put the child off, but she'd always prided herself on being honest with him. "Mitch was just suggesting that you might like to stay with him after school in the afternoons instead of going over to Mrs. Cohen's."

"Really?" Astonishment and excitement warred until he was bouncing with both. "Really, can I?"

"Well, I wanted to think about it and talk to you be-fore—"

"I'll behave." Radley rushed over to wrap his arms around his mother's waist. "I promise. Mitch is much better than Mrs. Cohen. Lots better. She smells like mothballs and pats me on the head."

"I rest my case," Mitch murmured.

Hester sent Mitch a smoldering look. She wasn't ac-customed to being outnumbered or to making a deci-sion without careful thought and consideration. "Now, Radley, you know Mrs. Cohen's very nice. You've been staying with her for over two years."

Radley squeezed harder and played his ace. "If I stayed with Mitch I could come right home. And I'd do my homework first." It was a rash promise, but it was a desperate situation. "You'd get home sooner, too, and everything. Please, Mom, say yes."

She hated to deny him anything, because there were too many things she'd already had to. He was looking up at her now with his cheeks rosy with pleasure. Bend-ing, she kissed him. "All right, Rad, we'll try it and see how it works out."

"It's going to be great." He locked his arms around her neck before he turned to Mitch. "It's going to be just great."

Chapter 3

Mitch liked to sleep late on weekends—whenever he thought of them as weekends. Because he worked in his own home, at his own pace, he often forgot that to the vast majority there was a big difference between Monday mornings and Saturday mornings. This particular Saturday, however, he was spending in bed, largely dead to the world.

He'd been restless the evening before after he'd left Hester's apartment. Too restless to go back to his own alone. On the spur of the moment he'd gone out to the little lounge where the staff of Universal Comics often got together. He'd run into his inker, another artist and one of the staff writers for *The Great Beyond,* Universal's bid for the supernatural market. The music had been loud and none too good, which had been exactly what his mood had called for.

From there he'd been persuaded to attend an all-night horror film festival in Times Square. It had been past six when he'd come home, a little drunk and with only enough energy left to strip and tumble into bed—where he'd promised himself he'd stay for the next twenty-four hours. When the phone rang eight hours later, he answered it mostly because it annoyed him.

"Yeah?"

"Mitch?" Hester hesitated. It sounded as though he'd been asleep. Since it was after two in the afternoon, she dismissed the thought. "It's Hester Wallace. I'm sorry to bother you."

"What? No, it's all right." He rubbed a hand over his face, then pushed at the dog, who had shifted to the middle of the bed. "Damn it, Taz, shove over. You're breathing all over me."

Taz? Hester thought as both brows lifted. She hadn't thought that Mitch would have a roommate. She caught her bottom lip between her teeth. That was something she should have checked out. For Radley's sake.

"I really am sorry," she continued in a voice that had cooled dramatically. "Apparently I've caught you at a bad time."

"No." Give the stupid mutt an inch and he took a mile, Mitch thought as he hefted the phone and climbed to the other side of the bed. "What's up?"

"Are you?"

It was the mild disdain in her voice that had him bristling. That and the fact that it felt as though he'd eaten a sandbox. "Yeah, I'm up. I'm talking to you, aren't I?"

"I only called to give you all the numbers and information you need if you watch Radley next week."

"Oh." He pushed the hair out of his eyes and glanced

around, hoping he'd left a glass of watered-down soda or something close at hand. No luck. "Okay. You want to wait until I get a pencil?"

"Well, I…" He heard her put her hand over the receiver and speak to someone—Radley, he imagined from the quick intensity of the voice. "Actually, if it wouldn't put you out, Radley was hoping we could come by for a minute. He wants to introduce you to his friend. If you're busy, I can just drop the information by later."

Mitch started to tell her to do just that. Not only could he go back to sleep, but he might just be able to wrangle five minutes alone with her. Then he thought of Radley standing beside his mother, looking up at her with those big dark eyes. "Give me ten minutes," he muttered, and hung up before Hester could say a word.

Mitch pulled on jeans, then went into the bath to fill the sink with cold water. He took a deep breath and stuck his face in it. He came up swearing but awake. Five minutes later he was pulling on a sweatshirt and wondering if he'd remembered to wash any socks. All the clothes that had come back from the laundry neatly folded had been dumped on the chair in the corner of the bedroom. He briefly considered pushing his way through them, then let it go when he heard the knock. Taz's tail thumped on the mattress.

"Why don't you pick up this place?" Mitch asked him. "It's a pigsty."

Taz grinned, showing a set of big white teeth, then made a series of growls and groans.

"Excuses. Always excuses. And get out of bed. Don't you know it's after two?" Mitch rubbed a hand over his unshaven chin, then went to open the door.

She looked great, just plain great, with a hand on a

shoulder of each boy and a half smile on her face. Shy? he thought, a little surprised as he realized it. He had thought her cool and aloof, but now he believed she used that to hide an innate shyness, which he found amazingly sweet.

"Hiya, Rad."

"Hi, Mitch," Radley returned, almost bursting with importance. "This is my friend Josh Miller. He doesn't believe you're Commander Zark."

"Is that so?" Mitch looked down at the doubting Thomas, a skinny towhead about two inches taller than Rad. "Come on in."

"It's nice of you to put up with this," Hester began. "We weren't going to have any peace until Rad and Josh had it settled." The living room looked as though it had exploded. That was Hester's first thought as Mitch closed the door behind them. Papers and clothes and wrappers were everywhere. She imagined there was furniture, too, but she couldn't have described it.

"Tell Josh you're Commander Zark," Radley insisted.

"I guess you could say that." The notion pleased him. "I created him, anyway." He looked down again at Josh, whose pout had gone beyond doubt to true suspicion. "You two go to school together?"

"Used to." Josh stood close to Hester as he studied Mitch. "You don't look like Commander Zark."

Mitch rubbed a hand over his chin again. "Rough night."

"He is too Zark. Hey, look, Mom. Mitch has a VCR." Radley easily overlooked the clutter and homed in on the entertainment center. "I'm saving up my allowance to buy one. I've got seventeen dollars."

"It adds up," Mitch murmured, and flicked a finger

down his nose. "Why don't we go into the office? I'll show you what's cooking in the spring issue."

"Wow."

Taking this as an assent, Mitch led the way.

The office, Hester noted, was big and bright and every bit as chaotic as the living room. She was a creature of order, and it was beyond her how anyone could produce under these conditions. Yet there was a drawing board set up, and tacked to it were sketches and captions.

"You can see Zark's going to have his hands full when Leilah teams up with the Black Moth."

"The Black Moth. Holy cow." Faced with the facts, Josh was duly impressed. Then he remembered his comic book history, and suspicion reared again. "I thought he destroyed the Moth five issues ago."

"The Moth only went into hibernation after Zark bombarded the Zenith with experimental ZT-5. Leilah used her scientific genius to bring him out again."

"Wow." This came from Josh as he stared at the oversized words and drawings. "How come you make this so big? It can't fit in a comic book."

"It has to be reduced."

"I read all about that stuff." Radley gave Josh a superior glance. "I got this book out of the library that gave the history of comic books, all the way back to the 1930s."

"The Stone Age." Mitch smiled as the boys continued to admire his work. Hester was doing some admiring of her own. Beneath the clutter, she was certain there was a genuine, French rococo cupboard. And books. Hundreds of them. Mitch watched her wander the room.

And would have gone on watching if Josh hadn't tugged on his arm.

"Please, can I have your autograph?"

Mitch felt foolishly delighted as he stared down at the earnest face. "Sure." Shuffling through papers, he found a blank one and signed it. Then, with a flourish, he added a quick sketch of Zark.

"Neat." Josh folded the paper reverently and slipped it in his back pocket. "My brother's always bragging because he's got an autographed baseball, but this is better."

"Told ya." With a grin, Radley moved closer to Mitch. "And I'm going to be staying with Mitch after school until Mom gets home from work."

"No kidding?"

"All right, guys, we've taken up enough of Mr. Dempsey's time." Hester started to shoo the boys along when Taz strolled into the room.

"Gee whiz, he's really big." Radley started forward, hand out, when Hester caught him.

"Radley, you know better than to go up to a strange dog."

"Your mom's right," Mitch put in. "But in this case it's okay. Taz is harmless."

And enormous, Hester thought, keeping a firm grip on both boys.

Taz, who had a healthy respect for little people, sat in the doorway and eyed them both. Small boys had a tendency to want to play rough and pull ears, which Taz suffered heroically but could do without. Waiting to see which way the wind blew, he sat and thumped his tail.

"He's anything but an aggressive dog," Mitch reassured Hester. He stepped around her and put a hand on Taz's head. Without, Hester noted, having to bend over.

"Does he do tricks?" Radley wanted to know. It was one of his most secret wishes to own a dog. A big one. But he never asked, because he knew they couldn't keep one shut in an apartment all day alone.

"No, all Taz does is talk."

"Talk?" Josh went into a fit of laughter. "Dogs can't talk."

"He means bark," Hester said, relaxing a little.

"No, I mean talk." Mitch gave Taz a couple of friendly pats. "How's it going, Taz?"

In answer, the dog pushed his head hard against Mitch's leg and began to groan and grumble. Eyes wide and sincere, he looked up at his master and howled and hooted until both boys were nearly rolling with laughter.

"He *does* talk." Radley stepped forward, palm up. "He really does." Taz decided Radley didn't look like an ear puller and nuzzled his long snout in the boy's hand. "He likes me. Look, Mom." It was love at first sight as Radley threw his arms around the dog's neck. Automatically Hester started forward.

"He's as gentle as they come, I promise you." Mitch put a hand on Hester's arm. Even though the dog was already grumbling out his woes in Radley's ear and allowing Josh to pet him, Hester wasn't convinced.

"I don't imagine he's used to children."

"He fools around with kids in the park all the time." As if to prove it, Taz rolled over to expose his belly for stroking. "Added to that is the fact that he's bone lazy. He wouldn't work up the energy to bite anything that hadn't been put in a bowl for him. You aren't afraid of dogs, are you?"

"No, of course not." Not really, she added to herself. Because she hated to show a weakness, Hester crouched down to pet the huge head. Unknowingly she hit the perfect spot, and Taz recognized a patsy when he saw one. He shifted to lay a paw on her thigh and, with his dark, sad eyes on hers, began to moan. Laughing, Hester rubbed behind his ears. "You're just a big baby, aren't you?"

"An operator's more like it," Mitch murmured, wondering what sort of trick he'd have to do to get Hester to touch him with such feeling.

"I can play with him every day, can't I, Mitch?"

"Sure." Mitch smiled down at Radley. "Taz loves attention. You guys want to take him for a walk?"

The response was immediate and affirmative. Hester straightened up, looking doubtfully at Taz. "I don't know, Rad."

"Please, Mom, we'll be careful. You already said me and Josh could play in the park for a little while."

"Yes, I know, but Taz is awfully big. I wouldn't want him to get away from you."

"Taz is a firm believer in conserving energy. Why run if strolling gets you to the same place?" Mitch went back into his office, rooted around and came up with Taz's leash. "He doesn't chase cars, other dogs or park police. He will, however, stop at every tree."

With a giggle, Radley took the leash. "Okay, Mom?"

She hesitated, knowing there was a part of her that wanted to keep Radley with her, within arm's reach. And, for his sake, it was something she had to fight. "A half hour." The words were barely out when he and Josh let out a whoop. "You have to get your coats— and gloves."

"We will. Come on, Taz."

The dog gave a huge sigh before gathering himself up. Grumbling only a little, he stationed himself between the two boys as they headed out.

"Why is it every time I see that kid I feel good?"

"You're very kind to him. Well, I should go upstairs and make sure they bundle up."

"I think they can handle it. Why don't you sit down?" He took advantage of her brief hesitation by taking her arm. "Come over by the window. You can watch them go out."

She gave in because she knew how Radley hated to be hovered over. "Oh, I have my office number for you, and the name and number of his doctor and the school." Mitch took the paper and stuck it in his pocket. "If there's any trouble at all, call me. I can be home in ten minutes."

"Relax, Hester. We'll get along fine."

"I want to thank you again. It's the first time since he started school, that Rad's looked forward to a Monday."

"I'm looking forward to it myself."

She looked down, waiting to see the familiar blue cap and coat. "We haven't discussed terms."

"What terms?"

"How much you want for watching him. Mrs. Cohen—"

"Good God, Hester, I don't want you to pay me."

"Don't be ridiculous. Of course I'll pay you."

He put a hand on her shoulder until she'd turned to face him. "I don't need the money, I don't want the money. I made the offer because Rad's a nice kid and I enjoy his company."

"That's very kind of you, but—"

His exasperated sigh cut her off. "Here come the buts again."

"I couldn't possibly let you do it for nothing."

Mitch studied her face. He'd thought her tough at their first meeting, and tough she was—at least on the outside. "Can't you accept a neighborly gesture?"

Her lips curved a bit, but her eyes remained solemn. "I guess not."

"Five bucks a day."

This time the smile reached her eyes. "Thank you."

He caught the ends of her hair between his thumb and forefinger. "You drive a hard bargain, lady."

"So I've been told." Cautiously she took a step away. "Here they come." He hadn't forgotten his gloves, she noted as she leaned closer to the window. Nor had he forgotten that he'd been taught to walk to the corner and cross at the light. "He's in heaven, you know. Rad's always wanted a dog." She touched a hand to the window and continued to watch. "He doesn't mention it because he knows we can't keep one in the apartment when no one's home all day. So he's settled for the promise of a kitten."

Mitch put a hand on her shoulder again, but gently this time. "He doesn't strike me as a deprived child, Hester. There's nothing for you to feel guilty about."

She looked at him then, her eyes wide and just a little sad. Mitch discovered he was just as drawn to that as he had been to her laughter. Without planning to, without knowing he'd needed to, he lifted a hand to her cheek. The pale gray of her irises deepened. Her skin warmed. Hester backed away quickly.

"I'd better go. I'm sure they'll want hot chocolate when they get back in."

"They have to bring Taz back here first," Mitch reminded her. "Take a break, Hester. Want some coffee?"

"Well, I—"

"Good. Sit down and I'll get it."

Hester stood in the center of the room a moment, a bit amazed at how smoothly he ran things—his way. She was much too used to setting her own rules to accept anyone else's. Still, she told herself it would be rude to leave, that her son would be back soon and that the least she could do after Mitch had been so good to the boy was bear his company for a little while.

She would have been lying if she'd denied that he interested her. In a casual way, of course. There was something about the way he looked at her, so deep and penetrating, while at the same time he appeared to take most of life as a joke. Yet there was nothing funny about the way he touched her.

Hester lifted fingertips to her cheek, where his had been. She would have to take care to avoid too much of that sort of contact. Perhaps, with effort, she could think of Mitch as a friend, as Radley did already. It might not sit well with her to be obliged to him, but she could swallow that. She'd swallowed worse.

He was kind. She let out a little breath as she tried to relax. Experience had given her a very sensitive antenna. She could recognize the kind of man who tried to ingratiate himself with the child to get to the mother. If she was sure of anything, it was that Mitch genuinely liked Radley. That, if nothing else, was a point in his favor.

But she wished he hadn't touched her that way, looked at her that way, made her feel that way.

"It's hot. Probably lousy, but hot." Mitch walked in with two mugs. "Don't you want to sit down?"

Hester smiled at him. "Where?"

Mitch set the mugs down on a stack of papers, then pushed magazines from the sofa. "Here."

"You know…" She stepped over a stack of old newspapers. "Radley's very good at tidying. He'd be glad to help you."

"I function best in controlled confusion."

Hester joined him on the sofa. "I can see the confusion, but not the controlled."

"It's here, believe me. I didn't ask if you wanted anything in the coffee, so I brought it black."

"Black's fine. This table—it's Queen Anne, isn't it?"

"Yeah." Mitch set his bare feet on it, then crossed them at the ankles. "You've got a good eye."

"One would have to under the circumstances." Because he laughed, she smiled as she took her first sip. "I've always loved antiques. I suppose it's the endurance. Not many things last."

"Sure they do. I once had a cold that lasted six weeks." He settled back as she laughed. "When you do that, you get a dimple at the corner of your mouth. Cute."

Hester was immediately self-conscious again. "You have a very natural way with children. Did you come from a large family?"

"No. Only child." He continued to study her, curious about her reaction to the most casual of compliments.

"Really? I wouldn't have guessed it."

"Don't tell me you're of the school who believes only a woman can relate to children?"

"No, not really," she hedged, because that had been

her experience thus far. "It's just that you're particularly good with them. No children of your own?" The question came out quickly, amazing and embarrassing her.

"No. I guess I've been too busy being a kid myself to think about raising any."

"That hardly makes you unusual," she said coolly.

He tilted his head as he studied her. "Tossing me in with Rad's father, Hester?"

Something flashed in her eyes. Mitch shook his head as he sipped again. "Damn, Hester, what did the bastard do to you?" She froze instantly. Mitch was quicker. Even as she started to rise, he put a restraining hand on her arm. "Okay, hands off that one until you're ready. I apologize if I hit a sore spot, but I'm curious. I've spent a couple of evenings with Rad now, and he's never mentioned his father."

"I'd appreciate it if you wouldn't ask him any questions."

"Fine." Mitch was capable of being just as snotty. "I didn't intend to grill the kid."

Hester was tempted to get up and excuse herself. That would be the easiest way. But the fact was that she was trusting her son to this man every afternoon. She supposed it would be best if he had some background.

"Rad hasn't seen his father in almost seven years."

"At all?" He couldn't help his surprise. His own family had been undemonstrative and distant, but he never went more than a year without seeing his parents. "Must be rough on the kid."

"They were never close. I think Radley's adjusted very well."

"Hold on. I wasn't criticizing you." He'd placed his hand over hers again, too firmly to be shaken off. "I know a happy, well-loved boy when I see one. You'd walk through fire for him. Maybe you don't think it shows, but it does."

"There's nothing that's more important to me than Radley." She wanted to relax again, but he was sitting too close, and his hand was still on hers. "I only told you this so that you wouldn't ask him questions that might upset him."

"Does that sort of thing happen often?"

"Sometimes." His fingers were linked with hers now. She couldn't quite figure out how he'd managed it. "A new friend, a new teacher. I really should go."

"How about you?" He touched her cheek gently and turned her face toward him. "How have you adjusted?"

"Just fine. I have Rad, and my work."

"And no relationships?"

She wasn't sure if it was embarrassment or anger, but the sensation was very strong. "That's none of your business."

"If people only talked about what was their business, they wouldn't get very far. You don't strike me as a man-hater, Hester."

She lifted a brow. When pushed, she could play the game by someone else's rules. And she could play it well. "I went through a period of time when I despised men on principle. Actually, it was a very rewarding time of my life. Then, gradually, I came to the opinion that some members of your species weren't lower forms of life."

"Sounds promising."

She smiled again, because he made it easy. "The point is, I don't blame all men for the faults of one."

"You're just cautious."

"If you like."

"The one thing I'm sure I like is your eyes. No, don't look away." Patiently, he turned her face back to his. "They're fabulous—take it from an artist's standpoint."

She had to stop being so jumpy, Hester ordered herself. With an effort, she remained still. "Does that mean they're going to appear in an upcoming issue?"

"They just might." He smiled, appreciating the thought and the fact that though tense, she was able to hold her own. "Poor old Zark deserves to meet someone who understands him. These eyes would."

"I'll take that as a compliment." And run. "The boys will be back in a minute."

"We've got some time yet. Hester, do you ever have fun?"

"What a stupid question. Of course I do."

"Not as Rad's mother, but as Hester." He ran a hand through her hair, captivated.

"I *am* Rad's mother." Though she managed to rise, he stood with her.

"You're also a woman. A gorgeous one." He saw the look in her eyes and ran his thumb along her jawline. "Take my word for it. I'm an honest man. You're one gorgeous bundle of nerves."

"That's silly. I don't have anything to be nervous about." Other than the fact that he was touching her, and his voice was quiet, and the apartment was empty.

"I'll take the shaft out of my heart later," he murmured. He bent to kiss her, then had to catch her when she nearly stumbled over the newspapers. "Take it easy. I'm not going to bite you. This time."

"I have to go." She was as close to panic as she ever allowed herself to come. "I have a dozen things to do."

"In a minute." He framed her face. She was trembling, he realized. It didn't surprise him. What did was that he wasn't steady himself. "What we have here, Mrs. Wallace, is called attraction, chemistry, lust. It doesn't really matter what label you put on it."

"Maybe not to you."

"Then we'll let you pick the label later." He stroked his thumbs over her cheekbones, gently, soothingly. "I already told you I'm not a maniac. I'll have to remember to get those references."

"Mitch, I told you I appreciate what you're doing for Rad, but I wish you'd—"

"Here and now doesn't concern Rad. This is you and me, Hester. When was the last time you let yourself be alone with a man who wanted you?" He casually brushed his thumb over her lips. Her eyes went to smoke. "When was the last time you let anyone do this?"

His mouth covered hers quickly, with a force that came as a shock. She hadn't been prepared for violence. His hands had been so gentle, his voice so soothing. She hadn't expected this edgy passion. But God, how she'd wanted it. With the same reckless need, she threw her arms around his neck and answered demand for demand.

"Too long," Mitch managed breathlessly when he tore his mouth from hers. "Thank God." Before she could utter more than a moan, he took her mouth again.

He hadn't been sure what he'd find in her—ice, anger, fear. The unrestrained heat came as much of a shock to his system as to hers. Her wide, generous mouth was warm and willing, with all traces of shyness swallowed by passion. She gave more than he would have asked for, and more than he'd been prepared to take.

His head spun, a fascinating and novel sensation he
couldn't fully appreciate as he struggled to touch and
taste. He dragged his hands through her hair, scattering the two thin silver pins she'd used to pull it back
from her face. He wanted it free and wild in his hands,
just as he wanted her free and wild in his bed. His plans
to go slowly, to test the waters, evaporated in an overwhelming desire to dive in headfirst. Thinking only of
this, he slipped his hands under her sweater. The skin
there was tender and warm. The silky little concoction
she wore was cool and soft. He slid his hands around
her waist and up to cup her breasts.

She stiffened, then shuddered. She hadn't known
how much she'd wanted to be touched like this. Needed
like this. His taste was so dark, so tempting. She'd forgotten what it was like to hunger for such things. It was
madness, the sweet release of madness. She heard him
murmur her name as he moved his mouth down her
throat and back again.

Madness. She understood it. She'd been there before,
or thought she had. Though it seemed sweeter now,
richer now, she knew she could never go there again.

"Mitch, please." It wasn't easy to resist what he was
offering. It surprised Hester how difficult it was to draw
away, to put the boundaries back. "We can't do this."

"We are," he pointed out, and drew the flavor from
her lips again. "And very well."

"*I* can't." With the small sliver of willpower she had
left, she struggled away. "I'm sorry. I should never have
let this happen." Her cheeks were hot. Hester put her
hands to them, then dragged them up through her hair.

His knees were weak. That was something to think about. But for the moment he concentrated on her. "You're taking a lot on yourself, Hester. It seems to be a habit of yours. I kissed you, and you just happened to kiss me back. Since we both enjoyed it, I don't see where apologies are necessary on either side."

"I should have made myself clear." She stepped back, hit the newspapers again, then skirted around them. "I do appreciate what you're doing for Rad—"

"Leave him out of this, for God's sake."

"I can't." Her voice rose, surprising her again. She knew better than to lose control. "I don't expect you to understand, but I can't leave him out of it." She took a deep breath, amazed that it did nothing to calm her pulse rate. "I'm not interested in casual sex. I have Rad to think about, and myself."

"Fair enough." He wanted to sit down until he'd recovered, but figured the situation called for an eye-to-eye discussion. "I wasn't feeling too casual about it myself."

That was what worried her. "Let's just drop it."

Anger was an amazing stimulant. Mitch stepped forward, and caught her chin in his hand. "Fat chance."

"I don't want to argue with you. I just think that—" The knock came as a blessed reprieve. "That's the boys."

"I know." But he didn't release her. "Whatever you're interested in, have time for, room for, might just have to be adjusted." He was angry, really angry, Mitch realized. It wasn't like him to lose his temper so quickly. "Life's full of adjustments, Hester." Letting her go, he opened the door.

"It was great." Rosy-cheeked and bright-eyed, Radley tumbled in ahead of Josh and the dog. "We even got Taz to run once, for a minute."

"Amazing." Mitch bent to unclip the leash. Grumbling with exhaustion, Taz walked to a spot by the window, then collapsed.

"You guys must be freezing." Hester kissed Radley's forehead. "It must be time for hot chocolate."

"Yeah!" Radley turned his beaming face to Mitch. "Want some? Mom makes real good hot chocolate."

It was tempting to put her on the spot. Perhaps it was a good thing for both of them that his temper was already fading. "Maybe next time." He pulled Radley's cap over his eyes. "I've got some things to do."

"Thanks a lot for letting us take Taz out. It was really neat, wasn't it, Josh?"

"Yeah. Thanks, Mr. Dempsey."

"Anytime. See you Monday, Rad."

"Okay." The boys fled, laughing and shoving. Mitch looked, but Hester was already gone.

Chapter 4

Mitchell Dempsey II had been born rich, privileged and, according to his parents, with an incorrigible imagination. Maybe that was why he'd taken to Radley so quickly. The boy was far from rich, not even privileged enough to have a set of parents, but his imagination was first-class.

Mitch had always liked crowds as much as one-on-one social situations. He was certainly no stranger to parties, given his mother's affection for entertaining and his own gregarious nature, and no one who knew him would ever have classed him as a loner. In his work, however, he had always preferred the solitary. He worked at home not because he didn't like distractions—he was really fond of them—but because he didn't care to have anyone looking over his shoulder or timing his progress. He'd never considered working any way other than alone. Until Radley.

They made a pact the first day. If Radley finished his homework, with or without Mitch's dubious help, he could then choose to either play with Taz or give his input into Mitch's latest story line. If Mitch had decided to call it quits for the day, they could entertain themselves with his extensive collection of videotapes or with Radley's growing army of plastic figures.

To Mitch, it was natural—to Radley, fantastic. For the first time in his young life he had a man who was part of his daily routine, one who talked to him and listened to him. He had someone who was not only as willing to spend time to set up a battle or wage a war as his mother was, but someone who understood his military strategy.

By the end of their first week, Mitch was not only a hero, creator of Zark and owner of Taz, but the most solid and dependable person in his life other than his mother. Radley loved, without guards or restrictions.

Mitch saw it, wondered at it and found himself just as captivated. He had told Hester no less than the truth when he'd said that he'd never thought about having children. He'd run his life on his own clock for so long that he'd never considered doing things differently. If he'd known what it was to love a small boy, to find pieces of himself in one, he might have done things differently.

Perhaps it was because of his discoveries that he thought of Radley's father. What kind of man could create something that special and then walk away from it? His own father had been stern and anything but understanding, but he'd been there. Mitch had never questioned the love.

A man didn't get to be thirty-five without knowing several contemporaries who'd been through divorces— many of them bitter. But he also was acquainted with several who'd managed to call a moratorium with their ex-wives in order to remain fathers. It was difficult enough to understand how Radley's father not only could have walked out, but could have walked away. After a week in Radley's company, it was all but impossible.

And what of Hester? What kind of man left a woman to struggle alone to raise a child they had brought into the world together? How much had she loved him? That was a thought that dug into his brain too often for comfort. The results of the experience were obvious. She was tense and overly cautious around men. Around him, certainly, Mitch thought with a grimace as he watched Radley sketch. So cautious that she'd stayed out of his path throughout the week.

Every day between 4:15 and 4:25, he received a polite call. Hester would ask him if everything had gone well, thank him for watching Radley, then ask him to send her son upstairs. That afternoon, Radley had handed him a neatly written check for twenty-five dollars drawn on the account of Hester Gentry Wallace. It was still crumpled in Mitch's pocket.

Did she really think he was going to quietly step aside after she'd knocked the wind out of him? He hadn't forgotten what she'd felt like pressed against him, inhibitions and caution stripped away for one brief, stunning moment. He intended to live that moment again, as well as the others his incorrigible imagination had conjured up.

If she did think he'd bow out gracefully, Mrs. Hester Wallace was in for a big surprise.

"I can't get the retro rockets right," Radley complained. "They never look right."

Mitch set aside his own work, which had stopped humming along the moment he'd started to think of Hester. "Let's have a look." He took the spare sketch pad he'd lent to Radley. "Hey, not bad." He grinned, foolishly pleased with Radley's attempt at the Defiance. It seemed the few pointers he'd given the kid had taken root. "You're a real natural, Rad."

The boy blushed with pleasure, then frowned again. "But see, the boosters and retros are all wrong. They look stupid."

"Only because you're trying to detail too soon. Look, light strokes, impressions first." He put a hand over the boy's to guide it. "Don't be afraid to make mistakes. That's why they make those big gum erasers."

"You don't make mistakes." Radley caught his tongue between his teeth as he struggled to make his hand move as expertly as Mitch's.

"Sure I do. This is my fifteenth eraser this year."

"You're the best artist in the whole world," Radley said, looking up, his heart in his eyes.

Moved and strangely humbled, Mitch ruffled the boy's hair. "Maybe one of the top twenty, but thanks." When the phone rang, Mitch felt a strange stab of disappointment. The weekend meant something different now—no Radley. For a man who had lived his entire adult life without responsibilities, it was a sobering thought to realize he would miss one. "That should be your mother."

"She said we could go out to the movies tonight 'cause it's Friday and all. You could come with us."

Giving a noncommittal grunt, Mitch answered the phone. "Hi, Hester."

"Mitch, I—everything okay?"

Something in her tone had his brows drawing together. "Just dandy."

"Did Radley give you the check?"

"Yeah. Sorry, I haven't had a chance to cash it yet."

If there was one thing she wasn't in the mood for at the moment, it was sarcasm. "Well, thanks. If you'd send Radley upstairs, I'd appreciate it."

"No problem." He hesitated. "Rough day, Hester?"

She pressed a hand to her throbbing temple. "A bit. Thank you, Mitch."

"Sure." He hung up, still frowning. Turning to Radley, he made the effort to smile. "Time to transfer your equipment, Corporal."

"Sir, yes, sir!" Radley gave a smart salute. The intergalactic army he'd left at Mitch's through the week was tossed into his backpack. After a brief search, both of his gloves were located and pushed in on top of the plastic figures. Radley stuffed his coat and hat in before kneeling down to hug Taz. "Bye, Taz. See ya." The dog rumbled a goodbye as he rubbed his snout into Radley's shoulder. "Bye, Mitch." He went to the door, then hesitated. "I guess I'll see you Monday."

"Sure. Hey, maybe I'll just walk up with you. Give your mom a full report."

"Okay!" Radley brightened instantly. "You left your keys in the kitchen. I'll get them." Mitch watched the tornado pass, then swirl back. "I got an A in spelling.

When I tell Mom, she'll be in a real good mood. We'll probably get sodas."

"Sounds like a good deal to me," Mitch said, and let himself be dragged along.

Hester heard Radley's key in the lock and set down the ice pack. Leaning closer, she checked her face in the bathroom mirror, saw a bruise was already forming, and swore. She'd hoped to be able to tell Radley about the mishap, gloss over it and make it a joke before any battle scars showed. Hester downed two aspirin and prayed the headache would pass.

"Mom! Hey, Mom!"

"Right here, Radley." She winced at her own raised voice, then put on a smile as she walked out to greet him. The smile faded when she saw her son had brought company.

"Mitch came up to report," Radley began as he shrugged out of his backpack.

"What the hell happened to you?" Mitch crossed over to her in two strides. He had her face in his hands and fury in his eyes. "Are you all right?"

"Of course I am." She shot him a quick warning look, then turned to Radley. "I'm fine."

Radley stared up at her, his eyes widening, then his bottom lip trembling as he saw the black-and-blue mark under her eye. "Did you fall down?"

She wanted to lie and say yes, but she'd never lied to him. "Not exactly." She forced a smile, annoyed to have a witness to her explanation. "It seems that there was a man at the subway station who wanted my purse. I wanted it, too."

"You were mugged?" Mitch wasn't sure whether to

swear at her or gather her close and check for injuries.
Hester's long, withering look didn't give him the chance
to do either.

"Sort of." She moved her shoulders ~~~~ Radley
it was of little consequence. "It wasn't ~~~~ ~~~cit-
ing, I'm afraid. The subway was crowde~~~ ~~~ ~e
saw what was going on and called security, s~ ~~~ n
changed his mind about my purse and ran aw~~

Radley looked closer. He'd seen a black eye ~~~ ~.
Joey Phelps had had a really neat one once. But ~~~
never seen one on his mother. "Did he hit you?"

"Not really. That part was sort of an accident." A~
accident that hurt like the devil. "We were having this~
tug-of-war over my purse, and his elbow shot up. I didn't
duck quick enough, that's all."

"Stupid," Mitch muttered loud enough to be heard.

"Did you hit him?"

"Of course not," Hester answered, and thought long-
ingly of her ice pack. "Go put your things away now,
Radley."

"But I want to know about—"

"Now," his mother interrupted in a tone she used
rarely and to great effect.

"Yes, ma'am," Radley mumbled, and lugged the
backpack off the couch.

Hester waited until he'd turned the corner into his
room. "I want you to know I don't appreciate your interference."

"You haven't begun to see interference. What the
hell's wrong with you? You know better than to fight
with a mugger over a purse. What if he'd had a knife?"
Even the thought of it had his reliable imagination working overtime.

"He didn't have a knife." Hester felt her knees begin to tremble. The damnedest thing was that the reaction had chosen the most inopportune moment to set in. "And he doesn't have my purse, either."

"Or a black eye. For God's sake, Hester, you could have been seriously hurt, and I doubt there's anything in your purse that would warrant it. Credit cards can be canceled, a compact or a lipstick replaced."

"I suppose if someone had tried to lift your wallet you'd have given him your blessing."

"That's different."

"The hell it is."

He stopped pacing long enough to give her a long study. Her chin was thrust out, in the same way he'd seen Radley's go a few times. He'd expected the stubbornness, but he had to admit he hadn't expected the ready temper, or his admiration for it. But that was beside the point, he reminded himself as his gaze swept over her bruised cheekbone again.

"Let's just back up a minute. In the first place, you've got no business taking the subway alone."

She let out what might have been a laugh. "You've got to be kidding."

The funny thing was, he couldn't remember ever having said anything quite that stupid. It brought his own temper bubbling over. "Take a cab, damn it."

"I have no intention of taking a cab."

"Why?"

"In the first place it would be stupid, and in the second I can't afford it."

Mitch dragged the check out of his pocket and pushed it into her hand. "Now you can afford it, along with a reasonable tip."

"I have no intention of taking this." She shoved the crumpled check back at him. "Or of taking a taxi when the subway is both inexpensive and convenient. And I have less intention of allowing you to take a small incident and blow it into a major calamity. I don't want Radley upset."

"Fine, then take a cab. For the kid's sake, if not your own. Think how it would have been for him if you'd really been hurt."

The bruise stood out darkly as her cheeks paled. "I don't need you or anyone to lecture me on the welfare of my son."

"No, you do just fine by him. It's when it comes to Hester that you've got a few loose screws." He jammed his hands into his pockets. "Okay, you won't take a cab. At least promise you won't play Sally Courageous the next time some lowlife decides he likes the color of your purse."

Hester brushed at the sleeve of her jacket. "Is that the name of one of your characters?"

"It might be." He told himself to calm down. He didn't have much of a temper as a rule, but when it started to perk, it could come to a boil in seconds. "Look, Hester, did you have your life savings in your bag?"

"Of course not."

"Family heirlooms?"

"No."

"Any microchips vital to national security?"

She let out an exasperated sigh and dropped onto the arm of a chair. "I left them at the office." She pouted as she looked up at him. "Don't give me that disgusting smile now."

"Sorry." He changed it to a grin.

"I just had such a rotten day." Without realizing it, she slipped off her shoe and began to massage her instep. "The first thing this morning, Mr. Rosen went on an efficiency campaign. Then there was the staff meeting, then the idiot settlement clerk, who made a pass at me."

"What idiot settlement clerk?"

"Never mind." Tired, she rubbed her temple. "Just take it that things went from bad to worse until I was ready to bite someone's head off. Then that jerk grabbed my purse, and I just exploded. At least I have the satisfaction of knowing he'll be walking with a limp for a few days."

"Got in a few licks, did you?"

Hester continued to pout as she gingerly touched her eye with her fingertips. "Yeah."

Mitch walked over, then bent down to her level. With a look more of curiosity than sympathy, he examined the damage. "You're going to have a hell of a shiner."

"Really?" Hester touched the bruise again. "I was hoping this was as bad as it would get."

"Not a chance. It's going to be a beaut."

She thought of the stares and the explanations that would be necessary the following week. "Terrific."

"Hurt?"

"Yes."

Mitch touched his lips to the bruise before she could evade him. "Try some ice."

"I've already thought of that."

"I put my things away." Radley stood in the hallway looking down at his shoes. "I had homework, but I already did it."

"That's good. Come here." Radley continued to look at his shoes as he walked to her. Hester put her arms around his neck and squeezed. "Sorry."

"'S okay. I didn't mean to make you mad."

"You didn't make me mad. Mr. Rosen made me mad. That man who wanted my purse made me mad, but not you, baby."

"I could get you a wet cloth the way you do when my head hurts."

"Thanks, but I think I need a hot bath and an ice pack." She gave him another squeeze, then remembered. "Oh, we had a date didn't we? Cheeseburgers and a movie."

"We can watch TV instead."

"Well, why don't we see how I feel in a little while?"

"I got an *A* on my spelling test."

"My hero," Hester said, laughing.

"You know, that hot bath's a good idea. Ice, too." Mitch was already making plans. "Why don't you get started on that while I borrow Rad for a little while."

"But he just got home."

"It'll only take a little while." Mitch took her arm and started to lead her toward the hall. "Put some bubbles in the tub. They're great for the morale. We'll be back in half an hour."

"But where are you going?"

"Just an errand I need to run. Rad can keep me company, can't you, Rad?"

"Sure."

The idea of a thirty-minute soak was too tempting. "No candy, it's too close to dinner."

"Okay, I won't eat any," Mitch promised, and scooted her into the bath. Putting a hand on Radley's shoulder, he marched back into the living room. "Ready to go out on a mission, Corporal?"

Radley's eyes twinkled as he saluted. "Ready and willing, sir."

The combination of ice pack, hot bath and aspirin proved successful. By the time the water had cooled in the tub, Hester's headache was down to dull and manageable. She supposed she owed Mitch for giving her a few minutes to herself, Hester admitted as she pulled on jeans. Along with most of the pain, the shakiness had drained away in the hot water. In fact, when she took the time to examine her bruised eye, she felt downright proud of herself. Mitch had been right, bubbles had been good for the morale.

She pulled a brush through her hair and wondered how disappointed Radley would be if they postponed their trip to the movies. Hot bath or no, the last thing she felt like doing at the moment was braving the cold to sit in a crowded theater. She thought a matinee the next day might satisfy him. It would mean adjusting her schedule a bit, but the idea of a quiet evening at home after the week she'd put in made doing the laundry after dinner a lot more acceptable.

And what a week, Hester thought as she pulled on slippers. Rosen was a tyrant and the settlement clerk was a pest. She'd spent almost as much time during the last five days placating one and discouraging the other as she had processing loans. She wasn't afraid of work, but she did resent having to account for every minute of her time. It was nothing personal; Hester had discovered that within the first eight-hour stretch.

Rosen was equally overbearing and fussy with everyone on his staff.

And that fool Cummings. Hester pushed the thought of the overamorous clerk out of her mind and sat on the edge of the bed. She'd gotten through the first two weeks, hadn't she? She touched her cheekbone gingerly. With the scars to prove it. It would be easier now. She wouldn't have the strain of meeting all those new people. The biggest relief of all was that she didn't have to worry about Radley.

She'd never admit it to anyone, but she'd waited for Mitch to call every day that week to tell her Radley was too much trouble, he'd changed his mind, he was tired of spending his afternoons with a nine-year-old. But the fact was that every afternoon when Radley had come upstairs the boy had been full of stories about Mitch and Taz and what they'd done.

Mitch had showed him a series of sketches for the big anniversary issue. They'd taken Taz to the park. They'd watched the original, uncut, absolutely classic *King Kong* on the VCR. Mitch had showed him his comic book collection, which included the first issues of *Superman* and *Tales From the Crypt,* which everyone knew, she'd been informed, were practically priceless. And did she know that Mitch had an original, honest-to-God *Captain Midnight* decoder ring? Wow.

Hester rolled her eyes, then winced when the movement reminded her of the bruise. The man might be odd, she decided, but he was certainly making Radley happy. Things would be fine as long as she continued to think of him as Radley's friend and forgot about that unexpected and unexplainable connection they'd made last weekend.

Hester preferred to think about it as a connection rather than any of the terms Mitch had used. Attraction, chemistry, lust. No, she didn't care for any of those words, or for her immediate and unrestrained reaction to him. She knew what she'd felt. Hester was too honest to deny that for one crazed moment she'd welcomed the sensation of being held and kissed and desired. It wasn't something to be ashamed of. A woman who'd been alone as long as she had was bound to feel certain stirrings around an attractive man.

Then why didn't she feel any of those stirrings around Cummings?

Don't answer that, she warned herself. Sometimes it was best not to dig too deeply when you really didn't want to know.

Think about dinner, she decided. Poor Radley was going to have to make do with soup and a sandwich instead of his beloved cheeseburger tonight. With a sigh, she rose as she heard the front door open.

"Mom! Mom, come see the surprise."

Hester made sure she was smiling, though she wasn't sure she could take any more surprises that day. "Rad, did you thank Mitch for…oh." He was back, Hester saw, automatically adjusting her sweater. The two of them stood just inside the doorway with identical grins on their faces. Radley carried two paper bags, and Mitch hefted what looked suspiciously like a tape machine with cables dangling.

"What's all this?"

"Dinner and a double feature," Mitch informed her. "Rad said you like chocolate shakes."

"Yes, I do." The aroma finally carried to her. Sniffing, she eyed Radley's bags. "Cheeseburgers?"

"Yeah, and fries. Mitch said we could have double orders. We took Taz for a walk. He's eating his downstairs."

"He's got lousy table manners." Mitch carried the unit over to Hester's television.

"And I helped Mitch unhook the VCR. We got *Raiders of the Lost Ark*. Mitch has millions of movies."

"Rad said you like musical junk."

"Well, yes, I—"

"We got one of them, too." Rad set the bags down to go over and sit with Mitch on the floor. "Mitch said it's pretty funny, so I guess it'll be okay." He put a hand on Mitch's leg and leaned closer to watch the hookup.

"Singin' in the Rain." Handing Radley a cable, Mitch sat back to let him connect it.

"Really?"

He had to smile. There were times she sounded just like the kid. "Yeah. How's the eye?"

"Oh, it's better." Unable to resist, Hester walked over to watch. How odd it seemed to see her son's small hands working with those of a man.

"It's a tight squeeze, but the VCR just about fits under your television stand." Mitch gave Radley's shoulder a quick squeeze before he rose. "Colorful." With a finger under her chin, he turned Hester's face to the side to examine her eye. "Rad and I thought you looked a little beat, so we figured we'd bring the movie to you."

"I was." She touched her hand to his wrist a moment. "Thanks."

"Anytime." He wondered what her reaction, and Radley's, would be if he kissed her right now. Hester must have seen the question in his eyes, because she backed up quickly.

"Well, I guess I'd better get some plates so the food doesn't get cold."

"We've got plenty of napkins." He gestured toward the couch. "Sit down while my assistant and I finish up."

"I did it." Flushed with success, Radley scrambled back on all fours. "It's all hooked up."

Mitch bent to check the connections. "You're a regular mechanic, Corporal."

"We get to watch *Raiders* first, right?"

"That was the deal." Mitch handed him the tape. "You're in charge."

"It looks like I have to thank you again," Hester said when Mitch joined her on the couch.

"What for? I figured to wangle myself in on your date with Rad tonight." He pulled a burger out of the bag. "This is cheaper."

"Most men wouldn't choose to spend a Friday night with a small boy."

"Why not?" He took a healthy bite, and after swallowing continued, "I figure he won't eat half his fries, and I'll get the rest."

Radley took a running leap and plopped onto the couch between them. He gave a contented and very adult sigh as he snuggled down. "This is better than going out. Lots better."

He was right, Hester thought as she relaxed and let herself become caught up in Indiana Jones's adventures. There had been a time when she'd believed life could be that thrilling, romantic, heart-stopping. Circumstances had forced her to set those things aside, but she'd never lost her love of the fantasy of films. For a couple of hours it was possible to close off reality and the pressures that went with it and be innocent again.

Radley was bright-eyed and full of energy as he switched tapes. Hester had no doubt his dreams that night would revolve around lost treasures and heroic deeds. Snuggling against her, he giggled at Donald O'Connor's mugging and pratfalls, but began to nod off soon after Gene Kelly's marvelous dance through the rain.

"Fabulous, isn't it?" Mitch murmured. Radley had shifted so that his head rested against Mitch's chest.

"Absolutely. I never get tired of this movie. When I was a little girl, we'd watch it whenever it came on TV. My father's a big movie buff. You can name almost any film, and he'll tell you who was in it. But his first love was always the musical."

Mitch fell silent again. It took very little to learn how one person felt about another—a mere inflection in their voice, a softening of their expression. Hester's family had been close, as he'd always regretted his hadn't been. His father had never shared Mitch's love of fantasy or film, as he had never shared his father's devotion to business. Though he would never have considered himself a lonely child—his imagination had been company enough—he'd always missed the warmth and affection he'd heard so clearly in Hester's voice when she'd spoken of her father.

When the credits rolled, he turned to her again. "Your parents live in the city?"

"Here? Oh, no." She had to laugh as she tried to picture either of her parents coping with life in New York. "No, I grew up in Rochester, but my parents moved to the Sunbelt almost ten years ago—Fort Worth. Dad's still in banking and my mother has a part-time job in a bookstore. We were all amazed when she went to work.

I guess all of us thought she didn't know how to do anything but bake cookies and fold sheets."

"How many's we?"

Hester sighed a little as the screen went blank. She couldn't honestly remember when she'd enjoyed an evening more. "I have a brother and a sister. I'm the oldest. Luke's settled in Rochester with a wife and a new baby on the way, and Julia's in Atlanta. She's a disc jockey."

"No kidding?"

"Wake up, Atlanta, it's 6:00 a.m., time for three hits in a row." She laughed a little as she thought of her sister. "I'd give anything to take Rad down for a visit."

"Miss them?"

"It's just hard thinking how spread out we all are. I know how nice it would be for Rad to have more family close by."

"What about Hester?"

She looked over at him, a bit surprised to see how natural Radley looked dozing in the crook of his arm. "I have Rad."

"And that's enough?"

"More than." She smiled; then, uncurling her legs, she rose. "And speaking of Rad, I'd better take him in to bed."

Mitch picked the boy up and settled him over his shoulder. "I'll carry him."

"Oh, that's all right. I do it all the time."

"I've got him." Radley turned his face into Mitch's neck. What an amazing feeling, he thought, a little shaken by it. "Just show me where."

Telling herself it was silly to feel odd, Hester led him into Radley's bedroom. The bed had been made à la Rad, which meant the *Star Wars* spread was pulled up over rumpled sheets. Mitch narrowly missed stepping on a pint-size robot and a worn rag dog. There was a night-light burning by the dresser, because for all Radley's bravado he was still a bit leery about what might or might not be in the closet.

Mitch laid him down on the bed, then began to help Hester take off the boy's sneakers. "You don't have to bother." Hester untangled a knot in the laces with the ease of experience.

"It's not a bother. Does he use pajamas?" Mitch was already tugging off Radley's jeans. In silence, Hester moved over to Radley's dresser and took out his favorites. Mitch studied the bold imprint of Commander Zark. "Good taste. It always ticked me off they didn't come in my size."

The laugh relaxed her again. Hester bundled the top over Radley's head while Mitch pulled the bottoms over his legs.

"Kid sleeps like a rock."

"I know. He always has. He rarely woke up during the night even as a baby." As a matter of habit, she picked up the rag dog and tucked it in beside him before kissing his cheek. "Don't mention Fido," she murmured. "Radley's a bit sensitive about still sleeping with him."

"I never saw a thing." Then, giving in to the need, he brushed a hand over Radley's hair. "Pretty special, isn't he?"

"Yes, he is."

"So are you." Mitch turned and touched her hair in turn. "Don't close up on me, Hester," he said as she shifted her gaze away from his. "The best way to accept a compliment is to say thank you. Give it a shot."

Embarrassed more by her reaction to him than by his words, she made herself look at him. "Thank you."

"That's a good start. Now let's try it again." He slipped his arms around her. "I've been thinking about kissing you again for almost a week."

"Mitch, I—"

"Did you forget your line?" She'd lifted her hands to his shoulders to hold him off. But her eyes… He much preferred the message he read in them. "That was another compliment. I don't make a habit of thinking about a woman who goes out of her way to avoid me."

"I haven't been. Exactly."

"That's okay, because I figured it was because you couldn't trust yourself around me."

That had her eyes locking on his again, strong and steady. "You have an amazing ego."

"Thanks. Let's try another angle, then." As he spoke, he moved his hand up and down her spine, lighting little fingers of heat. "Kiss me again, and if the bombs don't go off this time I'll figure I was wrong."

"No." But despite herself she couldn't dredge up the will to push him away. "Radley's—"

"Sleeping like a rock, remember?" He touched his lips, very gently, to the swelling under her eye. "And even if he woke up, I don't think the sight of me kissing his mother would give him nightmares."

She started to speak again, but the words were only a sigh as his mouth met hers. He was patient this time, even…tender. Yet the bombs went off. She would have sworn they shook the floor beneath her as she dug her fingers hard into his shoulders.

It was incredible. Impossible. But the need was there, instant, incendiary. It had never been so strong before, not for anyone. Once, when she'd been very young, she'd had a hint of what true, ripe passion could be. And then it had been over. She had come to believe that, like so many other things, such passions were only temporary. But this—this felt like forever.

He'd thought he knew all there was to know about women. Hester was proving him wrong. Even as he felt himself sliding down that warm, soft tunnel of desire, he warned himself not to move too quickly or take too much. There was a hurricane in her, one he had already realized had been channeled and repressed for a long, long time. The first time he'd held her he'd known he had to be the one to free it. But slowly. Carefully. Whether she knew it or not, she was as vulnerable as the child sleeping beside them.

Then her hands were in his hair, pulling him closer. For one mad moment, he dragged her hard against him and let them both taste of what might be.

"Bombs, Hester." She shuddered as he traced his tongue over her ear. "The city's in shambles."

She believed him. With his mouth hot on hers, she believed him. "I have to think."

"Yeah, maybe you do." But he kissed her again. "Maybe we both do." He ran his hands down her body in one long, possessive stroke. "But I have a feeling we're going to come up with the same answer."

Shaken, she backed away. And stumbled over the robot. The crash didn't penetrate Radley's dreams.

"You know, you run into things every time I kiss you." He was going to have to go now or not at all. "I'll pick up the VCR later."

There was a little breath of relief as she nodded. She'd been afraid he'd ask her to sleep with him, and she wasn't at all sure what her answer would have been. "Thank you for everything."

"Good, you're learning." He stroked a finger down her cheek. "Take care of the eye."

Cowardly or not, Hester stayed by Radley's bed until she heard the front door shut. Then, easing down, she put a hand on her sleeping son's shoulder. "Oh, Rad, what have I gotten into?"

Chapter 5

When the phone rang at 7:25, Mitch had his head buried under a pillow. He would have ignored it, but Taz rolled over, stuck his snout against Mitch's cheek and began to grumble in his ear. Mitch swore and shoved at the dog, then snatched up the receiver and dragged it under the pillow.

"What?"

On the other end of the line, Hester bit her lip. "Mitch, it's Hester."

"So?"

"I guess I woke you up."

"Right."

It was painfully obvious that Mitch Dempsey wasn't a morning person. "I'm sorry. I know it's early."

"Is that what you called to tell me?"

"No...I guess you haven't looked out the window yet."

"Honey, I haven't even looked past my eyelids yet."

"It's snowing. We've got about eight inches, and it's not expected to let up until around midday. They're calling for twelve to fifteen inches."

"Who are they?"

Hester switched the phone to her other hand. Her hair was still wet from the shower, and she'd only had a chance to gulp down one cup of coffee. "The National Weather Service."

"Well, thanks for the bulletin."

"Mitch! Don't hang up."

He let out a long sigh, then shifted away from Taz's wet nose. "Is there more news?"

"The schools are closed."

"Whoopee."

She was tempted, very tempted to hang up the phone in his ear. The trouble was, she needed him. "I hate to ask, but I'm not sure I can get Radley all the way over to Mrs. Cohen's. I'd take the day off, but I have back-to-back appointments most of the day. I'm going to try to shift things around and get off early, but—"

"Send him down."

There was the briefest of hesitations. "Are you sure?"

"Did you want me to say no?"

"I don't want to interfere with any plans you had."

"Got any hot coffee?"

"Well, yes, I—"

"Send that, too."

Hester stared at the phone after it clicked in her ear, and tried to remind herself to be grateful.

Radley couldn't have been more pleased. He took Taz for his morning walk, threw snowballs—which the dog,

Nora Roberts 197

on principle, refused to chase—and rolled in the thick blanket of snow until he was satisfactorily covered.

Since Mitch's supplies didn't run to hot chocolate, Radley raided his mother's supply, then spent the rest of the morning happily involved with Mitch's comic books and his own sketches.

As for Mitch, he found the company appealing rather than distracting. The boy lay sprawled on the floor of his office and, between his reading or sketching, rambled on about whatever struck his fancy. Because he spoke to either Mitch or Taz, and seemed to be content to be answered or not, it suited everyone nicely.

By noon the snow had thinned to occasional flurries, dashing Radley's fantasy about another holiday. In tacit agreement, Mitch pushed away from his drawing board.

"You like tacos?"

"Yeah." Radley turned away from the window. "You know how to make them?"

"Nope. But I know how to buy them. Get your coat, Corporal, we've got places to go."

Radley was struggling into his boots when Mitch walked out with a trio of cardboard tubes. "I've got to stop by the office and drop these off."

Radley's mouth dropped down to his toes. "You mean the place where they make the comics?"

"Yeah." Mitch shrugged into his coat. "I guess I could do it tomorrow if you don't want to bother."

"No, I want to." The boy was up and dragging Mitch's sleeve. "Can we go today? I won't touch anything, I promise. I'll be real quiet, too."

"How can you ask questions if you're quiet?" He pulled the boy's collar up. "Get Taz, will you?"

It was always a bit of a trick, and usually an expensive one, to find a cabdriver who didn't object to a hundred-and-fifty pound dog as a passenger. Once inside, however, Taz sat by the window and morosely watched New York pass by.

"It's a mess out here, isn't it?" The cabbie shot a grin in the rearview mirror, pleased with the tip Mitch had given him in advance. "Don't like the snow myself, but my kids do." He gave a tuneless whistle to accompany the big-band music on his radio. "I guess your boy there wasn't doing any complaining about not going to school. No, sir," the driver continued, without any need for an answer. "Nothing a kid likes better than a day off from school, is there? Even going to the office with your dad's better than school, isn't it, kid?" The cabbie let out a chuckle as he pulled to the curb. The snow there had already turned gray. "Here you go. That's a right nice dog you got there, boy." He gave Mitch his change and continued to whistle as they got out. He had another fare when he pulled away.

"He thought you were my dad," Radley murmured as they walked down the sidewalk.

"Yeah." He started to put a hand on Radley's shoulder, then waited. "Does that bother you?"

The boy looked up, wide-eyed and, for the first time, shy. "No. Does it bother you?"

Mitch bent down so they were at eye level. "Well, maybe it wouldn't if you weren't so ugly."

Radley grinned. As they continued to walk, he slipped his hand into Mitch's. He'd already begun to fantasize about Mitch as his father. He'd done it once before with his second grade teacher, but Mr. Stratham hadn't been nearly as neat as Mitch.

"Is this it?" He stopped as Mitch walked toward a tall, scarred brownstone.

"This is it."

Radley struggled with disappointment. It looked so—ordinary. He'd thought they would at least have the flag of Perth or Ragamond flying. Understanding perfectly, Mitch led him inside.

There was a guard in the lobby who lifted a hand to Mitch and continued to eat his pastrami sandwich. Acknowledging the greeting, Mitch took Radley to an elevator and drew open the iron gate.

"This is pretty neat," Radley decided.

"It's neater when it works." Mitch pushed the button for the fifth floor, which housed the editorial department. "Let's hope for the best."

"Has it ever crashed?" The question was half wary, half hopeful.

"No, but it has been known to go on strike." The car shuddered to a stop on 5. Mitch swung the gate open again. He put a hand on Radley's head. "Welcome to bedlam."

It was precisely that. Radley forgot his disappointment with the exterior in his awe at the fifth floor. There was a reception area of sorts. In any case, there was a desk and a bank of phones manned by a harassed-looking black woman in a Princess Leilah sweatshirt. The walls around her were crammed with posters depicting Universal's most enduring characters: the Human Scorpion, the Velvet Saber, the deadly Black Moth and, of course, Commander Zark.

"How's it going, Lou?"

"Don't ask." She pushed a button on a phone. "I ask you, is it my fault the deli won't deliver his corned beef?"

"If I put him in a good mood, will you dig up some samples for me?"

"Universal Comics, please hold." The receptionist pushed another button. "You put him in a good mood, you've got my firstborn."

"Just the samples, Lou. Put on your helmet, Corporal. This could be messy." He led Radley down a short hall into the big, brightly lit hub of activity. It was a series of cubicles with a high noise level and a look of chaos. Pinned to the corkboard walls were sketches, rude messages and an occasional photograph. In a corner was a pyramid made of empty soda cans. Someone was tossing wadded-up balls of paper at it.

"Scorpion's never been a joiner. What's his motivation for hooking up with Worldwide Law and Justice?"

A woman with pencils poking out of her wild red hair at dangerous angles shifted in her swivel chair. Her eyes, already huge, were accented by layers of liner and mascara. "Look, let's be real. He can't save the world's water supply on his own. He needs someone like Atlantis."

A man sat across from her, eating an enormous pickle. "They hate each other. Ever since they bumped heads over the Triangular Affair."

"That's the point, dummy. They'll have to put personal feelings aside for the sake of mankind. It's a moral." Glancing over, she caught sight of Mitch. "Hey, Dr. Deadly's poisoned the world's water supply. Scorpion's found an antidote. How's he going to distribute it?"

"Sounds like he'd better mend fences with Atlantis," Mitch replied. "What do you think, Radley?"

For a moment, Rad was so tongue-tied he could only stare. Then, taking a deep breath, he let the words blurt out. "I think they'd make a neat team, 'cause they'd always be fighting and trying to show each other up."

"I'm with you, kid." The redhead held out her hand. "I'm M. J. Jones."

"Wow, really?" He wasn't sure whether he was more impressed with meeting M. J. Jones or with discovering she was a woman. Mitch didn't see the point in mentioning that she was one of the few in the business.

"And this grouch over here is Rob Myers. You bring him as a shield, Mitch?" she asked without giving Rob time to swallow his pickle. They'd been married for six years, and she obviously enjoyed frustrating him.

"Do I need one?"

"If you don't have something terrific in those tubes, I'd advise you to slip back out again." She shoved aside a stack of preliminary sketches. "Maloney just quit, defected to Five Star."

"No kidding?"

"Skinner's been muttering about traitors all morning. And the snow didn't help his mood. So if I were you... Oops, too late." Respecting rats who deserted tyrannically captained ships, M.J. turned away and fell into deep discussion with her husband.

"Dempsey, you were supposed to be in two hours ago."

Mitch gave his editor an ingratiating smile. "My alarm didn't go off. This is Radley Wallace, a friend of mine. Rad, this is Rich Skinner."

Radley stared. Skinner looked exactly like Hank

Wheeler, the tanklike and overbearing boss of Joe David, alias the Fly. Later, Mitch would tell him that the resemblance was no accident. Radley switched Taz's leash to his other hand.

"Hello, Mr. Skinner. I really like your comics. They're lots better than Five Star. I hardly ever buy Five Star, because the stories aren't as good."

"Right." Skinner dragged a hand through his thinning hair. "Right," he repeated with more conviction. "Don't waste your allowance on Five Star, kid."

"No, sir."

"Mitch, you know you're not supposed to bring that mutt in here."

"You know how Taz loves you." On cue, Taz lifted his head and howled.

Skinner started to swear, then remembered the boy. "You got something in those tubes, or did you just come by to brighten up my dull day?"

"Why don't you take a look for yourself?"

Grumbling, Skinner took the tubes and marched off. As Mitch started to follow, Radley grabbed at his hand. "Is he really mad?"

"Sure. He likes being mad best."

"Is he going to yell at you like Hank Wheeler yells at the Fly?"

"Maybe."

Radley swallowed and buried his hand in Mitch's. "Okay."

Amused, Mitch led Radley into Skinner's office, where the venetian blinds had been drawn to shut off any view of the snow. Skinner unrolled the contents of the first tube and spread them over his already cluttered desk. He didn't sit, but loomed over them while Taz plopped down on the linoleum and went to sleep.

"Not bad," Skinner announced after he had studied the series of sketches and captions. "Not too bad. This new character, Mirium, you have plans to expand her?"

"I'd like to. I think Zark's ready to have his heart tugged from a different direction. Adds more emotional conflict. He loves his wife, but she's his biggest enemy. Now he runs into this empath and finds himself torn up all over again because he has feelings for her, as well."

"Zark never gets much of a break."

"I think he's the best," Radley piped in, forgetting himself.

Skinner lifted his bushy brows and studied Radley carefully. "You don't think he gets carried away with this honor and duty stuff?"

"Uh-uh." He wasn't sure if he was relieved or disappointed that Skinner wasn't going to yell. "You always know Zark's going to do the right thing. He doesn't have any super powers and stuff, but he's real smart."

Skinner nodded, accepting the opinion. "We'll give your Mirium a shot, Mitch, and see what the reader response is like." He let the papers roll into themselves again. "This is the first time I can remember you being this far ahead of deadline."

"That's because I have an assistant now." Mitch laid a hand on Radley's shoulder.

"Good work, kid. Why don't you take your assistant on a tour?"

It would take Radley weeks to stop talking about his hour at Universal Comics. When they left, he carried a shopping bag full of pencils with Universal's logo, a Mad Matilda mug that had been unearthed from someone's storage locker, a half dozen rejected sketches and a batch of comics fresh off the presses.

"This was the best day in my whole life," Radley said, dancing down the snow-choked sidewalk. "Wait until I show Mom. She won't believe it."

Oddly enough, Mitch had been thinking of Hester himself. He lengthened his stride to keep up with Radley's skipping pace. "Why don't we go by and pay her a visit?"

"Okay." He slipped his hand into Mitch's again. "The bank's not nearly as neat as where you work, though. They don't let anyone play radios or yell at each other, but they have a vault where they keep lots of money—millions of dollars—and they have cameras everywhere so they can see anybody who tries to rob them. Mom's never been in a bank that's been robbed."

Since the statement came out as an apology, Mitch laughed. "We can't all be blessed." He ran a hand over his stomach. He hadn't put anything into it in at least two hours. "Let's grab that taco first."

Inside the staid and unthreatened walls of National Trust, Hester dealt with a stack of paperwork. She enjoyed this part of her job, the organized monotony of it. There was also the challenge of sorting through the facts and figures and translating them into real estate, automobiles, business equipment, stage sets or college funds. Nothing gave her greater pleasure than to be able to stamp a loan with her approval.

She'd had to teach herself not to be softhearted. There were times the facts and figures told you to say no, no matter how earnest the applicant might be. Part of her job was to dictate polite and impersonal letters of refusal.

Hester might not have cared for it, but she accepted that responsibility, just as she accepted the occasional irate phone call from the recipient of a loan refusal.

At the moment she was stealing half an hour, with the muffin and coffee that would be her lunch, to put together three loan packages she wanted approved by the board when they met the following day. She had another appointment in fifteen minutes. And, with that and a lack of interruptions, she could just finish. She wasn't particularly pleased when her assistant buzzed through.

"Yes, Kay."

"There's a young man out here to see you, Mrs. Wallace."

"His appointment isn't for fifteen minutes. He'll have to wait."

"No, it isn't Mr. Greenburg. And I don't think he's here for a loan. Are you here for a loan, honey?"

Hester heard the familiar giggle and hurried to the door. "Rad? Is everything all right—oh."

He wasn't alone. Hester realized she'd been foolish to think Radley would have made the trip by himself. Mitch was with him, along with the huge, mild-eyed dog.

"We just ate tacos."

Hester eyed the faint smudge of salsa on Radley's chin. "So I see." She bent to hug him, then glanced up at Mitch. "Is everything okay?"

"Sure. We were just out taking care of a little business and decided to drop by." He took a good long look. She'd covered most of the colorful bruise with makeup. Only a hint of yellow and mauve showed through. "The eye looks better."

"I seem to have passed the crisis."

"That your office?" Without invitation, he strolled

over to stick his head inside. "God, how depressing. Maybe you can talk Radley into giving you one of his posters."

"You can have one," Radley agreed immediately. "I got a bunch of them when Mitch took me to Universal. Wow, Mom you should see it. I met M. J. Jones and Rich Skinner and I saw this room where they keep zillions of comics. See what I got." He held up his shopping bag. "For free. They said I could."

Her first feeling was one of discomfort. It seemed her obligation to Mitch grew with each day. Then she looked down at Radley's eager, glowing face. "Sounds like a pretty great morning."

"It was the best ever."

"Yellow alert," Kay murmured. "Rosen at three o'clock."

It didn't take words to show Mitch that Rosen was a force to be reckoned with. He saw Hester's face poker up instantly as she smoothed a hand over her hair to be sure it was in place.

"Good afternoon, Mrs. Wallace." He glanced meaningfully at the dog, who sniffed the toe of his shoe. "Perhaps you've forgotten that pets are not permitted inside the bank."

"No, sir. My son was just—"

"Your son?" Rosen gave Radley a brief nod. "How do you do, young man. Mrs. Wallace, I'm sure you remember that bank policy frowns on personal visits during working hours."

"Mrs. Wallace, I'll just put these papers on your desk for your signature—when your lunch break is over." Kay shuffled some forms importantly, then winked at Radley.

"Thank you, Kay."

Rosen harrumphed. He couldn't argue with a lunch break, but it was his duty to deal with other infractions of policy. "About this animal—"

Finding Rosen's tone upsetting, Taz pushed his nose against Radley's knee and moaned. "He's mine." Mitch stepped forward, his smile charming, his hand outstretched. Hester had time to think that with that look he could sell Florida swampland. "Mitchell Dempsey II. Hester and I are good friends, very good friends. She's told me so much about you and your bank." He gave Rosen's hand a hearty political shake. "My family has several holdings in New York. Hester's convinced me I should use my influence to have them transfer to National Trust. You might be familiar with some of the family companies. Trioptic, D and H Chemicals, Dempsey Paperworks?"

"Well, of course, of course." Rosen's limp grip on Mitch's hand tightened. "It's a pleasure to meet you, a real pleasure."

"Hester persuaded me to come by and see for myself how efficiently National Trust ticked." He definitely had the man's number, Mitch thought. Dollar signs were already flitting through the pudgy little brain. "I am impressed. Of course, I could have taken Hester's word for it." He gave her stiff shoulder an intimate little squeeze. "She's just a whiz at financial matters. I can tell you, my father would snatch her up as a corporate adviser in a minute. You're lucky to have her."

"Mrs. Wallace is one of our most valued employees."

"I'm glad to hear it. I'll have to bring up National Trust's advantages when I speak with my father."

"I'll be happy to take you on a tour personally. I'm sure you'd like to see the executive offices."

"Nothing I'd like better, but I am a bit pressed for time." If he'd had days stretching out before him, he wouldn't have spent a minute of them touring the stuffy corners of a bank. "Why don't you work up a package I can present at the next board meeting?"

"Delighted." Rosen's face beamed with pleasure. Bringing an account as large and diversified as Dempsey's to National Trust would be quite a coup for the stuffy bank manager.

"Just send it through Hester. You don't mind playing messenger, do you, darling?" Mitch said cheerfully.

"No," she managed.

"Excellent," Rosen said, the excitement evident in his voice. "I'm sure you'll find we can serve all your family's needs. We are the bank to grow with, after all." He patted Taz's head. "Lovely dog," he said and strode off with a new briskness in his step.

"What a fusty old snob," Mitch decided. "How do you stand it?"

"Would you come into my office a moment?" Hester's voice was as stiff as her shoulders. Recognizing the tone, Radley rolled his eyes at Mitch. "Kay, if Mr. Greenburg comes in, please have him wait."

"Yes, ma'am."

Hester led the way into her office, then closed the door and leaned against it. There was a part of her that wanted to laugh, to throw her arms around Mitch and howl with delight over the way he'd handled Rosen. There was another part, the part that needed a job, a regular salary and employee benefits, that cringed.

"How could you do that?"

"Do what?" Mitch took a look around the office. "The brown carpet has to go. And this paint. What do you call this?"

"Yuk," Radley ventured as he settled in a chair with Taz's head in his lap.

"Yeah, that's it. You know, your work area has a lot to do with your work production. Try that on Rosen."

"I won't be trying anything with Rosen once he finds out what you did. I'll be fired."

"Don't be silly. I never promised my family would move their interests to National Trust. Besides, if he puts together an intriguing enough package, they just might." He shrugged, indicating it made little difference to him. "If it'll make you happier, I can move my personal accounts here. A bank's a bank as far as I'm concerned."

"Damn it." It was very rare for her to swear out loud and with heat. Radley found the fur on Taz's neck of primary interest. "Rosen's got corporate dynasty on his mind, thanks to you. He's going to be furious with me when he finds out you made all that up."

Mitch tapped a hand on a tidy stack of papers. "You're obsessively neat, did you know that? And I didn't make anything up. I could have," he said thoughtfully. "I'm good at it, but there didn't seem to be any reason to."

"Would you stop?" Frustrated, she moved to him to slap his hands away from her work. "All that business about Trioptic and D and H Chemicals." Letting out a long sigh, she dropped down on the edge of the desk. "I know you did it to try to help me, and I appreciate the thought, but—"

"You do?" With a smile, he fingered the lapel of her suit jacket.

"You mean well, I suppose," Hester murmured.

"Sometimes." He leaned a little closer. "You smell much too good for this office."

"Mitch." She put a hand on his chest and glanced nervously at Radley. The boy had an arm hooked around Taz and was already deeply involved in one of his new comic books.

"Do you really think it would be a traumatic experience if the kid saw me kiss you?"

"No." At his slight movement, she pressed harder. "But that's beside the point."

"What *is* the point?" He took his hand from her jacket to fiddle with the gold triangle at her ear.

"The point is I'm going to have to see Rosen and explain to him that you were just…" What was the word she wanted? "Fantasizing."

"I've done a lot of that," he admitted as he moved his thumb down her jawline. "But I'm damned if I think it's any of his business. Want me to tell you the one about you and me in the life raft on the Indian Ocean?"

"No." This time she had to laugh, though the reaction in her stomach had more to do with heat than humor. Curiosity pricked at her so that she met his eyes, then looked quickly away again. "Why don't you and Rad go home? I have another appointment, then I'll go and explain things to Mr. Rosen."

"You're not mad anymore?"

She shook her head and gave in to the urge to touch his face. "You were just trying to help. It was sweet of you."

He imagined she'd have taken the same attitude with Radley if he'd tried to wash the dishes and had smashed her violet-edged china on the floor. Telling himself it was a kind of test, he pressed his lips firmly to hers. He felt each layer of reaction—the shock, the tension, the need. When he drew back, he saw more than indulgence in her eyes. The fire flickered briefly, but with intensity.

"Come on, Rad, your mom has to get back to work. If we're not in the apartment when you get home, we're in the park."

"Fine." Unconsciously she pressed her lips together to seal in the warmth. "Thanks."

"Anytime."

"Bye, Rad, I'll be home soon."

"Okay." He lifted his arms to squeeze her neck. "You're not mad at Mitch anymore?"

"No," she answered in the same carrying whisper. "I'm not mad at anyone."

She was smiling when she straightened, but Mitch saw the worried look in her eye. He paused with his hand on the knob. "You're really going to go up to Rosen and tell him I made that business up?"

"I have to." Then, because she felt guilty about launching her earlier attack, she smiled. "Don't worry. I'm sure I can handle him."

"What if I told you I didn't make it up, that my family founded Trioptic forty-seven years ago?"

Hester lifted a brow. "I'd say don't forget your gloves. It's cold out there."

"Okay, but do yourself a favor before you bare your soul to Rosen. Look it up in *Who's Who.*"

With her hands in her pockets, Hester walked to her office door. From there she saw Radley reach up to put a gloved hand into Mitch's bare one.

"Your son's adorable," Kay said, offering Hester

a file. The little skirmish with Rosen had completely changed her opinion of the reserved Mrs. Wallace.

"Thanks." When Hester smiled, Kay's new opinion was cemented. "And I do appreciate you covering for me that way."

"That's no big deal. I don't see what's wrong with your son dropping by for a minute."

"Bank policy," Hester murmured under her breath, and Kay let out a snort.

"Rosen policy, you mean. Beneath that gruff exterior is a gruff interior. But don't worry about him. I happen to know he considers your work production far superior to your predecessor's. As far as he's concerned, that's the bottom line."

Kay hesitated a moment as Hester nodded and flipped through the file. "It's tough raising a kid on your own. My sister has a little girl, she's just five. I know some nights Annie's just knocked out from wearing all the badges, you know."

"Yes, I do."

"My parents want her to move back home so Mom can watch Sarah while Annie works, but Annie's not sure it's the best thing."

"Sometimes it's hard to know if accepting help's right," Hester murmured, thinking of Mitch. "And sometimes we forget to be grateful that someone's there to offer it." She shook herself and tucked the file under her arm. "Is Mr. Greenburg here?"

"Just came in."

"Fine, send him in, Kay." She started for her office, then stopped. "Oh, and Kay, dig me up a copy of *Who's Who.*"

Chapter 6

He was loaded.

Hester was still dazed when she let herself into her apartment. Her downstairs neighbor with the bare feet and the holes in his jeans was an heir to one of the biggest fortunes in the country.

Hester took off her coat and, out of habit, went to the closet to hang it up. The man who spent his days writing the further adventures of Commander Zark came from a family who owned polo ponies and summer houses. Yet he lived on the fourth floor of a very ordinary apartment building in Manhattan.

He was attracted to her. She'd have had to be blind and deaf not to be certain of that, and yet she'd known him for weeks and he hadn't once mentioned his family or his position in an effort to impress her.

Who was he? she wondered. She'd begun to think

she had a handle on him, but now he was a stranger all over again.

She had to call him, tell him she was home and to send Radley up. Hester looked at the phone with a feeling of acute embarrassment. She'd lectured him about spinning a tale to Mr. Rosen; then, in her soft-hearted and probably condescending way, she'd forgiven him. It all added up to her doing what she hated most. Making a fool of herself.

Swearing, Hester snatched up the phone. She would have felt much better if she could have rapped Mitchell Dempsey II over the head with it.

She'd dialed half the numbers when she heard Radley's howl of laughter and the sound of stomping feet in the hall outside. She opened the door just as Radley was digging his key out of his pocket.

Both of them were covered with snow. Some that was beginning to melt dripped from Radley's ski cap and boot tops. They looked unmistakably as if they'd been rolling in it.

"Hi, Mom. We've been in the park. We stopped by Mitch's to get my bag, then came on up because we thought you'd be home. Come on out with us."

"I don't think I'm dressed for snow wars."

She smiled and peeled off her son's snow-crusted cap but, Mitch noted, she didn't look up. "So change." He leaned against the doorjamb, ignoring the snow that fell at his feet.

"I built a fort. Please come out and see. I already started a snow warrior, but Mitch said we should check in so you wouldn't worry."

His consideration forced her to look up. "I appreciate that."

He was watching her thoughtfully—too thoughtfully, Hester decided. "Rad says you build a pretty good snow warrior yourself."

"Please, Mom. What if we got a freak heat wave and the snow was all gone tomorrow? It's like the green-house effect, you know. I read all about it."

She was trapped and knew it. "All right, I'll change. Why don't you fix Mitch some hot chocolate and warm up?"

"All right!" Radley dropped down on the floor just inside the door. "You have to take off your boots," he told Mitch. "She gets mad if you track up the carpet."

Mitch unbuttoned his coat as Hester walked away. "We wouldn't want to make her mad."

Within fifteen minutes, Hester had changed into cor-duroys, a bulky sweater and old boots. In place of her red coat was a blue parka that showed some wear. Mitch kept one hand on Taz's leash and the other in his pocket as they walked across to the park. He couldn't say why he enjoyed seeing her dressed casually with Radley's hand joined tight with hers. He couldn't say for certain why he'd wanted to spend this time with her, but it had been he who'd planted the idea of another outing in Radley's head, and he who'd suggested that they go up together to persuade her to come outside.

He liked the winter. Mitch took a deep gulp of cold air as they walked through the soft, deep snow of Cen-tral Park. Snow and stinging air had always appealed to him, particularly when the trees were draped in white and there were snow castles to be built.

When he'd been a boy, his family had often win-tered in the Caribbean, away from what his mother had termed the "mess and inconvenience." He'd picked up an affection for scuba and white sand, but had never felt that a palm tree replaced a pine at Christmas.

The winters he'd liked best had been spent in his uncle's country home in New Hampshire, where there'd been woods to walk in and hills to sled. Oddly enough, he'd been thinking of going back there for a few weeks—until the Wallaces popped up two floors above, that is. He hadn't realized until today that he'd shuffled those plans to the back of his mind as soon as he'd seen Hester and her son.

Now she was embarrassed, annoyed and uncomfortable. Mitch turned to study her profile. Her cheeks were already rosy with cold, and she'd made certain that Radley walked between them. He wondered if she realized how obvious her strategies were. She didn't use the boy, not in the way some parents used their offspring for their own ambitions or purposes. He respected her for that more than he could have explained. But she had, by putting Radley in the center, relegated Mitch to the level of her son's friend.

And so he was, Mitch thought with a smile. But he'd be damned if he was going to let it stop there.

"There's the fort. See?" Radley tugged on Hester's hand, then let it go to run, too impatient to wait any longer.

"Pretty impressive, huh?" Before she could avoid it, Mitch draped a casual arm over her shoulder. "He's really got a knack."

Hester tried to ignore the warmth and pressure of his arm as she looked at her son's handiwork. The walls of the fort were about two feet high, smooth as stone, with one end sloping nearly a foot higher in the shape of a round tower. They'd made an arched doorway high enough for Radley to crawl through. When Hester reached the fort, she saw him pass through on his hands and knees and pop up inside, his arms held high.

"It's terrific, Rad. I imagine you had a great deal to do with it," she said quietly to Mitch.

"Here and there." Then he smiled, as though he was laughing at himself. "Rad's a better architect than I'll ever be."

"I'm going to finish my snow warrior." Belly down, Rad crawled through the opening again. "Build one, Mom, on the other side of the fort. They'll be the sentries." Rad began to pack and smooth snow on his already half-formed figure. "You help her, Mitch, 'cause I've got a head start."

"Fair's fair." Mitch scooped up a handful of snow. "Any objections to teamwork?"

"No, of course not." Still avoiding giving him a straight look, Hester knelt in the snow. Mitch dropped the handful of snow on her head.

"I figured that was the quickest way to get you to look at me." She glared, then began to push the snow into a mound. "Problem, Mrs. Wallace?"

Seconds ticked by as she pushed at the snow. "I got a copy of *Who's Who.*"

"Oh?" Mitch knelt down beside her.

"You were telling the truth."

"I've been known to from time to time." He shoved some more snow on the mound she was forming. "So?"

Hester frowned and punched the snow into shape. "I feel like an idiot."

"I told the truth, and you feel like an idiot." Patiently Mitch smoothed over the base she was making. "Want to explain the correlation?"

"You let me lecture you."

"It's kinda hard to stop you when you get rolling."

Hester began to dig out snow with both hands to form the legs. "You let me think you were some poor, eccentric Good Samaritan. I was even going to offer to put patches on your jeans."

"No kidding." Incredibly touched, Mitch caught her chin in his snow-covered glove. "That's sweet."

There was no way she was going to let his charm brush away the discomfort of her embarrassment. "The fact is, you're a rich, eccentric Good Samaritan." She shoved his hand away and began to gather snow for the torso.

"Does this mean you won't patch my jeans?"

Hester's long-suffering breath came out in a white plume. "I don't want to talk about it."

"Yes, you do." Always helpful, Mitch packed on more snow and succeeded in burying her up to the elbows. "Money shouldn't bother you, Hester. You're a banker."

"Money doesn't bother me." She yanked her arms free and tossed two good-sized hunks of snow into his face. Because she had to fight back a giggle, she turned her back. "I just wish the situation had been made clear earlier, that's all."

Mitch wiped the snow from his face, then scooped up more, running his tongue along the inside of his lip. He'd had a lot of experience in forming what he considered the ultimate snowball. "What's the situation, Mrs. Wallace?"

"I wish you'd stop calling me that in that tone of voice." She turned, just in time to get the snowball right between the eyes.

"Sorry." Mitch smiled, then began to brush off her coat. "Must've slipped. About this situation…"

"There is no situation between us." Before she realized it, she'd shoved him hard enough to send him sprawling in the snow. "Excuse me." Her laughter came out in hitches that were difficult to swallow. "I didn't mean to do that. I don't know what it is about you that makes me do things like that." He sat up and continued to stare at her. "I *am* sorry," she repeated. "I think it's best if we just let this other business drop. Now, if I help you up, will you promise not to retaliate?"

"Sure." Mitch held out a gloved hand. The moment he closed it over hers, he yanked her forward. Hester went down, face first. "I don't *always* tell the truth, by the way." Before she could respond, he wrapped his arms around her and began to roll.

"Hey, you're supposed to be building another sentry."

"In a minute," Mitch called to Rad, while Hester tried to catch her breath. "I'm teaching your mom a new game. Like it?" he asked her as he rolled her underneath him again.

"Get off me. I've got snow down my sweater, down my jeans—"

"No use trying to seduce me here. I'm stronger than that."

"You're crazy." She tried to sit up, but he pinned her beneath him.

"Maybe." He licked a trace of snow from her cheek and felt her go utterly still. "But I'm not stupid." His voice had changed. It wasn't the easy, carefree voice of her neighbor now, but the slow, soft tones of a lover. "You feel something for me. You may not like it, but you feel it."

It wasn't the unexpected exercise that had stolen her breath, and she knew it. His eyes were so blue in the lowering sunlight, and his hair glistened with a dusting of snow. And his face was close, temptingly close. Yes, she felt something, she felt something almost from the first minute she saw him, but she wasn't stupid, either.

"If you let go of my arms I'll show you just how I feel."

"Why do I think I wouldn't like it? Never mind." He brushed his lips over hers before she could answer. "Hester, the situation is this. You have feelings for me that have nothing to do with my money, because you didn't know until a few hours ago that I had any to speak of. Some of those feelings don't have anything to do with the fact that I'm fond of your son. They're very personal, as in you and me."

He was right, absolutely and completely right. She could have murdered him for it. "Don't tell me how I feel."

"All right." After he spoke, he surprised her by rising and helping her to her feet. Then he took her in his arms again. "I'll tell you how *I* feel then. I care for you—more than I'd counted on."

She paled beneath her cold-tinted cheeks. There was more than a hint of desperation in her eyes as she shook her head and tried to back away. "Don't say that to me."

"Why not?" He struggled against impatience as he lowered his brow to hers. "You'll have to get used to it. I did."

"I don't want this. I don't want to feel this way."

He tipped her head back, and his eyes were very serious. "We'll have to talk about that."

"No. There's nothing to talk about. This is just getting out of hand."

"It's not out of hand yet." He tangled his fingers in the tips of her hair, but his eyes never left hers. "I'm almost certain it will be before long, but it isn't yet. You're too smart and too strong for that."

She'd be able to breathe easier in a moment. She was sure of it. She'd be able to breathe easier as soon as she was away from him. "No, I'm not afraid of you." Oddly, she discovered that much was true.

"Then kiss me." His voice was coaxing now, gentle. "It's nearly twilight. Kiss me, once, before the sun goes down."

She found herself leaning into him, lifting her lips up and letting her lashes fall without questioning why it should seem so right, so natural to do as he asked. There would be questions later, though she was certain the answers wouldn't come as easily. For now, she touched her lips to his and found them cool, cool and patient.

The world was all ice and snow, forts and fairylands, but his lips were real. They fit on hers firmly, warming her soft, sensitive skin while the racing of her heart heated her body. There was the rushing whoosh of traffic in the distance, but closer, more intimate, was the whisper of her coat sliding against his as they pressed tighter together.

He wanted to coax, to persuade, and just once to see her lips curve into a smile as he left them. He knew there were times when a man who preferred action and impulse had to go step by step. Especially when the prize at the top was precious.

He hadn't been prepared for her, but he knew he could accept what was happening between them with

more ease than she. There were still secrets tucked inside her, hurts that had only partially healed. He knew
better than to wish for the power to wipe all that aside.
How she'd lived and what had happened to her were all
part of the woman she was. The woman he was very,
very close to falling in love with.

So he would take it step by step, Mitch told himself
as he placed her away from him. And he would wait.

"That might have cleared up a few points, but I think
we still have to talk." He took her hand to keep her close
another moment. "Soon."

"I don't know." Had she ever been this confused
before? She'd thought she'd left these feelings, these
doubts behind her long ago.

"I'll come up or you can come down, but we'll talk."

He was jockeying her into a corner, one she knew
she'd be backed into sooner or later. "Not tonight," she
said, despising herself for being a coward. "Rad and I
have a lot to do."

"Procrastination's not your style."

"It is this time," she murmured, and turned away
quickly. "Radley, we have to go in."

"Look, Mom, I just finished, isn't it great?" He stood
back to show off his warrior. "You hardly started yours."

"Maybe we'll finish it tomorrow." She walked to him
quickly and took him by the hand. "We have to go in
and fix dinner now."

"But can't we just—"

"No, it's nearly dark."

"Can Mitch come?"

"No, he can't." She shot a glance over her shoulder as
they walked. He was hardly more than a shadow now,
standing beside her son's fort. "Not tonight."

Mitch put a hand on his dog's head as Taz whined and started forward. "Nope. Not this time."

There didn't seem any way of avoiding him, Hester thought as she started down to Mitch's apartment at her son's request. She had to admit it had been foolish of her to try. On the surface, anyone would think that Mitch Dempsey was the solution to many of her problems. He was genuinely fond of Radley, and gave her son both a companion and a safe and convenient place to stay while she worked. His time was flexible, and he was very generous with it.

The truth was, he'd complicated her life. No matter how much she tried to look at him as Radley's friend or her slightly odd neighbor, he brought back feelings she hadn't experienced in almost ten years. Fluttery pulses and warm surges were things Hester had attributed to the very young or the very optimistic. She'd stopped being either when Radley's father had left them.

In all the years that had followed that moment, she'd devoted herself to her son—to making the best possible home for him, to make his life as normal and well balanced as possible. If Hester the woman had gotten lost somewhere in the shuffle, Radley's mother figured it was a fair exchange. Now Mitch Dempsey had come along and made her feel and, worse, had made her wish.

Taking a deep breath, Hester knocked on Mitch's door. Radley's friend's door, she told herself firmly. The only reason she was here was because Radley had been so excited about showing her something. She wasn't here to see Mitch; she wasn't hoping he would reach out and run his fingertips along her cheek as he sometimes did. Hester's skin warmed at the thought of it.

Hester linked her hands together and concentrated on Radley. She would see whatever it was he was so anxious for her to see, and then she would get them both back upstairs to their own apartment—and safety.

Mitch answered the door. He wore a sweatshirt sporting a decal of a rival super hero across the chest, and sweatpants with a gaping hole in one knee. There was a towel slung over his shoulders. He used one end of it to dry the sweat off his face.

"You haven't been out running in this weather?" she asked before she'd allowed herself to think, immediately regretting the question and the obvious concern in her voice.

"No." He took her hand to draw her inside. She smelled like the springtime that was still weeks and weeks away. Her dark blue suit gave her a look of uncreased professionalism he found ridiculously sexy. "Weights," he told her. The fact was, he'd been lifting weights a great deal since he'd met Hester Wallace. Mitch considered it the second best way to decrease tension and rid the body of excess energy.

"Oh." So that explained the strength she'd felt in his arms. "I didn't realize you went in for that sort of thing."

"The Mr. Macho routine?" he said, laughing. "No, I don't, actually. The thing is, if I don't work out regularly, my body turns into a toothpick. It's not a pretty sight." Because she looked nervous enough to jump out of her skin, Mitch couldn't resist. He leered and flexed his arm. "Want to feel my pecs?"

"I'll pass, thanks." Hester kept her hands by her sides. "Mr. Rosen sent this package." She slipped the fat bank portfolio out from where she'd held it at her side. "Just remember, you asked for it."

"So I did." Mitch accepted it, then tossed it on a pile of magazines on the coffee table. "Tell him I'll pass it along."

"And will you?"

He lifted a brow. "I usually keep my word."

She was certain of that. It reminded her that he'd said they would talk, and soon. "Radley called and said there was something he had to show me."

"He's in the office. Want some coffee?"

It was such a casual offer, so easy and friendly, that she nearly agreed. "Thanks, but we really can't stay. I had to bring some paperwork home with me."

"Fine. Just go on in. I need a drink."

"Mom!" The minute she stepped into the office, Radley jumped up and grabbed her hands. "Isn't it great? It's the neatest present I ever got in my life." With his hands still locked on hers, Radley dragged her over to a scaled-down drawing board.

It wasn't a toy. Hester could see immediately that it was top-of-the-line equipment, if child-sized. The small swivel stool was worn, but the seat was leather. Radley already had graph paper tacked to the board, and with compass and ruler had begun what appeared to be a set of blueprints.

"Is this Mitch's?"

"It was, but he said I could use it now, for as long as I wanted. See, I'm making the plans for a space station. This is the engine room. And over here and here are the living quarters. It's going to have a greenhouse, sort of like the one they had in this movie Mitch let me watch. Mitch showed me how to draw things to scale with these squares."

"I see." Pride in her son overshadowed any tension

as she crouched down for a better look. "You catch on fast, Rad. This is wonderful. I wonder if NASA has an opening."

He chuckled, facedown, as he did when he was both pleased and embarrassed. "Maybe I could be an engineer."

"You can be anything you want." She pressed a kiss to his temple. "If you keep drawing like this, I'm going to need an interpreter to know what you're doing. All these tools." She picked up a square. "I guess you know what they're for."

"Mitch told me. He uses them sometimes when he draws."

"Oh?" She turned the square over in her hand. It looked so—professional.

"Even comic art needs a certain discipline," Mitch said from the doorway. He held a large glass of orange juice, which was already half-gone. Hester rose. He looked—virile, she realized.

There was a faint vee of dampness down the center of his shirt. His hair had been combed through with no more than his fingers and, not for the first time, he hadn't bothered to shave off the night's growth of beard. Beside her, her son was happily remodeling his blueprint.

Virile, dangerous, nerve-wracking he might be, but a kinder man she'd never met. Concentrating on that, Hester stepped forward. "I don't know how to thank you."

"Rad already has."

She nodded, then laid a hand on Radley's shoulder. "You finish that up, Rad. I'll be in the other room with Mitch."

Hester walked into the living room. It was, as she'd

come to expect, cluttered and chaotic. Taz nosed around the carpet looking for cookie crumbs. "I thought I knew Rad inside and out," Hester began. "But I didn't know a drawing board would mean so much to him. I guess I would have thought him too young to appreciate it."

"I told you once he had a natural talent."

"I know." She gnawed on her lip. She wished she had accepted the offer of coffee so that she'd have something to do with her hands. "Rad told me that you were giving him some art lessons. You've done more for him than I ever could have expected. Certainly much more than you're obligated to."

He gave her a long, searching look. "It hasn't got anything to do with obligation. Why don't you sit down?"

"No." She linked her hands together, then pulled them apart again. "No, that's all right."

"Would you rather pace?"

It was the ease of his smile that had her unbending another notch. "Maybe later. I just wanted to tell you how grateful I am. Rad's never had..." A father. The words had nearly come out before Hester had swallowed them in a kind of horror. She hadn't meant that, she assured herself. "He's never had anyone to give him so much attention—besides me." She let out a little breath. That was what she'd meant to say. Of course it was. "The drawing board was very generous. Rad said it was yours."

"My father had it made for me when I was about Rad's age. He'd hoped I'd stop sketching monsters and start doing something productive." He said it without bitterness, but with a trace of amusement. Mitch had long since stopped resenting his parents' lack of understanding.

"It must mean a great deal to you for you to have kept it all this time. I know Rad loves it, but shouldn't you keep it for your own children?"

Mitch took a sip of juice and glanced around the apartment. "I don't seem to have any around at the moment."

"But still—"

"Hester, I wouldn't have given it to him if I hadn't wanted him to have it. It's been in storage for years, gathering dust. It gives me a kick to see Rad putting it to use." He finished off the juice, then set the glass down before he crossed to her. "The present's for Rad, with no strings attached to his mother."

"I know that, I didn't mean—"

"No, I don't think you did, exactly." He was watching her now, unsmiling, with that quiet intensity he drew out at unexpected moments. "I doubt if it was even in the front of your mind, but it was milling around in there somewhere."

"I don't think you're using Radley to get to me, if that's what you mean."

"Good." He did as she'd imagined he might, and ran a finger along her jawline. "Because the fact is, Mrs. Wallace, I'd like the kid without you, or you without the kid. It just so happens that in this case, you came as a set."

"That's just it. Radley and I are a unit. What affects him affects me."

Mitch tilted his head as a new thought began to dawn. "I think I'm getting a signal here. You don't think I'm playing pals and buddies with Rad to get Rad's mother between the sheets?"

"Of course not." She drew back sharply, looking toward the office. "If I had thought that, Radley wouldn't be within ten feet of you."

"But…" He laid his arms on her shoulders, linking his hands loosely behind her neck. "You're wondering if your feelings for me might be residual of Radley's feelings."

"I never said I had feelings for you."

"Yes, you did. And you say it again every time I manage to get this close. No, don't pull away, Hester." He tightened his hands. "Let's be upfront. I want to sleep with you. It has nothing to do with Rad, and less than I figured to do with the primal urge I felt the first time I saw your legs." Her eyes lifted warily to his, but held. "It has to do with the fact that I find you attractive in a lot of ways. You're smart, you're strong and you're stable. It might not sound very romantic, but the fact is, your stability is very alluring. I've never had a lot of it myself."

He brushed his linked hands up the back of her neck. "Now, maybe you're not ready to take a step like this at the moment. But I'd appreciate it if you'd take a straight look at what you want, at what you feel."

"I'm not sure I can. You only have yourself. I have Rad. Whatever I do, whatever decisions I make, ripple down to affect him. I promised myself years ago that he would never be hurt by another one of his parents. I'm going to keep that promise."

He wanted to demand that she tell him about Radley's father then and there, but the boy was just in the next room. "Let me tell you what I believe. You could never make a decision that could hurt Rad. But I do think you could make one that could hurt yourself. I want to be with you, Hester, and I don't think our being together is going to hurt Radley."

"It's all done." Radley streamed out of the office, the graph paper in both hands. Hester immediately started to move away. To prove a point to both of them, Mitch held her where she was. "I want to take it and show Josh tomorrow. Okay?"

Knowing a struggle would be worse than submission, Hester stayed still with Mitch's arms on her shoulders. "Sure you can."

Radley studied them a moment. He'd never seen a man with his arms around his mother, except his grandpa or his uncle. He wondered if this made Mitch like family. "I'm going over to Josh's tomorrow afternoon and I'm staying for a sleepover. We're going to stay up all night."

"Then I'll just have to look after your mom, won't I?"

"I guess." Radley began to roll the graph paper into a tube as Mitch had shown him.

"Radley knows I don't have to be looked after."

Ignoring her, Mitch continued to speak to Radley. "How about if I took your mom on a date?"

"You mean get dressed up and go to a restaurant and stuff?"

"Something like that."

"That'd be okay."

"Good. I'll pick her up at seven."

"I really don't think—"

"Seven's not good?" Mitch interrupted Hester. "All right, seven-thirty, but that's as late as it gets. If I don't eat by eight I get nasty." He gave Hester a quick kiss on the temple before releasing her. "Have a good time at Josh's."

"I will." Radley gathered up his coat and backpack. Then he walked to Mitch and hugged him. The words that had been on the tip of Hester's tongue dried up. "Thanks for the drawing board and everything. It's really neat."

"You're welcome. See you Monday." He waited until Hester was at the door. "Seven-thirty."

She nodded and closed the door quietly behind her.

Chapter 7

She could have made excuses, but the fact was, Hester didn't want to. She knew Mitch had hustled her into this dinner date, but as she crossed the wide leather belt at her waist and secured it, she discovered she didn't mind. In fact, she was relieved that he'd made the decision for her—almost.

The nerves were there. She stood in front of the bureau mirror and took a few long, deep breaths. Yes, there were nerves, but they weren't the stomach-roiling sort she experienced when she went on job interviews. Though she wasn't quite sure where her feelings lay when it came to Mitch Dempsey, she was glad to be certain she wasn't afraid.

Picking up her brush, she studied her reflection as she smoothed her hair. She didn't look nervous, Hester decided. That was another point in her favor. The black wool dress was flattering with its deep cowl neck and nipped-in waist. The red slash of belt accented the line before the skirt flared out. For some reason, red gave her confidence. She considered the bold color another kind of defense for a far-from-bold person.

She fixed oversized scarlet swirls at her ears. Like most of her wardrobe, the dress was practical. It could go to the office, to a PTA meeting or a business lunch. Tonight, she thought with a half smile, it was going on a date.

Hester tried not to dwell on how long it had been since she'd been on a date, but comforted herself with the fact that she knew Mitch well enough to keep up an easy conversation through an evening. An adult evening. As much as she adored Radley, she couldn't help but look forward to it.

When she heard the knock, she gave herself a last quick check, then went to answer. The moment she opened the door, her confidence vanished.

He didn't look like Mitch. Gone were the scruffy jeans and baggy sweatshirts. This man wore a dark suit with a pale blue shirt. And a tie. The top button of the shirt was open, and the tie of dark blue silk was knotted loose and low, but it was still a tie. He was clean-shaven, and though some might have thought he still needed a trim, his hair waved dark and glossy over his ears and the collar of his shirt.

Hester was suddenly and painfully shy.

She looked terrific. Mitch felt a moment's awkwardness himself as he looked at her. Her evening shoes put her to within an inch of his height so that they were eye to eye. It was the wariness in hers that had him relaxing with a smile.

"Looks like I picked the right color." He offered her an armful of red roses.

She knew it was foolish for a woman of her age to be flustered by something as simple as flowers. But her heart rushed up to her throat as she gathered them to her.

"Did you forget your line again?" he murmured.

"My line?"

"Thank you."

The scent of the roses flowed around her, soft and sweet. "Thank you."

He touched one of the petals. He already knew her skin felt much the same. "Now you're supposed to put them in water."

Feeling a great deal more than foolish, Hester stepped back. "Of course. Come in."

"The apartment feels different without Rad," he commented when Hester went to get a vase.

"I know. Whenever he goes to a sleepover, it takes me hours to get used to the quiet." He'd followed her into the kitchen. Hester busied herself with arranging the roses. I am a grown woman, she reminded herself, and just because I haven't been on a date since high school doesn't mean I don't remember how.

"What do you usually do when you have a free evening?"

"Oh, I read, watch a late movie." She turned with the vase and nearly collided with him. Water sloshed dangerously close to the top of the vase.

"The eye's barely noticeable now." He lifted a fingertip to where the bruise had faded to a shadow.

"It wasn't such a calamity." Her throat had tightened. Grown woman or not, she found herself enormously glad that the vase of roses was between them. "I'll get my coat."

After carrying the roses to the table beside the sofa, Hester went to the closet. She slipped one arm into the sleeve before Mitch came up behind her to help her finish. He made such an ordinary task sensual, she thought as she stared straight ahead. He brushed his hands over her shoulders, lingered, then trailed them down her arms before bringing them up again to gently release her hair from the coat collar.

Hester's hands were balled into fists as she turned her head. "Thank you."

"You're welcome." With his hands on her shoulders, Mitch turned her to face him. "Maybe you'll feel better if we get this out of the way now." He kept his hands where they were and touched his lips, firm and warm, to hers. Hester's rigid hands went lax. There was nothing demanding or passionate in the kiss. It moved her unbearably with its understanding.

"Feel better?" Mitch murmured.

"I'm not sure."

With a laugh, he touched his lips to hers again. "Well, I do." Linking his hand with hers, he walked to the door.

The restaurant was French, subdued and very exclusive. The pale flowered walls glowed in the quiet light and the flicker of candles. Diners murmured their private conversations over linen cloths and crystal stemware. The hustle and bustle of the streets were shut out by beveled glass doors.

"Ah, Monsieur Dempsey, we haven't seen you in some time." The maitre d' stepped forward to greet him.

"You know I always come back for your snails."

With a laugh, the maitre d' waved a waiter aside. "Good evening, *mademoiselle*. I'll take you to your table."

The little booth was candlelit and secluded, a place for hand-holding and intimate secrets. Hester's leg brushed Mitch's as they settled.

"The sommelier will be right with you. Enjoy your evening."

"No need to ask if you've been here before."

"From time to time I get tired of frozen pizza. Would you like champagne?"

"I'd love it."

He ordered a bottle, pleasing the wine steward with the vintage. Hester opened her menu and sighed over the elegant foods. "I'm going to remember this the next time I'm biting into half a tuna sandwich between appointments."

"You like your job?"

"Very much." She wondered if *soufflé de crabe* was what it sounded like. "Rosen can be a pain, but he does push you to be efficient."

"And you like being efficient."

"It's important to me."

"What else is, other than Rad?"

"Security." She looked over at him with a half smile. "I suppose that has to do with Rad. The truth is, anything that's been important to me over the last few years has to do with Rad."

She glanced up as the steward brought the wine and began his routine for Mitch's approval. Hester watched the wine rise in her fluted glass, pale gold and frothy. "To Rad, then," Mitch said as he lifted his glass to touch hers. "And his fascinating mother."

Hester sipped, a bit stunned that anything could taste so good. She'd had champagne before, but like everything that had to do with Mitch, it hadn't been quite like this. "I've never considered myself fascinating."

"A beautiful woman raising a boy on her own in one of the toughest cities in the world fascinates me." He sipped and grinned. "Added to that, you do have terrific legs, Hester."

She laughed, and even when he slipped his hand over hers, felt no embarrassment. "So you said before. They're long, anyway. I was taller than my brother until he was out of high school. It infuriated him, and I had to live down the name Stretch."

"Mine was String."

"String?"

"You know those pictures of the eighty-pound weakling? That was me."

Over the rim of her glass, Hester studied the way he filled out the suit jacket. "I don't believe it."

"One day, if I'm drunk enough, I'll show you pictures."

Mitch ordered in flawless French that had Hester staring. This was the comic-book writer, she thought, who built snow forts and talked to his dog. Catching the look, Mitch lifted a brow. "I spent a couple of summers in Paris during high school."

"Oh." It reminded her forcefully where he'd come from. "You said you didn't have any brothers or sisters. Do your parents live in New York?"

"No." He broke off a hunk of crusty French bread. "My mother zips in from time to time to shop or go to the theater, and my father might come in occasionally on business, but New York isn't their style. They still live most of the year in Newport, where I grew up."

"Oh, Newport. We drove through once when I was a kid. We'd always take these rambling car vacations in the summer." She tucked her hair behind her ear in an unconscious gesture that gave him a tantalizing view of her throat. "I remember the houses, the enormous mansions with the pillars and flowers and ornamental trees. We even took pictures. It was hard to believe anyone really lived there." Then she caught herself up abruptly and glanced over at Mitch's amused face. "You did."

"It's funny. I spent some time with binoculars watching the tourists in the summer. I might have homed in on your family."

"We were the ones in the station wagon with the suitcases strapped to the roof."

"Sure, I remember you." He offered her a piece of bread. "I envied you a great deal."

"Really?" She paused with her butter knife in midair. "Why?"

"Because you were going on vacation and eating hot dogs. You were staying in motels with soda machines outside the door and playing car bingo between cities."

"Yes," she murmured. "I suppose that sums it up."

"I'm not pulling poor-little-rich boy," he added when he saw the change in her eyes. "I'm just saying that having a big house isn't necessarily better than having a station wagon." He added more wine to her glass. "In any case, I finished my rebellious money-is-beneath-me stage a long time ago."

"I don't know if I can believe that from someone who lets dust collect on his Louis Quinze."

"That's not rebellion, that's laziness."

"Not to mention sinful," she put in. "It makes me itch for a polishing cloth and lemon oil."

"Any time you want to rub my mahogany, feel free."

She lifted a brow when he smiled at her. "So what did you do during your rebellious stage?"

Her fingertips grazed his. It was one of the few times she'd touched him without coaxing. Mitch lifted his gaze from their hands to her face. "You really want to know?"

"Yes."

"Then we'll make a deal. One slightly abridged life story for another."

It wasn't the wine that was making her reckless, Hester knew, but him. "All right. Yours first."

"We'll start off by saying my parents wanted me to be an architect. It was the only practical and acceptable profession they could see me using my drawing abilities for. The stories I made up didn't really appall them, they merely baffled them—so they were easily ignored. Straight out of high school, I decided to sacrifice my life to art."

Their appetizers were served. Mitch sighed approvingly over his escargots.

"So you came to New York?"

"No, New Orleans. At that time my money was still in trusts, though I doubt I would have used it, in any case. Since I refused to use my parents' financial backing, New Orleans was as close to Paris as I could afford to get. God, I loved it. I starved, but I loved the city. Those dripping, steamy afternoons, the smell of the river. It was my first great adventure. Want one of these? They're incredible."

"No, I—"

"Come on, you'll thank me." He lifted his fork to her lips. Reluctantly, Hester parted them and accepted.

"Oh." The flavor streamed, warm and exotic, over her tongue. "It's not what I expected."

"The best things usually aren't."

She lifted her glass and wondered what Radley's reaction would be when she told him she'd eaten a snail. "So what did you do in New Orleans?"

"I set up an easel in Jackson Square and made my living sketching tourists and selling watercolors. For three years I lived in one room where I baked in the summer and froze in the winter and considered myself one lucky guy."

"What happened?"

"There was a woman. I thought I was crazy about her and vice versa. She modeled for me when I was going through my Matisse period. You should have seen me then. My hair was about your length, and I wore it pulled back and fastened with a leather thong. I even had a gold earring in my left ear."

"You wore an earring?"

"Don't smirk, they're very fashionable now. I was ahead of my time." Appetizers were cleared away to make room for green salads. "Anyway, we were going to play house in my miserable little room. One night, when I'd had a little too much wine, I told her about my parents and how they'd never understood my artistic drive. She got absolutely furious."

"She was angry with your parents?"

"You are sweet," he said unexpectedly, and kissed her hand. "No, she was angry with me. I was rich and hadn't told her. I had piles of money and expected her to be satisfied with one filthy little room in the Quarter where she had to cook red beans and rice on a hot plate. The funny thing was she really cared for me when she'd thought I was poor, but when she found out I wasn't, and that I didn't intend to use what was available to me—and, by association, to her—she was infuriated. We had one hell of a fight, where she let me know what she really thought of me and my work."

Hester could picture him, young, idealistic and struggling. "People say things they don't mean when they're angry."

He lifted her hand and kissed her fingers. "Yes, very sweet." His hand remained on hers as he continued. "Anyway, she left and gave me the opportunity to take stock of myself. For three years I'd been living day to day, telling myself I was a great artist whose time was coming. The truth was I wasn't a great artist. I was a clever one, but I'd never be a great one. So I left New Orleans for New York and commercial art. I was good. I worked fast tucked in my little cubicle and generally made the client happy—and I was miserable. But my credentials there got me a spot at Universal, originally as an inker, then as an artist. And then—" he lifted his glass in salute "—there was Zark. The rest is history."

"You're happy." She turned her hand under his so their palms met. "It shows. Not everyone is as content with themselves as you are, as at ease with himself and what he does."

"It took me awhile."

"And your parents? Have you reconciled with them?"

"We came to the mutual understanding that we'd never understand each other. But we're family. I have my stock portfolio, so they can tell their friends the comic-book business is something that amuses me. Which is true enough."

Mitch ordered another bottle of champagne with the main course. "Now it's your turn."

She smiled and let the delicate soufflé melt on her tongue. "Oh, I don't have anything so exotic as an artist's garret in New Orleans. I had a very average childhood with a very average family. Board games on Saturday nights, pot roast on Sundays. Dad had a good job, Mom stayed home and kept the house. We loved each other very much, but didn't always get along. My sister was very outgoing, head cheerleader, that sort of thing. I was miserably shy."

"You're still shy," Mitch murmured as he wound his fingers around hers.

"I didn't think it showed."

"In a very appealing way. What about Rad's father?" He felt her hand stiffen in his. "I've wanted to ask, Hester, but we don't have to talk about it now if it upsets you."

She drew her hand from his to reach for her glass. The champagne was cold and crisp. "It was a long time ago. We met in high school. Radley looks a great deal like his father, so you can understand that he was very attractive. He was also just a little wild, and I found that magnetic."

She moved her shoulders a little, restlessly, but was determined to finish what she'd started. "I really was painfully shy and a bit withdrawn, so he seemed like something exciting to me, even a little larger than life. I fell desperately in love with him the first time he noticed me. It was as simple as that. In any case, we went together for two years and were married a few weeks after graduation. I wasn't quite eighteen and was absolutely sure that marriage was going to be one adventure after another."

"And it wasn't?" he asked when she paused.

"For a while it was. We were young, so it never seemed terribly important that Allan moved from one job to another, or quit altogether for weeks at a time. Once he sold the living room set that my parents had given us as a wedding present so that we could take a trip to Jamaica. It seemed impetuous and romantic, and at that time we didn't have any responsibilities except to ourselves. Then I got pregnant."

She paused again and, looking back, remembered her own excitement and wonder and fear at the idea of carrying a child. "I was thrilled. Allan got a tremendous kick out of it and started buying strollers and high chairs on credit. Money was tight, but we were optimistic, even when I had to cut down to part-time work toward the end of my pregnancy and then take maternity leave after Radley was born. He was beautiful." She laughed a little. "I know all mothers say that about their babies, but he was honestly the most beautiful, the most precious thing I'd ever seen. He changed my life. He didn't change Allan's."

She toyed with the stem of her glass and tried to work out in her mind what she hadn't allowed herself to think about for a very long time. "I couldn't understand it at the time, but Allan resented having the burden of responsibility. He hated it that we couldn't just stroll out of the apartment and go to the movies or go dancing whenever we chose. He was still unbelievably reckless with money, and because of Rad I had to compensate."

"In other words," Mitch said quietly, "you grew up."

"Yes." It surprised her that he saw that so quickly, and it relieved her that he seemed to understand. "Allan wanted to go back to the way things were, but we weren't children anymore. As I look back, I can see that he was jealous of Radley, but at the time I just wanted him to grow up, to be a father, to take charge. At twenty he was still the sixteen-year-old boy I'd known in high school, but I wasn't the same girl. I was a mother. I'd gone back to work because I'd thought the extra income would ease some of the strain. One day I'd come home after picking Radley up at the sitter's, and Allan was gone. He'd left a note saying he just couldn't handle being tied down any longer."

"Did you know he was leaving?"

"No, I honestly didn't. In all probability it was done on impulse, the way Allan did most things. It would never have occurred to him that it was desertion, to him it would've meant moving on. He thought he was being fair by taking only half the money, but he left all the bills. I had to get another part-time job in the evenings. I hated that, leaving Rad with a sitter and not seeing him. That six months was the worst time of my life."

Her eyes darkened a moment; then she shook her head and pushed it all back into the past. "After a while I'd straightened things out enough to quit the second job. About that time, Allan called. It was the first I'd heard from him since he'd left. He was very amiable, as if we'd been nothing more than passing acquaintances. He told me he was heading up to Alaska to work. After he hung up, I called a lawyer and got a very simple divorce."

"It must have been difficult for you." Difficult? he

thought—he couldn't even imagine what kind of hell it had been. "You could have gone home to your parents."

"No. I was angry for a long, long time. The anger made me determined to stay right here in New York and make it work for me and Radley. By the time the anger had died down, I was making it work."

"He's never come back to see Rad?"

"No, never."

"His loss." He cupped her chin, then leaned over to kiss her lightly. "His very great loss."

She found it easy to lift a hand to his cheek. "The same can be said about that woman in New Orleans."

"Thanks." He nibbled her lips again, enjoying the faint hint of champagne. "Dessert?"

"Hmmm?"

He felt a wild thrill of triumph at her soft, distracted sigh. "Let's skip it." Moving back only slightly, he signaled the waiter for the check, then handed Hester the last of the champagne. "I think we should walk awhile."

The air was biting, almost as exhilarating as the wine. Yet the wine warmed her, making her feel as though she could walk for miles without feeling the wind. She didn't object to Mitch's arm around her shoulders or to the fact that he set the direction. She didn't care where they walked as long as the feelings that stirred inside her didn't fade.

She knew what it was like to fall in love—to be in love. Time slowed down. Everything around you went quickly, but not in a blur. Colors were brighter, sounds sharper, and even in midwinter you could smell flowers. She had been there once before, had felt this intensely once before, but had thought she would never find that place again. Even as a part of her mind struggled to remind her that this couldn't be love—or certainly shouldn't be—she simply ignored it. Tonight she was just a woman.

There were skaters at Rockefeller Center, swirling around and around the ice as the music flowed. Hester watched them, tucked in the warmth of Mitch's arms. His cheek rested on her hair, and she could feel the strong, steady rhythm of his heart.

"Sometimes I bring Rad here on Sundays to skate or just to watch like this. It seems different tonight." She turned her head, and her lips were barely a whisper from his. "Everything seems different tonight."

If she looked at him like that again, Mitch knew he'd break his vow to give her enough time to clear her head and would bundle her into the nearest cab so that he could have her home and in bed before the look broke. Calling on willpower, he shifted her so he could brush his lips over her temple. "Things look different at night, especially after champagne." He relaxed again, her head against his shoulder. "It's a nice difference. Not necessarily steeped in reality, but nice. You can get enough reality from nine to five."

"Not you." Unaware of the tug-of-war she was causing inside him, she turned in his arms. "You make fantasies from nine to five, or whatever hours you choose."

"You should hear the one I'm making up now." He drew another deep breath. "Let's walk some more, and you can tell me about one of yours."

"A fantasy?" Her stride matched his easily. "Mine isn't nearly as earth-shaking as yours, I imagine. It's just a house."

"A house." He walked toward the Park, hoping they'd

both be a little steadier on their feet by the time they reached home. "What kind of house?"

"A country house, one of those big old farmhouses with shutters at the windows and porches all around. Lots of windows so you could look at the woods— there would have to be woods. Inside there would be high ceilings and big fireplaces. Outside would be a garden with wisteria climbing on a trellis." She felt the sting of winter on her cheeks, but could almost smell the summer.

"You'd be able to hear the bees hum in it all summer long. There'd be a big yard for Radley, and he could have a dog. I'd have a swing on the porch so I could sit outside in the evening and watch him catch lightning bugs in a jar." She laughed and let her head rest on his shoulder. "I told you it wasn't earth-shaking."

"I like it." He liked it so well he could picture it, white shuttered and hip roofed, with a barn off in the distance. "But you need a stream so Rad could fish."

She closed her eyes a moment, then shook her head. "As much as I love him, I don't think I could bait a hook. Build a tree house maybe, or throw a curveball, but no worms."

"You throw a curveball?"

She tilted her head and smiled. "Right in the strike zone. I helped coach Little League last year."

"The woman's full of surprises. You wear shorts in the dugout?"

"You're obsessed with my legs."

"For a start."

He steered her into their building and toward the elevators. "I haven't had an evening like this in a very long time."

"Neither have I."

She drew back far enough to study him as they began the ride to her floor. "I've wondered about that, about the fact that you don't seem to be involved with anyone."

He touched her chin with his fingertip. "Aren't I?"

She heard the warning signal, but wasn't quite sure what to do about it. "I mean, I haven't noticed you dating or spending any time with women."

Amused, he flicked the finger down her throat. "Do I look like a monk?"

"No." Embarrassed and more than a little unsettled, she looked away. "No, of course not."

"The fact is, Hester, after you've had your share of wild oats, you lose your taste for them. Spending time with a woman just because you don't want to be alone isn't very satisfying."

"From the stories I hear around the office from the single women, there are plenty of men who disagree with you."

He shrugged as they stepped off the elevator. "It's obvious you haven't played the singles scene." Her brows drew together as she dug for her key. "That was a compliment, but my point is it gets to be a strain or a bore—"

"And this is the age of the meaningful relationship."

"You say that like a cynic. Terribly uncharacteristic, Hester." He leaned against the jamb as she opened the door. "In any case, I'm not big on catchphrases. Are you going to ask me in?"

She hesitated. The walk had cleared her head enough for the doubts to seep through. But along with the doubts was the echo of the way she'd felt when they'd stood together in the cold. The echo was stronger. "All right. Would you like some coffee?"

"No." He shrugged out of his coat as he watched her.

"It's no trouble. It'll only take a minute."

He caught her hands. "I don't want coffee, Hester. I want you." He slipped her coat from her shoulders. "And I want you so bad it makes me jumpy."

She didn't back away, but stood, waiting. "I don't know what to say. I'm out of practice."

"I know." For the first time his own nerves were evident as he dragged a hand through his hair. "That's given me some bad moments. I don't want to seduce you." Then he laughed and walked a few paces away. "The hell I don't."

"I knew—I tried to tell myself I didn't, but I knew when I went out with you tonight that we'd come back here like this." She pressed a hand to her stomach, surprised that it was tied in knots. "I think I was hoping you'd just sort of sweep me away so I wouldn't have to make a decision."

He turned to her. "That's a cop-out, Hester."

"I know." She couldn't look at him then, wasn't certain she dared. "I've never been with anyone but Rad's father. The truth is, I've never wanted to be."

"And now?" He only wanted a word, one word.

She pressed her lips together. "It's been so long, Mitch. I'm frightened."

"Would it help if I told you I am, too?"

"I don't know."

"Hester." He crossed to her to lay his hands on her shoulders. "Look at me." When she did, her eyes were wide and achingly clear. "I want you to be sure, because I don't want regrets in the morning. Tell me what you want."

It seemed her life was a series of decisions. There was no one to tell her which was right or which was wrong. As always, she reminded herself that once the decision was made, she alone would deal with the consequences and accept the responsibility.

"Stay with me tonight," she whispered. "I want you."

Chapter 8

He cupped her face in his hands and felt her tremble. He touched his lips to hers and heard her sigh. It was a moment he knew he would always remember. Her acceptance, her desire, her vulnerability.

The apartment was silent. He would have given her music. The scent of the roses she'd put in a vase was pale next to the fragrance of the garden he imagined for her. The lamp burned brightly. He wouldn't have chosen the secrets of the dark, but rather the mystery of candlelight.

How could he explain to her that there was nothing ordinary, nothing casual in what they were about to give each other? How could he make her understand that he had been waiting all his life for a moment like this? He wasn't certain he could choose the right words, or that the words he did choose would reach her.

So he would show her.

With his lips still lingering on hers, he swept her up into his arms. Though he heard her quick intake of breath, she wrapped her arms around him.

"Mitch—"

"I'm not much of a white knight." He looked at her, half smiling, half questioning. "But for tonight we can pretend."

He looked heroic and strong and incredibly, impossibly sweet. Whatever doubts had remained slipped quietly away. "I don't need a white knight."

"Tonight I need to give you one." He kissed her once more before he carried her into the bedroom.

There was a part of him that needed, ached with that need, so much so that he wanted to lay her down on the bed and cover her with his body. There were times that love ran swiftly, even violently. He understood that and knew that she would, too. But he set her down on the floor beside the bed and touched only her hand.

He drew away just a little. "The light."

"But—"

"I want to see you, Hester."

It was foolish to be shy. It was wrong, she knew, to want to have this moment pass in the dark, anonymously. She reached for the bedside lamp and turned the switch.

The light bathed them, capturing them both standing hand in hand and eye to eye. The quick panic returned, pounding in her head and her heart. Then he touched her and quieted it. He drew off her earrings and set them on the bedside table so that the metal clicked quietly against the wood. She felt a rush of heat, as though with that one simple, intimate move he had already undressed her.

He reached for her belt, then paused when her hands fluttered nervously to his. "I won't hurt you."

"No." She believed him and let her hands drop away. He unhooked her belt to let it slide to the floor. When he lowered his lips to hers again, she slipped her arms around his waist and let the power guide her.

This was what she wanted. She couldn't lie to herself or make excuses. For tonight, she wanted to think only as a woman, to be thought of only as a woman. To be desired, enjoyed, wondered over. When their lips parted, their eyes met. And she smiled.

"I've been waiting for that." He touched a finger to her lips, overcome with a pleasure that was so purely emotional even he couldn't describe it.

"For what?"

"For you to smile at me when I kiss you." He brought his hand to her face. "Let's try it again."

This time the kiss went deeper, edging closer to those uncharted territories. She lifted her hands to his shoulders, then slid them around to encircle his neck. He felt her fingers touch the skin there, shyly at first, then with more confidence.

"Still afraid?"

"No." Then she smiled again. "Yes, a little. I'm not—" she looked away, and he once more brought her face back to his.

"What?"

"I'm not sure what to do. What you like."

He wasn't stunned by her words so much as humbled. He'd said he'd cared for her, and that was true. But now his heart, which had been teetering on the edge, fell over into love.

"Hester, you leave me speechless." He drew her against him, hard, and just held her there. "Tonight, just do what seems right. I think we'll be fine."

He began by kissing her hair, drawing in the scent that had so appealed to him. The mood was already set, seduction on either side unnecessary. He felt her heart begin to race against his; then she turned her head and found his lips with her own.

His hands weren't steady as he drew down the long zipper at her back. He knew it was an imperfect world, but needed badly to give her one perfect night. No one would ever have called him a selfish man, but it was a fact that he'd never before put someone else's needs so entirely before his own.

He drew the wool from her shoulders, down her arms. She wore a simple chemise beneath it, plain white without frills or lace. No fantasy of silk or satin could have excited him more.

"You're lovely." He pressed a kiss to one shoulder, then the other. "Absolutely lovely."

She wanted to be. It had been so long since she'd felt the need to be any more than presentable. When she saw his eyes, she felt lovely. Gathering her courage together, she began to undress him in turn.

He knew it wasn't easy for her. She drew his jacket off, then began to unknot his tie before she was able to lift her gaze to his again. He could feel her fingers tremble lightly against him as she unbuttoned his shirt.

"You're lovely, too," she murmured. The last, the only man she had ever touched this way had been little more than a boy. Mitch's muscles were subtle but hard, and though his chest was smooth, it was that of a man. Her movements were slow, from shyness rather than a knowledge of arousal. His stomach muscles quivered as she reached for the hook of his slacks.

"You're driving me crazy."

She drew her hands back automatically. "I'm sorry."

"No." He tried to laugh, but it sounded like a groan. "I like it."

Her fingers trembled all the more as she slid his slacks over his hips. Lean hips, with the muscles long and hard. She felt a surge that was both fascination and delight as she brought her hands to them. Then she was against him, and the shock of flesh against flesh vibrated through her.

He was fighting every instinct that pushed him to move quickly, to take quickly. Her shy hands and wondering eyes had taken him to the brink and he had to claw his way back. She sensed a war going on inside him, felt the rigidity of his muscles and heard the raggedness of his breathing.

"Mitch?"

"Just a minute." He buried his face in her hair. The battle for control was hard won. He felt weakened by it, weakened and stunned. When he found the soft, sensitive skin of her neck, he concentrated on that alone.

She strained against him, turning her head instinctively to give him freer access. It seemed as though a veil had floated down over her eyes so that the room, which had become so familiar to her, was hazy. She could feel her blood begin to pound where his lips rubbed and nibbled; then it was throbbing hot, close to the skin, softening it, sensitizing it. Her moan sounded primitive in her own ears. Then it was she who was drawing him down to the bed.

He'd wanted another minute before he let his body spread over hers. There were explosions bombarding his system, from head to heart to loins. He knew he had to calm them before they shattered his senses. But her hands were moving over him, her hips straining upward. With an effort, Mitch rolled so that they were side by side.

He brought his lips down on her, and for a moment all the needs, the fantasies, the darker desires centered there. Her mouth was moist and hot, pounding into his brain how she would be when he filled her. He was already dragging the thin barrier of her chemise aside so that she gasped when her breasts met him unencumbered. As his lips closed over the first firm point, he heard her cry out his name.

This was abandonment. She'd been sure she'd never wanted it, but now, as her body went fluid in her movements against his, she thought she might never want anything else. The feelings of flesh against flesh, growing hot and damp, were new and exhilarating. As were the avid seeking of mouths and the tastes they found and drew in. His murmurs to her were hot and incoherent, but she responded. The light played over his hands as he showed her how a touch could make the soul soar.

She was naked, but the shyness was gone. She wanted him to touch and taste and look his fill, just as she was driven to. His body was a fascination of muscle and taut skin. She hadn't known until now that to touch another, to please another, could bring on such wild waves of passion. He cupped a hand over her, and the passion contracted into a ball of flame in her center that abruptly, almost violently, burst. Gasping for breath, she reached for him.

He'd never had a woman respond so utterly. Watching her rise and peak had given him a delirious thrust of pleasure. He wanted badly to take her up and over again and again, until she was limp and mindless. But his control was slipping, and she was calling for him.

His body covered hers, and he filled her.

He couldn't have said how long they moved together—minutes, hours. But he would never forget how her eyes had opened and stared into his.

He was a little shaken as he lay with her on top of the crumpled spread with drops of freezing rain striking the windows. He turned his head toward the hiss and wondered idly how long it had been going on. As far as he could remember, he'd never been so involved with a woman that the outside world, and all its sights and sounds, had simply ceased to exist.

He turned away again and drew Hester against him. His body was cooling rapidly, but he had no desire to move. "You're quiet," he murmured.

Her eyes were closed. She wasn't ready to open them again. "I don't know what to say."

"How about 'Wow'?"

She was surprised she could laugh after such intensity. "Okay. Wow."

"Try for more enthusiasm. How about 'Fantastic, incredible, earth-shattering?'"

She opened her eyes now and looked into his. "How about beautiful?"

He caught her hand in his and kissed it. "Yeah, that'll do." When he propped himself up on his elbow to look down at her, she shifted. "Too late to be shy now," he told her. Then he ran a hand, light and possessively, down her body. "You know, I was right about your legs. I don't suppose I could talk you into putting on a pair of shorts and those little socks that stop at the ankles."

"I beg your pardon?"

Her tone had him gathering her to him and covering her face with kisses. "I have a thing about long legs in shorts and socks. I drive myself crazy watching women jog in the park in the summer. When they color-coordinate them, I'm finished."

"You're crazy."

"Come on, Hester, don't you have some secret turn-on? Men in muscle shirts, in tuxedos with black tie and studs undone?"

"Don't be silly."

"Why not?"

Why not, indeed, she thought, catching her bottom lip between her teeth. "Well, there is something about jeans riding low on the hips with the snap undone."

"I'll never snap my jeans again as long as I live."

She laughed again. "That doesn't mean I'm going to start wearing shorts and socks."

"That's okay. I get excited when I see you in a business suit."

"You do not."

"Oh, yes, I do." He rolled her on top of him and began to play with her hair. "Those slim lapels and high-collar blouses. And you always wear your hair up." With it caught in his hands, he lifted it on top of her head. It wasn't the same look at all, but one that still succeeded in making his mouth dry. "The efficient and dependable Mrs. Wallace. Every time I see you dressed that way I imagine how fascinating it would be to peel off those professional clothes and take out those tidy little pins." He let her hair slide down through his fingers.

Thoughtful, Hester rested her cheek against his cheek. "You're a strange man, Mitch."

"More than likely."

"You depend so much on your imagination, on what it might be, on fantasies and make-believe. With me it's facts and figures, profit and loss, what is or what isn't."

"Are you talking about our jobs or our personalities?"

"Isn't one really the same as the other?"

"No. I'm not Commander Zark, Hester."

She shifted, lulled by the rhythm of his heart. "I suppose what I mean is that the artist in you, the writer in you, thrives on imagination or possibilities. I guess the banker in me looks for checks and balances."

He was silent for a moment, stroking her hair. Didn't she realize how much more there was to her? This was the woman who fantasized about a home in the country, the one who threw a curveball, the one who had just taken a man of flesh and blood and turned him into a puddle of need.

"I don't want to get overly philosophical, but why do you think you chose to deal with loans? Do you get the same feeling when you turn down an application as you do when you approve one?"

"No, of course not."

"Of course not," he repeated. "Because when you approve one, you've had a hand in the possibilities. I have no doubt that you play by the book, that's part of your charm, but I'd wager you get a great deal of personal satisfaction by being able to say, 'Okay, buy your home, start your business, expand.'"

She lifted her head. "You seem to understand me very well." No one else had, she realized with a jolt. Ever.

"I've been giving you a great deal of thought." He drew her to him, wondering if she could feel how well their bodies fit. "A very great deal. In fact, I haven't thought about another woman since I delivered your pizza."

She smiled at that, and would have settled against him again, but he held her back. "Hester…" It was one of the few times in his life he'd ever felt self-conscious. She was looking at him expectantly, even patiently, while he struggled for the right words. "The thing is, I don't want to think about another woman, or be with another woman—this way." He struggled again, then swore. "Damn, I feel like I'm back in high school."

Her smile was cautious. "Are you going to ask me to go steady?"

It wasn't exactly what he'd had in mind, but he could see by the look in her eyes that he'd better go slowly. "I could probably find my class ring if you want."

She looked down at her hand, which was resting so naturally on his heart. Was it foolish to be so moved? If not, it was certainly dangerous. "Maybe we can just leave it that there's no one else I want to be with this way, either."

He started to speak, then stopped himself. She needed time to be sure that was true, didn't she? There had only been one other man in her life, and she'd been no more than a girl then. To be fair, he had to give her room to be certain. But he didn't want to be fair. No, Mitch Dempsey was no self-sacrificing Commander Zark.

"All right." He'd devised and won enough wars to

know how to plan strategy. He'd win Hester before she realized there'd been a battle.

Drawing her down to him, he closed his mouth over hers and began the first siege.

It was an odd and rather wonderful feeling to wake up in the morning beside a lover—even one who nudged you over to the edge of the mattress. Hester opened her eyes and, lying very still, savored it.

His face was buried against the back of her neck, and his arm was wrapped tightly around her waist—which was fortunate, as without it she would have rolled onto the floor. Hester shifted slightly and experienced the arousing sensation of having her sleep-warmed skin rub cozily against his.

She'd never had a lover. A husband, yes, but her wedding night, her first initiation into womanhood, had been nothing like the night she'd just shared with Mitch. Was it fair to compare them? she wondered. Would she be human if she didn't?

That first night so long ago had been frenzied, complicated by her nerves and her husband's hurry. Last night the passion had built layer by layer, as though there'd been all the time in the world to enjoy it. She'd never known that making love could be so liberating. In truth, she hadn't known a man could sincerely want to give pleasure as much as he desired to take it.

She snuggled into the pillow and watched the thin winter light come through the windows. Would things be different this morning? Would there be an awkwardness between them or, worse, a casualness that would diminish the depth of what they'd shared? The simple fact was she didn't know what it was like to have a lover—or to be one.

She was putting too much emphasis on one evening, she told herself, sighing. How could she not, when the evening had been so special?

Hester touched a hand to his, let it linger a moment, then shifted to rise. Mitch's arm clamped down.

"Going somewhere?"

She tried to turn over, but discovered his legs had pinned her. "It's almost nine."

"So?" His fingers spread out lazily to stroke.

"I have to get up. I need to pick Rad up in a couple of hours."

"Hmmm." He watched his little dream bubble of a morning in bed with her deflate, then reconstructed it to fit two hours. "You feel so good." He released his hold, but only so he could turn her around so they were face-to-face. "Look good, too," he decided as he studied her face through half-closed eyes. "And taste—" he touched his lips to hers, and there was nothing awkward, nothing casual "—wonderful. Imagine this." He ran a hand down her flank. "We're on an island—the South Seas, let's say. The ship was wrecked a week ago, and we're the only survivors." His eyes closed as he pressed a kiss to her forehead. "We've been living on fruit and the fish I cleverly catch with my pointed stick."

"Who cleans them?"

"This is a fantasy, you don't worry about details like that. Last night there was a storm—a big, busting tropical storm—and we had to huddle together for warmth and safety under the lean-to I built."

"You built?" Her lips curved against his. "Do I do anything useful?"

"You can do all you want in your own fantasy. Now shut up." He snuggled closer and could almost smell the salt air. "It's morning, and the storm washed everything clean. There are gulls swooping down near the surf. We're lying together on an old blanket."

"Which you heroically salvaged from the wreck."

"Now you're catching on. When we wake up, we discover we'd tangled together during the night, drawn together despite ourselves. The sun's hot—it's already warmed our half-naked bodies. Still dazed with sleep, already aroused, we come together. And then…" His lips hovered a breath away from hers. Hester let her eyes close as she found herself caught up in the picture he painted. "And then a wild boar attacks, and I have to wrestle him."

"Half-naked and unarmed?"

"That's right. I'm badly bitten, but I kill him with my bare hands."

Hester opened her eyes again to narrow slits. "And while you're doing that, I put the blanket over my head and whimper."

"Okay." Mitch kissed the tip of her nose. "But afterward you're very, very grateful that I saved your life."

"Poor, defenseless female that I am."

"That's the ticket. You're so grateful you tear the rags of your skirt to make bandages for my wounds, and then…" He paused for impact. "You make me coffee."

Hester drew back, not certain whether to be amazed or amused. "You went through that whole scenario so I'd offer to make you coffee?"

"Not just coffee, morning coffee, the first cup of coffee. Life's blood."

"I'd have made it even without the story."

"Yeah, but did you like the story?"

She combed the hair away from her face as she considered. "Next time I get to catch the fish."

"Deal."

She rose and, though she knew it was foolish, wished that she'd had her robe within arm's reach. Going to the closet, she slipped it on with her back still to him. "Do you want some breakfast?"

He was sitting up, rubbing his hands over his face when she turned. "Breakfast? You mean likes eggs or something? Hot food?" The only time he managed a hot breakfast was when he had the energy to drag himself to the corner diner. "Mrs. Wallace, for a hot breakfast you can have the crown jewels of Perth."

"All that for bacon and eggs?"

"Bacon, too? God, what a woman."

She laughed, sure he was joking. "Go ahead and get a shower if you want. It won't take long."

He hadn't been joking. Mitch watched her walk from the room and shook his head. He didn't expect a woman to offer to cook for him, or for one to offer as though he had a right to expect it. But this, he remembered, was the woman who would have sewed patches on his jeans because she'd thought he couldn't afford new ones.

Mitch climbed out of bed, then slowly, thoughtfully ran a hand through his hair. The aloof and professional Hester Wallace was a very warm and special woman, and he had no intention of letting her get away.

She was stirring eggs in a skillet when he came into the kitchen. Bacon was draining on a rack, and coffee was already hot. He stood in the doorway a moment, more than a little surprised that such a simple domestic scene would affect him so strongly. Her robe was flannel and covered her from neck to ankle, but to him Hester had never looked more alluring. He hadn't realized he'd been looking for this—the morning smells, the morning sounds of the Sunday news on the radio on the counter, the morning sights of the woman who'd shared his night moving competently in the kitchen.

As a child, Sunday mornings had been almost formal affairs—brunch at eleven, served by a uniformed member of the staff. Orange juice in Waterford, shirred eggs on Wedgwood. He'd been taught to spread the Irish linen on his lap and make polite conversation. In later years, Sunday mornings had meant a bleary-eyed search through the cupboards or a dash down to the nearest diner.

He felt foolish, but he wanted to tell Hester that the simple meal at her kitchen counter meant as much to him as the long night in her bed. Crossing to her, he wrapped his arms around her waist and pressed a kiss to her neck.

Strange how a touch could speed up the heart rate and warm the blood. Absorbing the sensation, she leaned back against him. "It's almost done. You didn't say how you liked your eggs, so you've got them scrambled with a little dill and cheese."

She could have offered him cardboard and told him to eat it with a plastic fork. Mitch turned her to face him and kissed her long and hard. "Thanks."

He'd flustered her again. Hester turned to the eggs in time to prevent them from burning. "Why don't you sit down?" She poured coffee into a mug and handed it to him. "With your life's blood."

He finished half the mug before he sat. "Hester, you know what I said about your legs?"

She glanced over as she heaped eggs on a plate. "Yes?"

"Your coffee's almost as good as they are. Tremendous qualities in a woman."

"Thanks." She set the plate in front of him before moving to the toaster.

"Aren't you eating any of this?"

"No, just toast."

Mitch looked down at the pile of golden eggs and crisp bacon. "Hester, I didn't expect you to fix me all this when you aren't eating."

"It's all right." She arranged a stack of toast on a plate. "I do it for Rad all the time."

He covered her hand with his as she sat beside him. "I appreciate it."

"It's only a couple of eggs," she said, embarrassed. "You should eat them before they get cold."

"The woman's a marvel," Mitch commented as he obliged her. "She raises an interesting and well-balanced son, holds down a demanding job, and cooks." Mitch bit into a piece of bacon. "Want to get married?"

She laughed and added more coffee to both mugs. "If it only takes scrambled eggs to get you to propose, I'm surprised you don't have three or four wives hidden in the closet."

He hadn't been joking. She would have seen it in his eyes if she'd looked at him, but she was busy spreading butter on toast. Mitch watched her competent, ringless hands a moment. It had been a stupid way to propose and a useless way to make her see he was serious. It was also too soon, he admitted as he scooped up another forkful of eggs.

The trick would be first to get her used to having him around, then to have her trust him enough to believe he would stay around. Then there was the big one, he mused as he lifted his cup. She had to need him. She wouldn't ever need him for the roof over her head or the food in her cupboards. She was much too self-sufficient for that, and he admired it. In time, she might come to need him for emotional support and companionship. It would be a start.

The courting of Hester would have to be both complex and subtle. He wasn't certain he knew exactly how to go about it, but he was more than ready to start. Today was as good a time as any.

"Got any plans for later?"

"I've got to pick up Rad around noon." She lingered over her toast, realizing it had been years since she had shared adult company over breakfast and that it had an appeal all its own. "Then I promised that I'd take him and Josh to a matinee. *The Moon of Andromeda.*"

"Yeah? Terrific movie. The special effects are tremendous."

"You've seen it?" She felt a twinge of disappointment. She'd been wondering if he might be willing to come along.

"Twice. There's a scene between the mad scientist and the sane scientist that'll knock you out. And there's this mutant that looks like a carp. Fantastic."

"A carp." Hester sipped her coffee. "Sounds wonderful."

"A cinematic treat for the eyes. Can I tag along?"

"You just said you've seen it twice already."

"So? The only movies I see once are dogs. Besides, I'd like to see Rad's reaction to the laser battle in deep space."

"Is it gory?"

"Nothing Rad can't handle."

"I wasn't asking for him."

With a laugh, Mitch took her hand. "I'll be there to protect you. How about it? I'll spring for the popcorn." He brought her hand up to his lips. "Buttered."

"How could I pass up a deal like that?"

"Good. Look, I'll give you a hand with the dishes, then I've got to go down and take Taz out before his bladder causes us both embarrassment."

"Go on ahead. There isn't that much, and Taz is probably moaning at the door by this time."

"Okay." He stood with her. "But next time I cook."

Hester gathered up the plates. "Peanut butter and jelly?"

"I can do better than that if it impresses you."

She smiled and reached for his empty mug. "You don't have to impress me."

He caught her face in his hands while she stood with her hands full of dishes. "Yes, I do." He nibbled at her lips, then abruptly deepened the kiss until they were both breathless. She was forced to swallow when he released her.

"That's a good start."

He was smiling as he brushed his lips over her forehead. "I'll be up in an hour."

Hester stood where she was until she heard the door close, then quietly set the dishes down again. How in the world had it happened? she wondered. She'd fallen in love with the man. He'd be gone only an hour, yet she wanted him back already.

Taking a deep breath, she sat down again. She had to keep herself from overreacting, from taking this, as she took too many other things, too seriously. He was fun, he was kind, but he wasn't permanent. There was nothing permanent but her and Radley. She'd promised herself years ago that she would never forget that again. Now, more than ever, she had to remember it.

Chapter 9

"Rich, you know I hate business discussions before noon."

Mitch sat in Skinner's office with Taz snoozing at his feet. Though it was after ten and he'd been up working for a couple of hours, he hadn't been ready to venture out and talk shop. He'd had to leave his characters on the drawing board in a hell of a predicament, and Mitch imagined they resented being left dangling as much as he resented leaving them.

"If you're going to give me a raise, that's fine by me, but you could've waited until after lunch."

"You're not getting a raise." Skinner ignored the phone that rang on his desk. "You're already overpaid."

"Well, if I'm fired, you could definitely have waited a couple of hours."

"You're not fired." Skinner drew his brows together

until they met above his nose. "But if you keep bringing that hound in here, I could change my mind."

"I made Taz my agent. Anything you say to me you can say in front of him."

Skinner sat back in his chair and folded hands that were swollen at the knuckles from years of nervous cracking. "You know, Dempsey, someone who didn't know you so well would think you were joking. The problem is, I happen to know you're crazy."

"That's why we get along so well, right? Listen, Rich, I've got Mirium trapped in a roomful of wounded rebels from Zirial. Being an empath, she's not feeling too good herself. Why don't we wrap this up so I can get back and take her to the crisis point?"

"Rebels from Zirial," Skinner mused. "You aren't thinking of bringing back Nimrod the Sorceror?"

"It's crossed my mind, and I could get back and figure out what he's got up his invisible sleeve if you'd tell me why you dragged me in here."

"You work here," Skinner pointed out.

"That's no excuse."

Skinner puffed out his cheeks and let the subject drop. "You know Two Moon Pictures has been negotiating with Universal for the rights to product Zark as a full-length film?"

"Sure. That's been going on a year, a year and a half now." Since the wheeling and dealing didn't interest him, Mitch stretched out a leg and began to massage Taz's flank with his foot. "The last thing you told me was that the alfalfa sprouts from L.A. couldn't get out of their hot tubs long enough to close the deal." Mitch grinned. "You've got a real way with words, Rich."

"The deal closed yesterday," Rich said flatly. "Two Moon wants to go with Zark."

Mitch's grin faded. "You're serious?"

"I'm always serious," Rich said, studying Mitch's reaction. "I thought you'd be a little more enthusiastic. Your baby's going to be a movie star."

"To tell you the truth, I don't know how I feel." Pushing himself out of the chair, Mitch began to pace Rich's cramped office. As he passed the window, he pulled open the blinds to let in slants of hard winter light. "Zark's always been personal. I don't know how I feel about him going Hollywood."

"You got a kick out of when B.C. Toys made the dolls."

"Action figures," Mitch corrected automatically. "I guess that's because they stayed pretty true to the theme." It was silly, he knew. Zark didn't belong to him. He'd created him, true, but Zark belonged to Universal, just like all the other heroes and villains of the staff's fertile imaginations. If, like Maloney, Mitch decided to move on, Zark would stay behind, the responsibility of someone else's imagination. "Did we retain any creative leeway?"

"Afraid they're going to exploit your firstborn?"

"Maybe."

"Listen, Two Moon bought the rights to Zark because he has potential at the box office—the way he is. It wouldn't be smart businesswise to change him. Let's look at the bottom line—comics are big business. A hundred and thirty million a year isn't something to shrug off. The business is thriving now the way it hasn't since the forties, and even though it's bound to level off, it's going to stay hot. Those jokers on the coast might dress funny, but they know a winner when they see one. Still, if you're worried, you could take their offer."

"What offer?"

"They want you to write the screenplay."

Mitch stopped where he was. "Me? I don't write movies."

"You write Zark—apparently that's enough for the producers. Our publishers aren't stupid, either. Stingy," he added with a glance at his worn linoleum, "but not stupid. They wanted the script to come from in-house, and there's a clause in the contract that says we have a shot. Two Moon agreed to accept a treatment from you first. If it doesn't pan out, they still want you on the project as a creative consultant."

"Creative consultant." Mitch rolled the title around on his tongue.

"If I were you, Dempsey, I'd get myself a two-legged agent."

"I just might. Look, I'm going to have to think about it. How long are they giving me?"

"Nobody mentioned a time frame. I don't think the possibility of your saying no occurred to them. But then, they don't know you like I do."

"I need a couple of days. There's someone I have to talk to."

Skinner waited until he'd started out. "Mitch, opportunity doesn't often kick down your door this way."

"Just let me make sure I'm at home first. I'll be in touch."

When it rains it pours, Mitch thought as he and Taz walked. It had started off as a fairly normal, even ordinary new year. He'd planned to dig his heels in a bit and get ahead of schedule so that he could take three or

four weeks off to ski, drink brandy and kick up some
snow on his uncle's farm. He'd figured on meeting one
or two attractive women on the slopes to make the evenings interesting. He'd thought to sketch a little, sleep
a lot and cruise the lodges. Very simple.

Then, within weeks, everything had changed. In
Hester he'd found everything he'd ever wanted in his
personal life, but he'd only begun to convince her that
he was everything she'd ever wanted in hers. Now he
was being offered one of the biggest opportunities of
his professional life, but he couldn't think of one without considering the other.

In truth, he'd never been able to draw a hard line
of demarcation between his professional and personal
lives. He was the same man whether he was having a
couple of drinks with friends or burning the midnight
oil with Zark. If he'd changed at all, it had been Hester and Radley who had caused it. Since he'd fallen for
them, he wanted the strings he'd always avoided, the
responsibilities he'd always blithely shrugged off.

So he went to her first.

Mitch strolled into the bank with his ears tingling
from the cold. The long walk had given him time to
think through everything Skinner had told him, and
to feel the first twinges of excitement. Zark, in Tech-
nicolor, in stereophonic sound, in Panavision.

Mitch stopped at Kay's desk. "She had lunch yet?"

Kay rolled back from her terminal. "Nope."

"Anybody with her now?"

"Not a soul."

"Good. When's her next appointment?"

Kay ran her finger down the appointment book.
"Two-fifteen."

"She'll be back. If Rosen stops by, tell him I took Mrs. Wallace to lunch to discuss some refinancing."

"Yes, sir."

She was working on a long column of figures when Mitch opened the door. She moved her fingers quickly over the adding machine, which clicked as it spewed out a stream of tape. "Kay, I'm going to need Lorimar's construction estimate. And would you mind ordering me a sandwich? Anything as long as it's quick. I'd like to have these figures upstairs by the end of the day. Oh, and I'll need the barter exchange transactions on the Duberry account. Look up the 1099."

Mitch shut the door at his back. "God, all this bank talk excites me."

"Mitch." Hester glanced up with the last of the figures still rolling through her head. "What are you doing here?"

"Breaking you out, and we have to move fast. Taz'll distract the guards." He was already taking her coat from the rack behind the door. "Let's go. Just keep your head down and look natural."

"Mitch, I've got—"

"To eat Chinese take-out and make love with me. In whatever order you like. Here, button up."

"I've only half-finished with these figures."

"They won't run away." He buttoned her coat, then closed his hands over her collar. "Hester, do you know how long it's been since we had an hour alone? Four days."

"I know. I'm sorry, things have been busy."

"Busy." He nodded toward her desk. "No one's going to argue with you there, but you've also been holding me off."

"No, I haven't." The truth was she'd been holding herself off, trying to prove to herself that she didn't need him as badly as it seemed. It hadn't been working as well as she'd hoped. There was tangible proof of that now as she stood facing him with her heart beating fast. "Mitch, I explained how I felt about...being with you with Radley in the apartment."

"And I'm not arguing that point, either." Though he would have liked to. "But Rad's in school and you have a constitutional right to a lunch hour. Come with me, Hester." He let his brow rest on hers. "I need you."

She couldn't resist or refuse or pretend she didn't want to be with him. Knowing she might regret it later, she turned her back on her work. "I'd settle for a peanut butter and jelly. I'm not very hungry."

"You got it."

Fifteen minutes later, they were walking into Mitch's apartment. As usual, his curtains were open wide so that the sun poured through. It was warm, Hester thought as she slipped out of her coat. She imagined he kept the thermostat up so that he could be comfortable in his bare feet and short-sleeved sweatshirts. Hester stood with her coat in her hands and wondered what to do next.

"Here, let me take that." Mitch tossed her coat carelessly over a chair. "Nice suit, Mrs. Wallace," he murmured, fingering the lapel of the dark blue pin-stripe.

She put a hand over his, once again afraid that things were moving too fast. "I feel..."

"Decadent?"

Once again, it was the humor in his eyes that relaxed her. "More like I've just climbed out my bedroom window at midnight."

"Did you ever?"

"No. I thought about it a lot, but I could never figure out what I was supposed to do once I climbed down."

"That's why I'm nuts about you." He kissed her cautious smile and felt her lips soften and give under his. "Climb out the bedroom window to me, Hester. I'll show you what to do." Then his hands were in her hair, and her control scattered as quickly as the pins.

She wanted him. Perhaps it had a great deal to do with madness, but oh, how she wanted him. In the long nights since they'd been together like this, she'd thought of him, of how he touched her, where he touched her, and now his hands were there, just as she remembered. This time she moved faster than he, pulling his sweater up over his head to feast on the warm, taut flesh beneath. Her teeth nipped into his lip, insisting, inciting, until he was dragging the jacket from her and fumbling with the buttons that ranged down the back of her blouse.

His touch wasn't as gentle when he found her, nor was he as patient. But she had long since thrown caution aside. Now, pressed hard against him, she gripped passion with both hands. Whether it was day or night no longer mattered. She was where she wanted to be, where, no matter how she struggled to pretend otherwise, she needed to be.

Madness, yes, it was madness. She wondered how she'd lived so long without it.

He unfastened her skirt so that it flowed over her hips and onto the floor. With a groan of satisfaction he pressed his mouth to her throat. Four days? Had it only been four days? It seemed like years since he had had her close and alone. She was as hot and as desperate against him as he'd dreamed she would be. He could savor the feel of her even as desire clamped inside his gut and swam in his head. He wanted to spend hours touching, being touched, but the intensity of the moment, the lack of time and her urgent murmurs made it impossible.

"The bedroom," she managed as he pulled the thin straps of her lingerie over her shoulders.

"No, here. Right here." He fastened his mouth on hers and pulled her to the floor.

He would have given her more. Even though his own system was straining toward the breaking point, he would have given her more, but she was wrapped around him. Before he could catch his breath, her hands were on his hips, guiding her to him. She dug her fingers into his flesh as she murmured his name, and whole galaxies seemed to explode inside his head.

When she could think again, Hester stared at the dust motes that danced in a beam of sunlight. She was lying on a priceless Aubusson with Mitch's head pillowed between her breasts. It was the middle of the day, she had a pile of paperwork on her desk, and she'd just spent the better part of her lunch making love on the floor. She couldn't remember ever being more content.

She hadn't known life could be like this—an adventure, a carnival. For years she hadn't believed there was room for the madness of love and lovemaking in a world that revolved around responsibilities. Now, just now, she was beginning to realize she could have both. For how long, she couldn't be sure. Perhaps one day would be enough. She combed her fingers through his hair.

"I'm glad you came to take me to lunch."

"If this is any indication, we're going to have to make it a habit. Still want that sandwich?"

"Uh-uh. I don't need anything." But you. Hester sighed, realizing she was going to have to accept that. "I'm going to have to get back."

"You don't have an appointment until after two. I checked. Your barter exchange transactions can wait a few more minutes, can't they?"

"I suppose."

"Come on." He was up and pulling her to her feet.

"Where?"

"We'll have a quick shower, then I need to talk to you."

Hester accepted his offer of a robe and tried not to worry about what he had to say. She understood Mitch well enough to know he was full of surprises. The trouble was, she wasn't certain she was ready for another. Shoulders tense, she sat beside him on the couch and waited.

"You look like you're waiting for the blindfold and your last cigarette."

Hester shook back her still damp hair and tried to smile. "No, it's just that you sounded so serious."

"I've told you before, I have my serious moments." He shoved magazines off the table with his foot. "I had some news today, and I haven't decided how I feel about it. I wanted to see what you thought."

"Your family?" she began, instantly concerned.

"No." He took her hand. "I guess I'm making it sound like bad news, and it's not. At least I don't think it is. A production company in Hollywood just cut a deal with Universal to make a movie out of Zark."

Hester stared at him a moment, then blinked. "A

movie. Well, that's wonderful. Isn't it? I mean, I know he's very popular in comics, but a movie would be even bigger. You should be thrilled, and very proud that your work can translate that way."

"I just don't know if they can pull it off, if they can bring him to the screen with the right tone, the right emotion. Don't look at me that way."

"Mitch, I know how you feel about Zark. At least I think I do. He's your creation, and he's important to you."

"He's real to me," Mitch corrected. "Up here," he said, tapping his temple. "And, as corny as it might sound, in here." He touched a hand to his heart. "He made a difference in my life, made a difference in how I looked at myself and my work. I don't want to see them screw him up and make him into some cardboard hero or, worse, into something infallible and perfect."

Hester was silent a moment. She began to understand that giving birth to an idea might be as life-altering as giving birth to a child. "Let me ask you something: why did you create him?"

"I wanted to make a hero—a very human one—with flaws and vulnerabilities, and I guess with high standards. Someone kids could relate to because he was just flesh and blood, but powerful enough inside to fight back. Kids don't have a hell of a lot of choices, you know. I remember when I was young I wanted to be able to say 'no, I don't want to, I don't like that.' When I read, I could see there were possibilities, ways out. That's what I wanted Zark to be."

"Do you think you succeeded?"

"Yeah. On a personal level, I succeeded when I came up with the first issue. Professionally, Zark has pushed

Universal to the top. He translates into millions of dollars a year for the business."

"Do you resent that?"

"No, why should I?"

"Then you shouldn't resent seeing him take the next step."

Mitch fell silent, thinking. He might have known Hester would see things more clearly and be able to cut through everything to the most practical level. Wasn't that just one more reason he needed her?

"They offered to let me do the screenplay."

"What?" She was sitting straight up now, eyes wide. "Oh, Mitch, that's wonderful. I'm so proud of you."

He continued to play with her fingers. "I haven't done it yet."

"Don't you think you can?"

"I'm not sure."

She started to speak, then caught herself. After a moment, she spoke carefully. "Strange, if anyone had asked, I would have said you were the most self-confident man I'd ever met. Added to that, I'd have said that you'd be much too selfish with Zark to let anyone else write him."

"There's a difference between writing a story line for a comic series and writing a screenplay for a major motion picture."

"So?"

He had to laugh. "Tossing my own words back at me, aren't you?"

"You can write, I'd be the first to say that you have a very fluid imagination, and you know your character better than anyone else. I don't see the problem."

"Screwing up is the problem. Anyway, if I don't do the script, they want me as creative consultant."

"I can't tell you what to do, Mitch."

"But?"

She leaned forward, putting her hands on his shoulders. "Write the script, Mitch. You'll hate yourself if you don't try. There aren't any guarantees, but if you don't take the risk, there's no reward either."

He lifted a hand to hers and held it firmly as he watched her. "Do you really feel that way?"

"Yes, I do. I also believe in you." She leaned closer and touched her mouth to his.

"Marry me, Hester."

With her lips still on his, she froze. Slowly, very slowly, she drew away. "What?"

"Marry me." He took her hands in his to hold them still. "I love you."

"Don't. Please don't do this."

"Don't what? Don't love you?" He tightened his grip as she struggled to pull away. "It's a great deal too late for that, and I think you know it. I'm not lying when I tell you that I've never felt about anyone the way I feel about you. I want to spend my life with you."

"I can't." Her voice was breathless. It seemed each word she pushed out seared the back of her throat. "I can't marry you. I don't want to marry anyone. You don't understand what you're asking."

"Just because I haven't been there doesn't mean I don't know." He'd expected surprise, even some resistance. But he could see now he'd totally miscalculated. There was out-and-out fear in her eyes and full panic in her voice. "Hester, I'm not Allan and we both know you're not the same woman you were when you were married to him."

"It doesn't matter. I'm not going through that again, and I won't put Radley through it." She pulled away and started to dress. "You're not being reasonable."

"*I'm* not?" Struggling for calm, he walked behind her and began to do up her buttons. Her back went rigid. "You're the one who's basing her feelings now on something that happened years ago."

"I don't want to talk about it."

"Maybe not, and maybe now's not the best time, but you're going to have to." Though she resisted, he turned her around. "We're going to have to."

She wanted to get away, far enough that she could bury everything that had been said. But for the moment she had to face it. "Mitch, we've known each other for a matter of weeks, and we've just begun to be able to accept what's happening between us."

"What *is* happening?" he demanded. "Aren't you the one who said at the beginning that you weren't interested in casual sex?"

She paled a bit, then turned away to pick up her suit jacket. "There wasn't anything casual about it."

"No, there wasn't, not for either of us. You understand that?"

"Yes, but—"

"Hester, I said I loved you. Now I want to know how you feel about me."

"I don't know." She let out a gasp when he grabbed her shoulders again. "I tell you I don't know. I think I love you. Today. You're asking me to risk everything I've done, the life I've built for myself and Rad, over an emotion I already know can change overnight."

"Love doesn't change overnight," he corrected. "It can be killed or it can be nurtured. That's up to the people involved. I want a commitment from you, a family, and I want to give those things back to you."

"Mitch, this is all happening too fast, much too fast for both of us."

"Damn it, Hester, I'm thirty-five years old, not some kid with hot pants and no brains. I don't want to marry you so I can have convenient sex and a hot breakfast, but because I know we could have something together, something real, something important."

"You don't know what marriage is like, you're only imagining."

"And you're only remembering a bad one. Hester, look at me. Look at me," he demanded again. "When the hell are you going to stop using Radley's father as a yardstick?"

"He's the only one I've got." She shook him off again and tried to catch her breath. "Mitch, I'm flattered that you want me."

"The hell with that."

"Please." She dragged a hand through her hair. "I do care about you, and the only thing I'm really sure of is that I don't want to lose you."

"Marriage isn't the end of a relationship, Hester."

"I can't think about marriage. I'm sorry." The panic flowed in and out of her voice until she was forced to stop and calm it. "If you don't want to see me anymore, I'll try to understand. But I'd rather…I hope we can just let things go on the way they are."

He dug his hands into his pockets. He had a habit of pushing too far too fast, and knew it. But he hated to waste the time he could already imagine them having together. "For how long, Hester?"

"For as long as it lasts." She closed her eyes. "That sounds hard. I don't mean it to. You mean a great deal to me, more than I thought anyone ever would again."

Mitch brushed a finger over her cheek and brought it away wet. "A low blow," he murmured, studying the tear.

"I'm sorry. I don't mean to do this. I had no idea that you were thinking along these lines."

"I can see that." He gave a self-deprecating laugh. "In three dimensions."

"I've hurt you. I can't tell you how much I regret that."

"Don't. I asked for it. The truth is, I hadn't planned on asking you to marry me for at least a week."

She started to touch his hand, then stopped. "Mitch, can we just forget all this, go on as we were?"

He reached out and straightened the collar of her jacket. "I'm afraid not. I've made up my mind, Hester. That's something I try to do only once or twice a year. Once I've done it, there's no turning back." His gaze came up to hers with that rush of intensity she felt to the bone. "I'm going to marry you, sooner or later. If it has to be later, that's fine. I'll just give you some time to get used to it."

"Mitch, I won't change my mind. It wouldn't be fair if I let you think I would. It isn't a matter of a whim, but of a promise I made to myself."

"Some promises are best broken."

She shook her head. "I don't know what else to say. I just wish—"

He pressed his finger to her lips. "We'll talk about it later. I'll take you back to work."

"No, don't bother. Really," she said when he started to argue. "I'd like some time to think, anyway. Being with you makes that difficult."

"That's a good start." He took her chin in his hand and studied her face. "You look fine, but next time don't cry when I ask you to marry me. It's hell on the ego." He kissed her before she could speak. "See you later, Mrs. Wallace. Thanks for lunch."

A little dazed, she walked out into the hall. "I'll call you later."

"Do that. I'll be around."

He closed the door, then turned to lean back against it. Hurt? He rubbed a spot just under his heart. Damn right it hurt. If anyone had told him that being in love could cause the heart to twist, he'd have continued to avoid it. He'd had a twinge when his long-ago love in New Orleans had deserted him. It hadn't prepared him for this sledgehammer blow. What could possibly have?

But he wasn't giving up. What he had to do was figure out a plan of attack—subtle, clever and irresistible. Mitch glanced down at Taz consideringly.

"Where do you think Hester would like to go on our honeymoon?"

The dog grumbled, then rolled over on his back.

"No," Mitch decided. "Bermuda's overdone. Never mind, I'll come up with something."

Chapter 10

"Radley, you and your friends have to tone down the volume on the war, please." Hester took the measuring tape from around her neck and stretched it out over the wall space. Perfect, she thought with a satisfied nod. Then she took the pencil from behind her ear to mark two *X*s where the nails would go.

The little glass shelves she would hang were a present to herself, one that was completely unnecessary and pleased her a great deal. She didn't consider the act of hanging them herself a show of competence or independence, but simply one more of the ordinary chores she'd been doing on her own for years. With a hammer in one hand, she lined up the first nail. She'd given it two good whacks when someone knocked on the door.

"Just a minute." She gave the nail a final smack. From Radley's bedroom came the sounds of antiaircraft and whistling missiles. Hester took the second nail out of her mouth and stuck it in her pocket. "Rad, we're going to be arrested for disturbing the peace." She opened the door to Mitch. "Hi."

The pleasure showed instantly, gratifying him. It had been two days since he'd seen her, since he'd told her he loved her and wanted to marry her. In two days he'd done a lot of hard thinking, and could only hope that, despite herself, Hester had done some thinking, too.

"Doing some remodeling?" he asked with a nod at the hammer.

"Just hanging a shelf." She wrapped both hands around the handle of the hammer, feeling like a teenager. "Come in."

He glanced toward Radley's room as she shut the door. It sounded as though a major air strike was in progress. "You didn't mention you were opening a playground."

"It's been a lifelong dream of mine. Rad, they've just signed a treaty—hold your fire!" With a cautious smile for Mitch, she waved him toward a chair. "Radley has Josh over today, and Ernie—Ernie lives upstairs and goes to school with Rad."

"Sure, the Bitterman kid. I know him. Nice," he commented as he looked at the shelves.

"They're a present for completing a successful month at National Trust." Hester ran a finger along a beveled edge. She really did want this more than a new outfit.

"You're on the reward program?"

"Self-reward."

"The best kind. Want me to finish that for you?"

"Oh?" She glanced down at the hammer. "Oh, no,

thanks. I can do it. Why don't you sit down? I'll get you some coffee."

"You hang the shelf, I'll get the coffee." He kissed the tip of her nose. "And relax, will you?"

"Mitch." He'd taken only two steps away when she reached for his arm. "I'm awfully glad to see you. I was afraid, well, that you were angry."

"Angry?" He gave her a baffled look. "About what?"

"About…" She trailed off as he continued to stare at her in a half interested, half curious way that made her wonder if she'd imagined everything he'd said. "Nothing." She dug the nail out of her pocket. "Help yourself to the coffee."

"Thanks." He grinned at the back of her head. He'd done exactly what he'd set out to do—confuse her. Now she'd be thinking about him, about what had been said between them. The more she thought about it, the closer she'd be to seeing reason.

Whistling between his teeth, he strolled into the kitchen while Hester banged in the second nail.

He *had* asked her to marry him. She remembered everything he'd said, everything she'd said in return. And she knew that he'd been angry and hurt. Hadn't she spent two days regretting that she'd had to cause that? Now he strolled in as though nothing had happened.

Hester set down the hammer, then lifted the shelves. Maybe he'd cooled off enough to be relieved that she'd said no. That could be it, she decided, wondering why the idea didn't ease her mind as much as it should have.

"You made cookies." Mitch came in carrying two mugs, with a plate of fresh cookies balanced on top of one.

"This morning." She smiled over her shoulder as she adjusted the shelves.

"You want to bring that up a little on the right." He sat on the arm of a chair, then set her mug down so his hands would be free for the chocolate-chip cookies. "Terrific," he decided after the first bite. "And, if I say so myself, I'm an expert."

"I'm glad they pass." With her mind on her shelves, Hester stepped back to admire them.

"It's important. I don't know if I could marry a woman who made lousy cookies." He picked up a second one and examined it. "Yeah, maybe I could," he said as Hester turned slowly to stare at him. "But it would be tough." He devoured the second one and smiled at her. "Luckily, it won't have to be an issue."

"Mitch." Before she could work out what to say, Radley came barreling in, his two friends behind him.

"Mitch!" Delighted with the company, Radley screeched to a halt beside him so that Mitch's arm went naturally around his shoulders. "We just had the neatest battle. We're the only survivors."

"Hungry work. Have a cookie."

Radley took one and shoved it into his mouth. "We've got to go up to Ernie's and get more weapons." He reached for another cookie, then caught his mother's eye. "You didn't bring Taz up."

"He stayed up late watching a movie. He's sleeping in today."

"Okay." Radley accepted this before turning to his mother. "Is it okay if we go up to Ernie's for a while?"

"Sure. Just don't go outside unless you let me know."

"We won't. You guys go ahead. I gotta get something."

He raced back to the bedroom while his friends trooped to the door.

"I'm glad he's making some new friends," Hester commented as she reached for her mug. "He was worried about it."

"Radley's not the kind of kid who has trouble making friends."

"No, he's not."

"He's also fortunate to have a mother who lets them come around and bakes cookies for them." He took another sip of coffee. His mother's cook had baked little cakes. He thought Hester would understand it wasn't quite the same thing. "Of course, once we're married we'll have to give him some brothers and sisters. What are you going to put on the shelf?"

"Useless things," she murmured, staring at him. "Mitch, I don't want to fight, but I think we should clear this up."

"Clear what up? Oh, I meant to tell you I started on the script. It's going pretty well."

"I'm glad." And confused. "Really, that's wonderful, but I think we should talk about this business first."

"Sure, what business was that?"

She opened her mouth, and was once more interrupted by her son. When Radley came in, Hester walked away to put a small china cat on the bottom shelf.

"I made something for you in school." Embarrassed, Radley held his hands behind his back.

"Yeah?" Mitch set his coffee down. "Do I get to see it?"

"It's Valentine's Day, you know." After a moment's hesitation, he handed Mitch a card fashioned out of construction paper and blue ribbon. "I made Mom this heart with lace stuff, but I thought the ribbon was better for guys." Radley shuffled his feet. "It opens."

Not certain he could trust his voice, Mitch opened the card. Radley had used his very best block printing.

"To my best friend, Mitch. I love you, Radley." He had to clear his throat, and hoped he wouldn't make a fool out of himself. "It's great. I, ah, nobody ever made me a card before."

"Really?" Embarrassment faded with surprise. "I make them for Mom all the time. She says she likes them better than the ones you buy."

"I like this one a lot better," Mitch told him. He wasn't sure boys that were nearly ten tolerated being kissed, but he ran a hand over Radley's hair and kissed him anyway. "Thanks."

"You're welcome. See ya."

"Yeah." Mitch heard the door slam as he stared down at the little folded piece of construction paper.

"I didn't know he'd made it," Hester said quietly. "I guess he wanted to keep it a secret."

"He did a nice job." At the moment, he didn't have the capacity to explain what the paper and ribbon meant to him. Rising, he walked to the window with the card in his hands. "I'm crazy about him."

"I know." She moistened her lips. She did know it. If she'd ever doubted the extent of Mitch's feelings for her son, she'd just seen full proof of it. It only made things more difficult. "In just a few weeks, you've done so much for him. I know neither one of us have the right to expect you to be there, but I want you to know it means a lot that you are."

He had to clamp down on a surge of fury. He didn't want her gratitude, but one hell of a lot more. Keep cool,

Dempsey, he warned himself. "The best advice I can give you is to get used to it, Hester."

"That's exactly what I can't do." Driven, she went to him. "Mitch, I do care for you, but I'm not going to depend on you. I can't afford to expect or anticipate or rely."

"So you've said." He set the card down carefully on the table. "I'm not arguing."

"What were you saying before—"

"What did I say?"

"About when we were married."

"Did I say that?" He smiled at her as he wound her hair around his finger. "I don't know what I could have been thinking of."

"Mitch, I have a feeling you're trying to throw me off guard."

"Is it working?"

Treat it lightly, she told herself. If he wanted to make a game of it, she'd oblige him. "Only to the point that it confirms what I've always thought about you. You're a very strange man."

"In what context?"

"Okay, to begin with, you talk to your dog."

"He talks back, so that doesn't count. Try again." With her hair still wound around his finger, he tugged her a bit closer. Whether she realized it or not, they were talking about their relationship, and she was relaxed.

"You write comic books for a living. And you read them."

"Being a woman with banking experience, you should understand the importance of a good investment. Do you know what the double issue of my *Defenders of Perth* is worth to a collector? Modesty prevents me from naming figures."

"I bet it does."

He acknowledged this with a slight nod. "And, Mrs. Wallace, I'd be happy to debate the value of literature in any form with you. Did I mention that I was captain of the debating team in high school?"

"No." She had her hands on his chest, once again drawn to the tough, disciplined body beneath the tattered sweater. "There's also the fact that you haven't thrown out a newspaper or magazine in five years."

"I'm saving up for the big paper drive of the second millennium. Conservation is my middle name."

"You also have an answer for everything."

"There's only one I want from you. Did I mention that I fell for your eyes right after I fell for your legs?"

"No, you didn't." Her lips curved just a little. "I never told you that the first time I saw you, through the peephole, I stared at you for a long time."

"I know." He grinned back at her. "If you look in those things right, you can see a shadow."

"Oh," she said, and could think of nothing else to say.

"You know, Mrs. Wallace, those kids could come running back in here anytime. Do you mind if we stop talking for a few minutes?"

"No." She slipped her arms around him. "I don't mind at all."

She didn't want to admit even to herself that she felt safe, protected, with his arms around her. But she did. She didn't want to accept that she'd been afraid of losing him, terrified of the hole he would have left in her life. But the fear had been very real. It faded now as she lifted her lips to his.

She couldn't think about tomorrow or the future Mitch sketched so easily with talk of marriage and family. She'd been taught that marriage was forever, but she'd learned that it was a promise easily made and easily broken. There would be no more broken promises in her life, no more broken vows.

Feelings might rush through her, bringing with them longings and silver-dusted dreams. Her heart might be lost to him, but her will was still her own. Even as her hands gripped him tighter, pulled him closer, Hester told herself it was that will that would save them both unhappiness later.

"I love you, Hester." He murmured the words against her mouth, knowing she might not want to hear them but that it was something he had to say. If he said it enough, she might begin to believe the words and, more, the meaning behind them.

He wanted forever from her—forever for her—not just a moment like this, stolen in the sunlight that poured through the window, or other moments, taken in the shadows. Only once before had he wanted anything with something close to this intensity. That had been something abstract, something nebulous called art. The time had eventually come when he'd been forced to admit that dream would never be within reach.

But Hester was here in his arms. He could hold her like this and taste the sweet, warm longings that stirred in her. She wasn't a dream, but a woman he loved and wanted and would have. If keeping her meant playing games until the layers of her resistance were washed away, then he'd play.

He lifted his hands to her face, twining his fingers into her hair. "I guess the kids will be coming back."

"Probably." Her lips sought his again. Had she ever felt this sense of urgency before? "I wish we had more time."

"Do you?"

Her eyes were half-closed as he drew away. "Yes."

"Let me come back tonight."

"Oh, Mitch." She stepped into his arms to rest her head on his shoulder. For the first time in a decade, she found the mother and the woman at war. "I want you. You know that, don't you?"

Her heart was still pumping hard and fast against his. "I think I figured it out."

"I wish we could be together tonight, but there's Rad."

"I know how you feel about me staying here with Rad in the next room. Hester…" He ran his hands up her arms to rest them on her shoulders. "Why not be honest with him, tell him we care about each other and want to be together?"

"Mitch, he's only a baby."

"No, he's not. No, wait," he continued before she could speak again. "I'm not saying we should make it seem casual or careless, but that we should let Radley know how we feel about each other, and when two grown people feel this strongly about each other they need to show it."

It seemed so simple when he said it, so logical, so natural. Gathering her thoughts, she stepped back. "Mitch, Rad loves you, and he loves with the innocence and lack of restriction of a child."

"I love him, too."

She looked into his eyes and nodded. "Yes, I think you do, and if it's true, I hope you'll understand. I'm afraid that if I bring Radley into this at this point he'll come to depend on you even more than he already does. He'd come to look at you as…"

"As a father," Mitch finished. "You don't want a father in his life, do you, Hester?"

"That's not fair." Her eyes, usually so calm and clear, turned to smoke.

"Maybe not, but if I were you I'd give it some hard thought."

"There's no reason to say cruel things because I won't have sex with you when my son's sleeping in the next room."

He caught her by the shirt so fast she could only stare. She'd seen him annoyed, pushed close to the edge, but never furious. "Damn you, do you think that's all I'm talking about? If all I wanted was sex, I could go downstairs and pick up the phone. Sex is easy, Hester. All it takes is two people and a little spare time."

"I'm sorry." She closed her eyes, knowing she'd never said or done anything in her life she'd been more ashamed of. "That was stupid, Mitch, I just keep feeling as though my back's against the wall. I need some time, please."

"So do I. But the time I need is with you." He dropped his hands and stuck them in his pockets. "I'm pressuring you. I know it and I'm not going to stop, because I believe in us."

"I wish I could, also, honestly I do, but there's too much at stake for me."

And for himself, Mitch thought, but was calm enough now to hold off. "We'll let it ride for a while. Are you and Rad up to hitting a few arcades at Times Square tonight?"

"Sure. He'd love it." She stepped toward him again. "So would I."

"You say that now, but you won't after I humiliate you with my superior skill."

"I love you."

He let out a long breath, fighting back the urge to grab her again and refuse to let go. "You going to let me know when you're comfortable with that?"

"You'll be the first."

He picked up the card Radley had made him. "Tell Rad I'll see him later."

"I will." He was halfway to the door when she started after him. "Mitch, why don't you come to dinner tomorrow? I'll fix a pot roast."

He tilted his head. "The kind with the little potatoes and carrots all around?"

"Sure."

"And biscuits?"

She smiled. "If you want."

"Sounds great, but I'm tied up."

"Oh." She struggled with the need to ask how, but reminded herself she didn't have the right.

Mitch smiled, selfishly pleased to see her disappointment. "Can I have a rain check?"

"Sure." She tried to answer the smile. "I guess Radley told you about his birthday next week," she said when Mitch reached the door.

"Only five or six times." He paused, his hand on the knob.

"He's having a party next Saturday afternoon. I know he'd like you to come if you can."

"I'll be there. Look, why don't we take off about seven? I'll bring the quarters."

"We'll be ready." He wasn't going to kiss her goodbye, she thought. "Mitch, I—"

"I almost forgot." Casually he reached in his back pocket and pulled out a small box.

"What is it?"

"It's Valentine's Day, isn't it?" He put it in her hand. "So this is a Valentine's Day present."

"A Valentine's Day present," she repeated dumbly.

"Yeah, tradition, remember? I thought about candy, but I figured you'd spend a whole lot of time making sure Radley didn't eat too much of it. But look, if you'd rather have candy, I'll just take this back and—"

"No." She pulled the box out of his reach, then laughed. "I don't even know what it is."

"You'd probably find out if you open the box."

Flipping the lid, she saw the thin gold chain that held a heart no bigger than her thumbnail. It glittered with the diamonds that formed it. "Oh, Mitch, it's gorgeous."

"Something told me it'd be a bigger hit with you than candy. Candy would have made you think about oral hygiene."

"I'm not that bad," she countered, then lifted the heart out of the box. "Mitch, it's really beautiful, I love it, but it's too—"

"Conventional, I know," he interrupted as he took it from her. "But I'm just that kind of guy."

"You are?"

"Just turn around and let me hook it for you."

She obeyed, lifting one hand up under her hair. "I do love it, but I don't expect you to buy me expensive presents."

"Um-hmm." His brows were drawn together as he worked the clasp. "I didn't expect bacon and eggs, but you seemed to get a kick out of fixing them." The clasp secured, he turned her around to face him. "I get a kick out of seeing you wear my heart around your neck."

"Thank you." She touched a finger to the heart. "I didn't buy you any candy, either, but maybe I can give you something else."

She was smiling when she kissed him, gently, teasingly, with a power that surprised them both. It took only an instant, an instant to be lost, to need, to imagine. His back was to the door as he moved his hands from her face to her hair to her shoulders, then to her hips to mold her even more truly against him. The fire burned, hot and fast, so that even when she drew away he felt singed by it. With his eyes on hers, Mitch let out a very long, very slow breath.

"I guess those kids will be coming back."

"Any minute."

"Uh-huh." He kissed her lightly on the brow before he turned and opened the door. "See you later."

He would go down to get Taz, Mitch thought as he started down the hall. Then he was going for a walk. A long one.

True to his word Mitch's pockets were filled with quarters. The arcades were packed with people and echoed with the pings and whistles and machine-gun sound effects of the games. Hester stood to the side as Mitch and Radley used their combined talents to save the world from intergalactic wars.

"Nice shooting, Corporal." Mitch slapped the boy's shoulder as a Phaser II rocket disintegrated in a flash of colored light.

"It's your turn." Radley relinquished the controls to his superior officer. "Watch out for the sensor missiles."

"Don't worry. I'm a veteran."

"We're going to beat the high score." Radley tore his eyes away from the screen long enough to look at his mother. "Then we can put our initials up. Isn't this a neat place? It's got everything."

Everything, Hester thought, including some seamy-looking characters in leather and tattoos. The machine behind her let out a high-pitched scream. "Just stay close, okay?"

"Okay, Corporal, we're only seven hundred points away from the high score. Keep your eyes peeled for nuclear satellites."

"Aye, aye, sir." Radley clenched his jaw and took the controls.

"Good reflexes," Mitch said to Hester as he watched Radley control his ship with one hand and fire surface-to-air missiles with the other.

"Josh has one of those home video games. Rad loves to go over and play things like this." She caught her bottom lip between her teeth as Radley's ship barely missed annihilation. "I can never figure out how he can tell what's going on. Oh, look, he's passed the high score."

They continued to watch in tense silence as Radley fought bravely to the last man. As a finale, the screen exploded in brilliant fireworks of sound and light.

"A new record." Mitch hoisted Radley in the air. "This calls for a field promotion. Sergeant, inscribe your initials."

"But you got more points than I did."

"Who's counting? Go ahead."

Face flushed with pride, Radley clicked the button

that ran through the alphabet. R.A.W. A for Allan, Mitch thought, and said nothing.

"My initials spell raw, and backward they spell war—pretty neat, huh?"

"Pretty neat," Mitch agreed. "Want to give it a shot, Hester?"

"No, thanks. I'll just watch."

"Mom doesn't like to play," Radley confided. "Her palms sweat."

"Your palms sweat?" Mitch repeated with a grin.

Hester sent a telling look in Radley's direction. "It's the pressure. I can't take being responsible for the fate of the world. I know it's a game," she said before Mitch could respond. "But I get, well, caught up."

"You're terrific, Mrs. Wallace." He kissed her as Radley looked on and considered.

It made him feel funny to see Mitch kiss his mother. He wasn't sure if it was a good funny or a bad funny. Then Mitch dropped a hand to his shoulder. It always made Radley feel nice when Mitch put his hand there.

"Okay, what'll it be next, the Amazon jungles, medieval times, a search for the killer shark?"

"I like the one with the ninja. I saw a ninja movie at Josh's once—well, almost did. Josh's mom turned it off because one of the women was taking her clothes off and stuff."

"Oh, yeah?" Mitch stifled a laugh as Hester's mouth dropped open. "What was the name?"

"Never mind." Hester gripped Radley's hand. "I'm sure Josh's parents just made a mistake."

"Josh's father thought it was about throwing stars and kung fu. Josh's mom got mad and made him take it back to the video place and get something else. But I still like ninjas."

"Let's see if we can find a free machine." Mitch fell into step beside Hester. "I don't think he was marked for life."

"I'd still like to know what 'and stuff' means."

"Me, too." He swung an arm around her shoulders to steer her through a clutch of teenagers. "Maybe we could rent it."

"I'll pass, thanks."

"You don't want to see *Naked Ninjas from Nagasaki?*" When she turned around to stare at him, Mitch held out both hands, palms up. "I made it up. I swear."

"Hmmm."

"Here's one. Can I play this one?"

Mitch continued to grin at Hester as he dug out quarters.

The time passed so that Hester almost stopped hearing the noise from both machines and people. To placate Radley she played a few of the less intense games, ones that didn't deal with world domination or universal destruction. But for the most part she watched him, pleased to see him enjoying what was for him a real night on the town.

They must look like a family, she thought as Radley and Mitch bent over the controls in a head-to-head duel. She wished she still believed in such things. But to her, families and lifetime commitments were as fanciful as the machines that spewed out color and light around them.

Day-to-day, Hester thought with a little sigh. That was all she could afford to believe in now. In a few hours she would tuck Radley in bed and go to her room alone. That was the only way to make sure they were both safe. She heard Mitch laugh and shout encouragement to Radley, and looked away. It was the only way, she told herself again. No matter how much she wanted or was tempted to believe again, she couldn't risk it.

"How about the pinball machines?" Mitch suggested.

"They're okay." Though they rang with wild colors and lights, Radley didn't find them terribly exciting. "Mom likes them though."

"Are you any good?"

Hester pushed aside her uneasy thoughts. "Not bad."

"Care to go one-on-one?" He jingled the quarters in his pockets.

Though she'd never considered herself highly competitive, she was swayed by his smug look. "All right."

She'd always had a touch for pinball, a light enough, quick enough touch to have beaten her brother nine times out of ten. Though these machines were electronic and more sophisticated than the ones she'd played in her youth, she didn't doubt she could make a good showing.

"I could give you a handicap," Mitch suggested as he pushed coins into the slot.

"Funny, I was just going to say the same thing to you." With a smile, Hester took the controls.

It had something to do with black magic and white knights. Hester tuned out the sounds and concentrated on keeping the ball in play. Her timing was sharp. Mitch stood behind her with his hands tucked in his back pockets and nodded as she sent the ball spinning.

He liked the way she leaned into the machine, her lips slightly parted, her eyes narrowed and alert. Now and then she would catch her tongue between her teeth and push her body forward as if to follow the ball on its quick, erratic course.

The little silver ball rammed into rubber, sending bells ringing and lights flashing. By the time her first ball dropped, she'd already racked up an impressive score.

"Not bad for an amateur," Mitch commented with a wink at Radley.

"I'm just warming up." With a smile, she stepped back.

Radley watched the progress of the ball as Mitch took control. But he had to stand on his toes to get the full effect. It was pretty neat when the ball got hung up in the top of the machine where the bumpers sent it vibrating back and forth in a blur. He glanced behind him at the rows of other machines and wished he'd thought to ask for another quarter before they'd started to play. But if he couldn't play, he could watch. He edged away to get a closer look at a nearby game.

"Looks like I'm ahead by a hundred," Mitch said as he stepped aside for Hester.

"I didn't want to blow you away with the first ball. It seemed rude." She pulled back the plunger and let the ball rip.

This time she had the feel and the rhythm down pat. She didn't let the ball rest as she set it right, then left, then up the middle where it streaked through a tunnel and crashed into a lighted dragon. It took her back to her childhood, when her wants had been simple and her dreams still gilt-edged. As the machine rocked with noise, she laughed and threw herself into the competition.

Her score flashed higher and higher with enough

fanfare to draw a small crowd. Before her second ball dropped, people were choosing up sides.

Mitch took position. Unlike Hester, he didn't block out the sounds and lights, but used them to pump the adrenaline. He nearly lost the ball, causing indrawn breaths behind him, but caught it on the tip of his flipper to shoot it hard into a corner. This time he finished fifty points behind her.

The third and final turn brought more people. Hester thought she heard someone placing bets before she tuned them out and put all her concentration on the ball and her timing. She was nearly exhausted before she backed away again.

"You're going to need a miracle, Mitch."

"Don't get cocky." He flicked his wrists like a concert pianist and earned a few hoots and cheers from the crowd.

Hester had to admit as she watched his technique that he played brilliantly. He took chances that could have cost him his last ball, but turned them into triumph. He stood spread-legged and relaxed, but she saw in his eyes that kind of deep concentration that she'd come to expect from him, but had yet to become used to. His hair fell over his forehead, as careless as he was. There was a slight smile on his face that struck her as both pleased and reckless.

She found herself watching him rather than the ball as she toyed with the little diamond heart she'd worn over a plain black turtleneck.

This was the kind of man women dreamed about and made heroes of. This was the kind of man a woman could come to lean upon if she wasn't careful. With a man like him, a woman could have years of laughter.

The defenses around her heart weakened a bit with her sigh.

The ball was lost in the dragon's cave with a series of roars.

"She got you by ten points," someone in the crowd pointed out. "Ten points, buddy."

"Got yourself a free game," someone else said, giving Hester a friendly slap on the back.

Mitch shook his head as he wiped his hands on the thighs of his jeans. "About that handicap—" he began.

"Too late." Ridiculously pleased with herself, Hester hooked her thumbs in her belt loops and studied her score. "Superior reflexes. It's all in the wrist."

"How about a rematch?"

"I don't want to humiliate you again." She turned, intending to offer Radley the free game. "Rad, why don't you…Rad?" She nudged her way through the few lingering onlookers. "Radley?" A little splinter of panic shot straight up her spine. "He's not here."

"He was here a minute ago." Mitch put a hand on her arm and scanned what he could see of the room.

"I wasn't paying any attention." She brought a hand up to her throat, where the fear had already lodged, and began to walk quickly. "I know better than to take my eyes off him in a place like this."

"Stop." He kept his voice calm, but her fear had already transferred itself to him. He knew how easy it was to whisk one small boy away in a crowd. You couldn't pour your milk in the morning without being aware of it. "He's just wandering around the machines. We'll find him. I'll go around this way, you go down here."

She nodded and spun away without a word. They were six or seven deep at some of the machines. Hes-

ter stopped at each one, searching for a small blond boy
in a blue sweater. She called for him over the noise and
clatter of machines.

When she passed the big glass doors and looked
outside to the lights and crowded sidewalks of Times
Square, her heart turned over in her breast. He hadn't
gone outside, she told herself. Radley would never do
something so expressly forbidden. Unless someone had
taken him, or…

Gripping her hands together tightly, she turned away.
She wouldn't think like that. But the room was so big,
filled with so many people, all strangers. And the noise,
the noise was more deafening than she'd remembered.
How could she have heard him if he'd called out for her?

She started down the next row, calling. Once she
heard a young boy laugh and spun around. But it wasn't
Radley. She'd covered half the room, and ten minutes
was gone, when she thought she would have to call the
police. She quickened her pace and tried to look everywhere at once as she went from row to row.

There was so much noise, and the lights were so
bright. Maybe she should double back—she might have
missed him. Maybe he was waiting for her now by that
damn pinball machine, wondering where she'd gone.
He might be afraid. He could be calling for her. He
could be…

Then she saw him, hoisted in Mitch's arms. Hester
shoved two people aside as she ran for them. "Radley!"
She threw her arms around both of them and buried her
face in his hair.

"He'd gone over to watch someone play," Mitch
began as he stroked a hand up and down her back. "He
ran into someone he knew from school."

"It was Ricky Nesbit, Mom. He was with his big brother, and they lent me a quarter. We went to play a game. I didn't know it was so far away."

"Radley." She struggled with the tears and kept her voice firm. "You know the rules about staying with me. This is a big place with a lot of people. I have to be able to trust you not to wander away."

"I didn't mean to. It was just that Ricky said it would just take a minute. I was coming right back."

"Rules have reasons, Radley, and we've been through them."

"But, Mom—"

"Rad." Mitch shifted the boy in his arms. "You scared your mother and me."

"I'm sorry." His eyes clouded up. "I didn't mean to make you scared."

"Don't do it again." Her voice softened as she kissed his cheek. "Next time it's solitary confinement. You're all I've got, Rad." She hugged him again. Her eyes were closed so that she didn't see the change in Mitch's expression. "I can't let anything happen to you."

"I won't do it again."

All she had, Mitch thought as he set the boy down. Was she still so stubborn that she couldn't admit, even to herself, that she had someone else now, too? He jammed his hands into his pockets and tried to force back both anger and hurt. She was going to have to make room in her life soon, very soon, or he'd damn well make it for her.

Chapter 11

He wasn't sure if he was doing more harm than good by staying out of Hester's way for a few days, but Mitch needed time himself. It wasn't his style to dissect and analyze, but to feel and act. However, he'd never felt quite this strongly before or acted quite so rashly.

When possible, he buried himself in work and in the fantasies he could control. When it wasn't, he stayed alone in his rooms, with old movies flickering on the television or music blaring through the stereo. He continued to work on the screenplay he didn't know if he could write, in the hope that the challenge of it would stop him from marching two floors up and demanding that Hester Wallace came to her senses.

She wanted him, yet she didn't want him. She opened to him, yet kept the most precious part of her closed.

She trusted him, yet didn't believe in him enough to share her life with him.

You're all I've got, Rad. And all she wanted? Mitch was forced to ask himself the question. How could such a bright, giving woman base the rest of her life on a mistake she'd made over ten years before?

The helplessness of it infuriated him. Even when he'd hit bottom in New Orleans, he hadn't been helpless. He'd faced his limitations, accepted them, and had channeled his talents differently. Had the time come for him to face and accept his limitations with Hester?

He spent hours thinking about it, considering compromises and then rejecting them. Could he do as she asked and leave things as they were? They would be lovers, with no promises between them and no talk of a future. They could have a relationship as long as there was no hint of permanency or bonds. No, he couldn't do as she asked. Now that he had found the only woman he wanted in his life, he couldn't accept her either part-time or partway.

It was something of a shock to discover he was such an advocate of marriage. He couldn't say that he'd seen very many that had been made in heaven. His parents had been well suited—the same tastes, the same class, the same outlook—but he couldn't remember ever witnessing any passion between them. Affection and loyalty, yes, and a united front against their son's ambitions, but they lacked the spark and simmer that added excitement.

He asked himself if it was only passion he felt for Hester, but knew the answer already. Even as he sat alone he could imagine them twenty years in the future, sitting on the porch swing she'd described. He could see them growing older together, filing away memories and traditions.

He wasn't going to lose that. However long it took, however many walls he had to scale, he wasn't going to lose that.

Mitch dragged a hand through his hair, then gathered up the boxes he needed to lug upstairs.

She was afraid he wasn't coming. There had been some subtle change in Mitch since the night they'd gone to Times Square. He'd been strangely distant on the phone, and though she'd invited him up more than once, he'd always made an excuse.

She was losing him. Hester poured punch into paper cups and reminded herself that she'd known it was only temporary. He had the right to live his own life, to go his own way. She could hardly expect him to tolerate the distance she felt she had to put between them or to understand the lack of time and attention she could give him because of Radley and her job. All she could hope was that he would remain a friend.

Oh, God, she missed him. She missed having him to talk to, to laugh with, even to lean on—though she could only allow herself to lean a little. Hester set the pitcher on the counter and took a deep breath. It couldn't matter, she couldn't *let* it matter now. There were ten excited and noisy boys in the other room. Her responsibility, she reminded herself. She couldn't stand here listing her regrets when she had obligations.

As she carried the tray of drinks into the living room, two boys shot by her. Three more were wrestling on the floor, while the others shouted to be heard over the record player. Hester had already noted that one of Radley's newest friends wore a silver earring and spoke knowledgeably about girls. She set the tray down and glanced quickly at the ceiling.

Give me a few more years of comic books and erector sets. Please, I'm just not ready for the rest of it yet.

"Drink break," she said out loud. "Michael, why don't you let Ernie out of that headlock now and have some punch? Rad, set down the kitten. They get cranky if they're handled too much."

With reluctance, Radley set the little bundle of black-and-white fur in a padded basket. "He's really neat. I like him the best." He snatched a drink off the tray as several other hands reached out. "I really like my watch, too." He held it out, pushing a button that sent it from time mode to the first in a series of miniature video games.

"Just make sure you don't play with it when you should be paying attention in school."

Several boys groaned and elbowed Radley. Hester had just about convinced them to settle down with one of Radley's board games when the knock sounded at the door.

"I'll get it!" Radley hopped up and raced for the door. He had one more birthday wish. When he opened the door, it came true. "Mitch! I knew you'd come. Mom said you'd probably gotten real busy, but I knew you'd come. I got a kitten. I named him Zark. Want to see?"

"As soon as I get rid of some of these boxes." Even arms as well tuned as his were beginning to feel the strain. Mitch set them on the sofa and turned, only to have Zark's namesake shoved into his hands. The kitten purred and arched under a stroking finger. "Cute. We'll have to take him down and introduce him to Taz."

"Won't Taz eat him?"

"You've got to be kidding." Mitch tucked the kitten under his arm and looked at Hester. "Hi."

"Hi." He needed a shave, his sweater had a hole in the seam, and he looked wonderful. "We were afraid you wouldn't make it."

"I said I'd be here." Lazily he scratched between the kitten's ears. "I keep my promises."

"I got this watch, too." Radley held up his wrist. "It tells the time and the date and stuff, then you can play Dive Bomb and Scrimmage."

"Oh, yeah, Dive Bomb?" Mitch sat on the arm of the couch and watched Radley send the little dots spinning. "Never have to be bored on a long subway ride again, right?"

"Or at the dentist's office. You want to play?"

"Later. I'm sorry I'm late. I got hung up in the store."

"That's okay. We didn't have the cake yet 'cause I wanted to wait. It's chocolate."

"Great. Aren't you going to ask for your present?"

"I'm not supposed to." He sneaked a look at his mother, who was busy keeping some of his friends from wrestling again. "Did you really get me something?"

"Nah." Laughing at Radley's expression, he ruffled his hair. "Sure I did. It's right there on the couch."

"Which one?"

"All of them."

Radley's eyes grew big as saucers. "All of them?"

"They all sort of go together. Why don't you open that one first?"

Because of the lack of time and materials, Mitch hadn't wrapped the boxes. He'd barely had enough forethought to put tape over the name brand and model, but buying presents for young boys was a new experience, and one he'd enjoyed immensely. Radley began to pry open the heavy cardboard with assistance from his more curious friends.

"Wow, a PC." Josh craned his head over Radley's shoulder. "Robert Sawyer's got one just like it. You can play all kinds of things on it."

"A computer." Radley stared in amazement at the open box, then turned to Mitch. "Is it for me, really? To keep?"

"Sure you can keep it—it's a present. I was hoping you'd let me play with it sometime."

"You can play with it anytime, anytime you want." He threw his arms around Mitch's neck, forgetting to be embarrassed because his friends were watching. "Thanks. Can we hook it up right now?"

"I thought you'd never ask."

"Rad, you'll have to clear off the desk in your room. Hold it," Hester added when a flood of young bodies started by. "That doesn't mean shoving everything on the floor, okay? You take care of it properly, and Mitch and I will bring this in."

They streaked away with war whoops that warned her she'd be finding surprises under Radley's bed and under the rug for some time. She'd worry about that later. Now she crossed the room to stand beside Mitch.

"That was a terribly generous thing to do."

"He's bright. A kid that bright deserves one of these."

"Yes." She looked at the boxes yet to be opened. There'd be a monitor, disk drives, software. "I've wanted to get him one, but haven't been able to swing it."

"I didn't mean that as a criticism, Hester."

"I know you didn't." She gnawed at her lip in a gesture that told him her nerves were working at her. "I also know this isn't the time to talk, and that we have to. But before we take this in to Rad, I want to tell you how glad I am that you're here."

"It's where I want to be." He ran a thumb along her jawline. "You're going to have to start believing that."

She took his hand and turned her lips into his palm. "You might not feel the same way after you spend the next hour or so with ten fifth-graders." She smiled as the first minor crash sounded from Radley's bedroom. "'Once more unto the breach'?"

The crash was followed by several young voices raised in passionate argument. "How about, 'Lay on, MacDuff'?"

"Whatever." Drawing a deep breath, Hester lifted the first box.

It was over. The last birthday guest had been dragged away by his parents. A strange and wonderful silence lay over the living room. Hester sat in a chair, her eyes half-closed, while Mitch lay sprawled on the couch with his closed completely. In the silence Hester could hear the occasional click of Radley's new computer, and the mewing of Zark, who sat in his lap. With a contented sigh, she surveyed the living room.

It was in shambles. Paper cups and plates were strewn everywhere. The remains of potato chips and pretzels were in bowls, with a good portion of them crushed into the carpet. Scraps of wrapping paper were scattered among the toys the boys had decided worthy of attention. She didn't want to dwell on what the kitchen looked like.

Mitch opened one eye and looked at her. "Did we win?"

"Absolutely." Reluctantly, Hester dragged herself up. "It was a brilliant victory. Want a pillow?"

"No." Taking her hand, he flipped her down on top of him.

"Mitch, Radley is—"

"Playing with his computer," he finished, then nuzzled her bottom lip. "I'm betting he breaks down and puts some of the educational software in before it's over."

"It was pretty clever of you to mix those in."

"I'm a pretty clever kind of guy." He shifted her until she fit into the curve of his shoulder. "Besides, I figured I'd win you over with the machine's practicality, and Rad and I could play the games."

"I'm surprised you don't have one of your own."

"Actually...it seemed like such a good idea when I went in for Rad's that I picked up two. To balance my household accounts," he said when Hester looked up at him. "And modernize my filing system."

"You don't have a filing system."

"See?" He settled his cheek on her hair. "Hester, do you know what one of the ten greatest boons to civilization is?"

"The microwave oven?"

"The afternoon nap. This is a great sofa you've got here."

"It needs reupholstering."

"You can't see that when you're lying on it." He tucked his arm around her waist. "Sleep with me awhile."

"I really have to clean up." But she found it easy to close her eyes.

"Why? Expecting company?"

"No. But don't you have to go down and take Taz out?"

"I slipped Ernie a couple of bucks to walk him."

Hester snuggled into his shoulder. "You are clever."

"That's what I've been trying to tell you."

"I haven't even thought about dinner," she murmured as her mind began to drift.

"Let 'em eat cake."

With a quiet laugh, she slipped into sleep beside him.

Radley wandered in a few moments later, the kitten curled in his arms. He'd wanted to tell them about his latest score. Standing at the foot of the sofa, he scratched the kitten's ears and studied his mom and Mitch thoughtfully. Sometimes when he had a bad dream or wasn't feeling very good, his mom would sleep with him. It always made him feel better. Maybe sleeping with Mitch made his mom feel better.

He wondered if Mitch loved his mom. It made his stomach feel funny to think about it. He wanted Mitch to stay and be his friend. If they got married, did that mean Mitch would go away? He would have to ask, Radley decided. His mom always told him the truth. Shifting the kitten to one arm, he lifted the bowl of chips and carried it into his room.

It was nearly dark when she awoke. Hester opened her eyes and looked directly into Mitch's. She blinked, trying to orient herself. Then he kissed her, and she remembered everything.

"We must have slept for an hour," she murmured.

"Closer to two. How do you feel?"

"Groggy. I always feel groggy if I sleep during the day." She stretched her shoulders and heard Radley giggling in his room. "He must still be at that computer. I don't think I've ever seen him happier."

"And you?"

"Yes." She traced his lips with her fingertip. "I'm happy."

"If you're groggy and happy, this might be the perfect time for me to ask you to marry me again."

"Mitch."

"No? Okay, I'll wait until I can get you drunk. Any more of that cake left?"

"A little. You're not angry?"

Mitch combed his fingers through his hair as he sat up. "About what?"

Hester put her hands on his shoulders, then rested her cheek on his. "I'm sorry I can't give you what you want."

He tightened his arms around her; then with an effort, he relaxed. "Good. That means you're close to changing your mind. I'd like a double-ring ceremony."

"Mitch!"

"What?"

She drew back and, because she didn't trust his smile, shook her head. "Nothing. I think it's best to say nothing. Go ahead and help yourself to the cake. I'm going to get started in here."

Mitch glanced around the room, which looked to be in pretty good shape by his standards. "You really want to clean this up tonight?"

"You don't expect me to leave this mess until the

morning," she began, then stopped herself. "Forget I said that. I forgot who I was talking to."

Mitch narrowed his eyes suspiciously. "Are you accusing me of being sloppy?"

"Not at all. I'm sure there's a lot to be said for living in a 'junkyard' decor with a touch of 'paper drive' thrown in. It's uniquely you." She began to gather up paper plates. "It probably comes from having maids as a child."

"Actually, it comes from never being able to mess up a room. My mother couldn't stand disorder." He'd always been fond of it, Mitch mused, but there was something to be said for watching Hester tidy up. "For my tenth birthday, she hired a magician. We sat in little folding chairs—the boys in suits, the girls in organdy dresses—and watched the performance. Then we were served a light lunch on the terrace. There were enough servants around so that when it was over there wasn't a crumb to be picked up. I guess I'm overcompensating."

"Maybe a little." She kissed both of his cheeks. What an odd man he was, she thought, so calm and easygoing on one hand, so driven by demons on the other. She strongly believed that childhood affected adulthood, even to old age. It was the strength of that belief that made her so fiercely determined to do the best she could by Radley. "You're entitled to your dust and clutter, Mitch. Don't let anyone take it away from you."

He kissed her cheek in return. "I guess you're entitled to your neat and tidy. Where's your vacuum?"

She drew back, brow lifted. "Do you know what one is?"

"Cute. Very cute." He pinched her, hard, just under

the ribs. Hester jumped back with a squeal. "Ah, tick-lish, huh?"

"Cut it out," she warned, holding out the stack of paper plates like a shield. "I wouldn't want to hurt you."

"Come on." He crouched like a wrestler. "Two falls out of three."

"I'm warning you." Wary of the gleam in his eye, she backed up as he advanced. "I'll get violent."

"Promise?" He lunged, gripping her under the waist. In reflex, Hester lifted her arms. The plates, dripping with cake and ice cream, caught him full in the face. "Oh, God." Her own scream of laughter had her falling backward into a chair. She opened her mouth to speak, but only doubled up again.

Very slowly Mitch wiped a hand over his cheek, then studied the smear of chocolate. Watching, Hester let out another peal of laughter and held her sides helplessly.

"What's going on?" Radley came into the living room staring at his mother, who could do nothing but point. Shifting his gaze, Radley stared in turn at Mitch. "Jeez." Radley rolled his eyes and began to gig-gle. "Mike's little sister gets food all over her face like that. She's almost two."

The control Hester had been scratching for slipped out of her grip. Choking with laughter, she pulled Rad-ley against her. "It was—it was an accident," she man-aged, then collapsed again.

"It was a deliberate sneak attack," Mitch corrected. "And it calls for immediate retribution."

"Oh, please." Hester held out a hand, knowing she was too weak to defend herself. "I'm sorry. I swear. It was a reflex, that's all."

"So's this." He came closer, and though she ducked

behind Radley, Mitch merely sandwiched the giggling boy between them. And he kissed her, her mouth, her nose, her cheeks, while she squirmed and laughed and struggled. When he was finished, he'd transferred a satisfactory amount of chocolate to her face. Radley took one look at his mother and slipped, cackling, to the floor.

"Maniac," she accused as she wiped chocolate from her chin with the back of her hand.

"You look beautiful in chocolate, Hester."

It took more than an hour to put everything to rights again. By popular vote, they ended up sharing a pizza as they once had before, then spending the rest of the evening trying out Radley's birthday treasures. When he began to nod over the keyboard, Hester nudged him into bed.

"Quite a day." Hester set the kitten in his basket at the foot of Radley's bed, then stepped out into the hall.

"I'd say it's a birthday he'll remember."

"So will I." She reached up to rub at a slight stiffness at the base of her neck. "Would you like some wine?"

"I'll get it." He turned her toward the living room. "Go sit down."

"Thanks." Hester sat on the couch, stretched out her legs and slipped off her shoes. It was definitely a day she would remember. Sometime during it, she'd come to realize that she could also have a night to remember.

"Here you go." Mitch handed her a glass of wine, then slipped onto the sofa beside her. Holding his own glass up, he shifted her so that she rested against him.

"This is nice." With a sigh, she brought the wine to her lips.

"Very nice." He bent to brush his lips over her neck. "I told you this was a great sofa."

"Sometimes I forget what it's like to relax like this. Everything's done, Radley's happy and tucked into bed, tomorrow's Sunday and there's nothing urgent to think about."

"No restless urge to go out dancing or carousing?"

"No." She stretched her shoulders. "You?"

"I'm happy right here."

"Then stay." She pressed her lips together a moment. "Stay tonight."

He was silent. His hand stopped its easy massage of her neck, then began again, slowly. "Are you sure that's what you want?"

"Yes." She drew a deep breath before she turned to look at him. "I've missed you. I wish I knew what was right and what was wrong, what was best for all of us, but I know I've missed you. Will you stay?"

"I'm not going anywhere."

She settled back against him, content. For a long time they sat just as they were, half dreaming, in silence, with lamplight glowing behind them.

"Are you still working on the script?" she asked at length.

"Mmm-hmm." He could get used to this, he thought, very used to having Hester snuggled beside him in the late evening with the lamplight dim and the scent of her hair teasing his senses. "You were right. I'd have hated myself if I hadn't tried to write it. I guess I had to get past the nerves."

"Nerves?" She smiled over her shoulder. "You?"

"I've been known to have them, when something's

either unfamiliar or important. They were stretched pretty thin the first time I made love with you."

Hearing it not only surprised her but made the memory of it all the sweeter. "They didn't show."

"Take my word for it." He stroked the outside of her thigh, lightly and with a casualness that was its own kind of seduction. "I was afraid that I'd make the wrong move and screw up something that was more important than anything else in my life."

"You didn't make any wrong moves, and you make me feel very special."

When she rose, it felt natural to hold out a hand to him, to have his close over hers. She switched off lights as they walked to the bedroom.

Mitch closed the door. Hester turned down the bed. He knew it could be like this every night, for all the years they had left. She was on the edge of believing it. He knew it, he could see it in her eyes when he crossed to her. Her eyes remained on his while she unbuttoned her blouse.

They undressed in silence, but the air had already started to hum. Though nerves had relaxed, anticipation was edgier than ever. Now they knew what they could bring to each other. They slipped into bed together and turned to each other.

It felt so right, just the way his arms slipped around her to bring her close. Just the way their bodies met, merging warmth to warmth. She knew the feel of him now, the firmness, the strength. She knew how easily hers fit against it. She tipped her head back and, with her eyes still on his, offered her mouth.

Kissing him was like sliding down a cool river toward churning white water.

The sound of pleasure came deep in his throat as she pressed against him. The shyness was still there, but without the reserve and hesitation. Now there was only sweetness and an offering.

It was like this each time they came together. Exhilarating, stunning and right. He cupped the back of her head in his hand as she leaned over him. The light zing of the wine hadn't completely faded from her tongue. He tasted it, and her, as she explored his mouth. He sensed a boldness growing in her that hadn't been there before, a new confidence that caused her to come to him with her own demands and needs.

Her heart was open, he thought as her lips raced over his throat. And Hester was free. He'd wanted this for her—for them. With something like a laugh, he rolled over her and began to drive her toward madness.

She couldn't get enough of him. She took her hands, her mouth, over him quickly, almost fiercely, but found it impossible to assuage the greed. How could she have known a man could feel so good, so exciting? How could she have known that the scent of his skin would make her head reel and her desires sharpen? Just her name murmured in his voice aroused her.

Locked together, they tumbled over the sheets, tangling in the blanket, shoving it aside because the need for its warmth was long past. He moved as quickly as she, discovering new secrets to delight and torment her. She heard him gasp out her name as she ranged kisses over his chest. She felt his body tense and arch as she moved her hands lower.

Perhaps the power had always been there inside her, but Hester was certain it had been born in her that night. The power to arouse a man past the civilized, and perhaps past the wise. Wise or not, she gloried in it when he trapped her beneath him and let desire rule.

His mouth was hot and hungry as it raced over her. Demands, promises, pleas swirled through her head, but she couldn't speak. Even her breath was trapped as he drove her up and up. She caught him close, as though he were a lifeline in a sea that raged.

Then they both went under.

Chapter 12

The sky was cloudy and threatening snow. Half dozing, Hester turned away from the window to reach for Mitch. The bed beside her was rumpled but empty.

Had he left her during the night? she wondered as she ran her hand over the sheets where he'd slept. Her first reaction was disappointment. It would have been so sweet to have had him there to turn to in the morning. Then she drew her hand back and cupped it under her cheek.

Perhaps it was best that he'd gone. She couldn't be sure how Radley would feel. If Mitch was there to reach out to, she knew it would only become more difficult to keep herself from doing so again and again. No one knew how hard and painfully she'd worked to stop herself from needing anyone. Now, after all the years of struggling, she'd just begun to see real progress. She'd made a good home for Radley in a good neighborhood and had a strong, well-paying job. Security, stability.

She couldn't risk those things again for the emotional morass that came with depending on someone else. But she was already beginning to depend on him, Hester thought as she pushed back the blankets. No matter how much her head told her it was best that he wasn't here, she was sorry he wasn't. She *was* sorry, sorrier than he could ever know, that she was strong enough to stand apart from him.

Hester slipped on her robe and went to see if Radley wanted breakfast.

She found them together, hunched over the keyboard of Radley's computer while graphics exploded on the screen. "This thing's defective," Mitch insisted. "That was a dead-on shot."

"You missed by a mile."

"I'm going to tell your mother you need glasses. Look, this is definite interference. How am I supposed to concentrate when this stupid cat's chewing on my toes?"

"Poor sportsmanship," Radley said soberly as Mitch's last man was obliterated.

"Poor sportsmanship! I'll show you poor sportsmanship." With that he snatched Radley up and held him upside down. "Now is this machine defective, or what?"

"No." Giggling, Radley braced his hands on the floor. "Maybe *you* need glasses."

"I'm going to have to drop you on your head. You really leave me no choice. Oh, hi, Hester." With his arm hooked around Radley's legs, he smiled at her.

"Hi, Mom!" Though his cheeks were turning pink,

Radley was delighted with his upside-down position. "I beat Mitch three times. But he's not really mad."

"Says who?" Mitch flipped the boy upright, then dropped him lightly on the bed. "I've been humiliated."

"I destroyed him," Radley said with satisfaction.

"I can't believe I slept through it." She offered them both a cautious smile. It didn't seem as though Radley was anything but delighted to find Mitch here. As for herself, she wasn't having an easy time keeping the pleasure down, either. "I suppose after three major battles you'd both like some breakfast."

"We already ate." Radley leaned over the bed to reach for the kitten. "I showed Mitch how to make French toast. He said it was real good."

"That was before you cheated."

"I did not." Radley rolled on his back and let the kitten creep up his stomach. "Mitch washed the pan, and I dried it. We were going to fix you some, but you just kept on sleeping."

The idea of the two men in her life fiddling in the kitchen while she slept left her flustered. "I guess I didn't expect anyone to be up so early."

"Hester." Mitch stepped closer to swing an arm over her shoulders. "I hate to break this to you, but it's after eleven."

"Eleven?"

"Yeah. How about lunch?"

"Well, I..."

"You think about it. I guess I should go down and take care of Taz."

"I'll do it." Radley was up and bouncing. "I can give him his food and take him for a walk and everything. I know how, you showed me."

"It's okay with me. Hester?"

She was having trouble just keeping up. "All right. But you'll have to bundle up."

"I will." He was already reaching for his coat. "Can I bring Taz back with me? He hasn't met Zark yet."

Hester glanced at the tiny ball of fur, thinking of Taz's big white teeth. "I don't know if Taz would care for Zark."

"He loves cats," Mitch assured her as he picked up Radley's ski cap off the floor. "In a purely noncannibalistic way." He reached in his pocket for his keys.

"Be careful," she called as Radley rushed by, jingling Mitch's keys. The front door slammed with a vengeance.

"Good morning," Mitch said, and turned her into his arms.

"Good morning. You could have woken me up."

"It was tempting." He ran his hands up the back of her robe. "Actually, I was going to make some coffee and bring you in a cup. Then Radley came in. Before I knew it, I was up to my wrists in egg batter."

"He, ah, didn't wonder what you were doing here?"

"No." Knowing exactly how her mind was working, he kissed the tip of her nose. Then, shifting her to his side, he began to walk with her to the kitchen. "He came in while I was boiling water and asked if I was fixing breakfast. After a brief consultation, we decided he was the better qualified of the two. There's some coffee left, but I think you'd be better off pouring it out and starting again."

"I'm sure it's fine."

"I love an optimist."

She almost managed a smile as she reached in the refrigerator for the milk. "I thought you'd gone."

"Would you rather I had?"

She shook her head but didn't look at him. "Mitch, it's so hard. It just keeps getting harder."

"What does?"

"Trying not to want you here like this all the time."

"Say the word and I'll move in, bag and dog."

"I wish I could. I really wish I could. Mitch, when I walked into Rad's bedroom this morning and saw the two of you together, something just clicked. I stood there thinking this is the way it could be for us."

"That's the way it *will* be for us, Hester."

"You're so sure." With a small laugh, she turned to lean her palms on the counter. "You're so absolutely sure, and have been almost from the beginning. Maybe that's one of the things that frightens me."

"A light went on for me when I saw you, Hester." He came closer to put his hands on her shoulders. "I haven't gone through my life knowing exactly what I wanted, and I can't claim that everything always goes the way I'd planned, but with you I'm sure." He pressed his lips to her hair. "Do you love me, Hester?"

"Yes." With a long sigh, she shut her eyes. "Yes, I love you."

"Then marry me." Gently he turned her around to face him. "I won't ask you to change anything but your name."

She wanted to believe him, to believe it was possible to start a new life just once more. Her heart was thudding hard against her ribs as she wrapped her arms around him. *Take the chance,* it seemed to be telling her. *Don't throw love away.* Her fingers tensed against him. "Mitch, I—" When the phone rang, Hester let out a pent-up breath. "I'm sorry."

"So am I," he muttered, but released her.

Her legs were still unsteady as she picked up the receiver to the wall phone. "Hello." The giddiness fled, and with it all the blossoming pleasure. "Allan."

Mitch looked around quickly. Her eyes were as flat as her voice. She'd already twisted the phone cord around her hand as if she wanted to anchor herself. "Fine," she said. "We're both fine. Florida? I thought you were in San Diego."

So he'd moved again, Hester thought as she listened to the familiar voice, restless as ever. She listened with the cold patience of experience as he told her how wonderful, how terrific, how incredibly he was doing.

"Rad isn't here at the moment," she told him, though Allan hadn't asked. "If you want to wish him a happy birthday, I can have him call you back." There was a pause, and Mitch saw her eyes change and the anger come. "Yesterday." She set her teeth, then took a long breath through them. "He's ten, Allan. Radley was ten yesterday. Yes, I'm sure it's difficult for you to imagine."

She fell silent again, listening. The dull anger lodged itself in her throat, and when she spoke again, her voice was hollow. "Congratulations. Hard feelings?" She didn't care for the sound of her own laugh. "No, Allan, there are no feelings whatsoever. All right, then, good luck. I'm sorry, that's as enthusiastic as it gets. I'll tell Radley you called."

She hung up, careful to bolt down the need to slam down the receiver. Slowly she unwound the cord which was biting into her hand.

"You okay?"

She nodded and walked to the stove to pour coffee

she didn't want. "He called to tell me he's getting married again. He thought I'd be interested."

"Does it matter?"

"No." She sipped it black and welcomed the bitterness. "What he does stopped mattering years ago. He didn't know it was Radley's birthday." The anger came bubbling to the surface no matter how hard she tried to keep it submerged. "He didn't even know how old he was." She slammed the cup down so that coffee sloshed over the sides. "Radley stopped being real for him the minute he walked out the door. All he had to do was shut it behind him."

"What difference does it make now?"

"He's Radley's father."

"No." His own anger sprang out. "That's something you've got to work out of your system, something you've got to start accepting. The only part he played in Rad's life was biological. There's no trick to that, and no automatic bond of loyalty comes with it."

"He has a responsibility."

"He doesn't want it, Hester." Struggling for patience, he took her hands. "He's cut himself off from Rad completely. No one's going to call that admirable, and it's obvious it wasn't done for the boy's sake. But would you rather have him strolling in and out of Radley's life at his own whim, leaving the kid confused and hurting?"

"No, but I—"

"You want him to care, and he doesn't care." Though her hands remained in his, he felt the change. "You're pulling back from me."

It was true. She could regret it, but she couldn't stop it. "I don't want to."

"But you are." This time, it was he who pulled away. "It only took a phone call."

"Mitch, please try to understand."

"I've been trying to understand." There was an edge to his voice now that she hadn't heard before. "The man left you, and it hurt, but it's been over a long time."

"It's not the hurt," she began, then dragged a hand through her hair. "Or maybe it is, partly. I don't want to go through that ever again, the fear, the emptiness. I loved him. You have to understand that maybe I was young, maybe I was stupid, but I loved him."

"I've always understood that," he said, though he didn't like to hear it. "A woman like you doesn't make promises lightly."

"No, when I make them I mean to keep them. I wanted to keep this one." She picked up the coffee again, wrapping both hands around the cup to keep them warm. "I can't tell you how badly I wanted to keep my marriage together, how hard I tried. I gave up part of myself when I married Allan. He told me we were going to move to New York, we were going to do things in a big way, and I went. Leaving my home, my family and friends was the most terrifying thing I'd ever done, but I went because he wanted it. Almost everything I did during our marriage I did because he wanted it. And because it was easier to go along than to refuse. I built my life around his. Then, at the age of twenty, I discovered I didn't have a life at all."

"So you made one, for yourself and for Radley. That's something to be proud of."

"I am. It's taken me eight years, eight years to feel I'm really on solid ground again. Now there's you."

"Now there's me," he said slowly, watching her. "And

you just can't get past the idea that I'll pull the rug out from under you again."

"I don't want to be that woman again." She said the words desperately, searching for the answers even as she struggled to give them to him. "A woman who focuses all her needs and goals around someone else. If I found myself alone this time, I'm not sure I could stand up again."

"Listen to yourself. You'd rather be alone now than risk the fact that things might not work out for the next fifty years? Take a good look at me, Hester, I'm not Allan Wallace. I'm not asking you to bury yourself to make me happy. It's the woman you are today who I love, the woman you are today who I want to spend my life with."

"People change, Mitch."

"And they can change together." He drew a deep breath. "Or they can change separately. Why don't you let me know when you make up your mind what you want to do?"

She opened her mouth, then closed it again when he walked away. She didn't have the right to call him back.

He shouldn't complain, Mitch thought as he sat at his new keyboard and toyed with the next scene in his script. The work was going better than he'd expected— and faster. It was becoming easy for him to bury himself in Zark's problems and let his own stew.

At this point, Zark was waiting by Leilah's bedside, praying that she would survive the freak accident that had left her beauty intact but her brain damaged. Of course, when she awoke she would be a stranger. His wife of two years would become his greatest enemy, her mind as brilliant as ever but warped and evil. All his plans and dreams would be shattered forever. Whole galaxies would be in peril.

"You think you've got problems?" Mitch muttered. "Things aren't exactly bouncing along for me, either."

Eyes narrowed, he studied the screen. The atmosphere was good, he thought as he tipped back. Mitch didn't have any problem imagining a twenty-third-century hospital room. He didn't have any trouble imagining Zark's distress or the madness brewing in Leilah's unconscious brain. What he did have trouble imagining was his life without Hester.

"Stupid." The dog at his feet yawned in agreement. "What I should do is go down to that damn bank and drag her out. She'd love that, wouldn't she?" he said with a laugh as he pushed away from the machine and stretched. "I could beg." Mitch rolled that around in his mind and found it uncomfortable. "I could, but we'd probably both be sorry. There's not much left after reasoning, and I've tried that. What would Zark do?"

Mitch rocked back on his heels and closed his eyes. Would Zark, hero and saint, back off? Would Zark, defender of right and justice, bow out gracefully? Nope, Mitch decided. When it came to love, Zark was a patsy. Leilah kept kicking astrodust in his face, but he was still determined to win her back.

At least Hester hadn't tried to poison him with nerve gas. Leilah had pulled that and more, but Zark was still nuts about her.

Mitch studied the poster of Zark he'd tacked to the wall for inspiration. We're in the same boat, buddy, but I'm not going to pull out the oars and start rowing, either. And Hester's going to find herself in some turbulent waters.

He glanced at the clock on his desk, but remembered it had stopped two days before. He was pretty sure he'd sent his watch to the laundry along with his socks. Because he wanted to see how much time he had before Hester was due home, he walked into the living room. There, on the table, was an old mantel clock that Mitch was fond enough of to remember to wind. Just as he glanced at it, he heard Radley at the door.

"Right on time," Mitch said when he swung the door open. "How cold is it?" He grazed his knuckles down Radley's cheek in a routine they'd developed. "Forty-three degrees."

"It's sunny," Radley said, dragging off his backpack.

"Shooting for the park, are you?" Mitch waited until Radley had folded his coat neatly over the arm of the sofa. "Maybe I can handle it after I fortify myself. Mrs. Jablanski next door made cookies. She feels sorry for me because no one's fixing me hot meals, so I copped a dozen."

"What kind?"

"Peanut butter."

"All right!" Radley was already streaking into the kitchen. He liked the ebony wood and smoked glass table Mitch had set by the wall. Mostly because Mitch didn't mind if the glass got smeared with fingerprints. He settled down, content with milk and cookies and Mitch's company. "We have to do a dumb state project," he said with his mouth full. "I got Rhode Island. It's the smallest state. I wanted Texas."

"Rhode Island." Mitch smiled and munched on a cookie. "Is that so bad?"

"Nobody cares about Rhode Island. I mean, they've got the Alamo and stuff in Texas."

"Well, maybe I can give you a hand with it. I was born there."

"In Rhode Island? Honest?" The tiny state took on a new interest.

"Yeah. How long do you have?"

"Six weeks," Radley said with a shrug as he reached for another cookie. "We've got to do illustrations, which is okay, but we've got to do junk like manufacturing and natural resources, too. How come you moved away?"

He started to make some easy remark, then decided to honor Hester's code of honesty. "I didn't get along with my parents very well. We're better friends now."

"Sometimes people go away and don't come back."

The boy spoke so matter-of-factly that Mitch found himself responding the same way. "I know."

"I used to worry that Mom would go away. She didn't."

"She loves you." Mitch ran a hand along the boy's hair.

"Are you going to marry her?"

Mitch paused in midstroke. "Well, I..." Just how did he handle this one? "I guess I've been thinking about it." Feeling ridiculously nervous, he rose to heat up his coffee. "Actually, I've been thinking about it a lot. How would you feel if I did?"

"Would you live with us all the time?"

"That's the idea." He poured the coffee, then sat down beside Radley again. "Would that bother you?"

Radley looked at him with dark and suddenly inscrutable eyes. "One of my friends' moms got married again. Kevin says since they did his stepfather isn't his friend anymore."

"Do you think if I married your mom I'd stop being your friend?" He caught Radley's chin in his hand. "I'm not your friend because of your mom, but because of you. I can promise that won't change when I'm your stepfather."

"You wouldn't be my stepfather. I don't want one of those." Radley's chin trembled in Mitch's hand. "I want a real one. Real ones don't go away."

Mitch slipped his hands under Radley's arms and lifted him onto his lap. "You're right. Real ones don't." Out of the mouth of babes, he thought, and nuzzled Radley against him. "You know, I haven't had much practice being a father. Are you going to get mad at me if I mess up once in a while?"

Radley shook his head and burrowed closer. "Can we tell Mom?"

Mitch managed a laugh. "Yeah, good idea. Get your coat, Sergeant, we're going on a very important mission."

Hester was up to her elbows in numbers. For some reason, she was having a great deal of trouble adding two and two. It didn't seem terribly important anymore. That, she knew, was a sure sign of trouble. She went through files, calculated and assessed, then closed them again with no feeling at all.

His fault, she told herself. It was Mitch's fault that she was only going through the motions, and thinking about going through the same motions day after day for the next twenty years. He'd made her question herself. He'd made her deal with the pain and anger she'd tried to bury. He'd made her want what she'd once sworn never to want again.

And now what? She propped her elbows on the stack of files and stared into space. She was in love, more deeply and more richly in love than she'd ever been before. The man she was in love with was exciting, kind and committed, and he was offering her a new beginning.

That was what she was afraid of, Hester admitted. That was what she kept heading away from. She hadn't fully understood before that she had blamed herself, not Allan, all these years. She had looked on the breakup of her marriage as a personal mistake, a private failure. Rather than risk another failure, she was turning away her first true hope.

She said it was because of Radley, but that was only partly true. Just as the divorce had been a private failure, making a full commitment to Mitch had been a private fear.

He'd been right, she told herself. He'd been right about so many things all along. She wasn't the same woman who had loved and married Allan Wallace. She wasn't even the same woman who had struggled for a handhold when she'd found herself alone with a small child.

When was she going to stop punishing herself? Now, Hester decided, picking up the phone. Right now. Her hand was steady as she dialed Mitch's number, but her heart wasn't. She caught her bottom lip between her teeth and listened to the phone ring—and ring.

"Oh, Mitch, won't we ever get the timing right?" She hung up the receiver and promised herself she wouldn't lose her courage. In an hour she would go home and tell him she was ready for that new beginning.

At Kay's buzz, Hester picked up the receiver again. "Yes, Kay."

"Mrs. Wallace, there's someone here to see you about a loan."

With a frown, Hester checked her calendar. "I don't have anything scheduled."

"I thought you could fit him in."

"All right, but buzz me in twenty minutes. I've got to clear some things up before I leave."

"Yes, ma'am."

Hester tidied her desk and was preparing to rise when Mitch walked in. "Mitch? I was just… What are you doing here? Rad?"

"He's waiting with Taz in the lobby."

"Kay said I had someone waiting to see me."

"That's me." He stepped up to the desk and set down a briefcase.

She started to reach for his hand, but his face seemed so set. "Mitch, you didn't have to say you'd come to apply for a loan."

"That's just what I'm doing."

She smiled and settled back. "Don't be silly."

"Mrs. Wallace, you *are* the loan officer at this bank?"

"Mitch, really, this isn't necessary."

"I'd hate to tell Rosen you sent me to a competitor." He flipped open the briefcase. "I've brought the financial information usual in these cases. I assume you have the necessary forms for a mortgage application?"

"Of course, but—"

"Then why don't you get one out?"

"All right, then." If he wanted to play games, she'd

oblige him. "So you're interested in securing a mortgage. Are you purchasing the property for investment purposes, for rental or for a business?"

"No, it's purely personal."

"I see. Do you have a contract of sale?"

"Right here." It pleased him to see her mouth drop open.

Taking the papers from him, Hester studied them. "This is real."

"Of course it's real. I put a bid on the place a couple of weeks ago." He scratched at his chin as if thinking back. "Let's see, that would have been the day I had to forgo pot roast. You haven't offered it again."

"You bought a house?" She scanned the papers again. "In Connecticut?"

"They accepted my offer. The papers just came through. I believe the bank will want to get its own appraisal. There is a fee for that, isn't there?"

"What? Oh, yes, I'll fill out the papers."

"Fine. In the meantime, I do have some snapshots and a blueprint." He slipped them out of the briefcase and placed them on her desk. "You might want to look them over."

"I don't understand."

"You might begin to if you look at the pictures."

She lifted them and stared at her fantasy house. It was big and sprawling, with porches all around and tall, wide windows. Snow mantled the evergreens beside the steps and lay stark and white on the roof.

"There are a couple of outbuildings you can't see. A barn, a henhouse—both unoccupied at the moment. The lot is about five acres, with woods and a stream. The real estate agent claims the fishing's good. The roof needs some work and the gutters have to be replaced, and inside it could use some paint or paper and a little help with the plumbing. But it's sound." He watched her as he spoke. She didn't look up at him, but continued to stare, mesmerized by the snapshots. "The house has been standing for a hundred and fifty years. I figure it'll hold up a while longer."

"It's lovely." Tears pricked the back of her eyes, but she blinked them away. "Really lovely."

"Is that from the bank's point of view?"

She shook her head. He wasn't going to make it easy. And he shouldn't, she admitted to herself. She'd already made it difficult enough for both of them. "I didn't know you were thinking of relocating. What about your work?"

"I can set up my drawing board in Connecticut just as easily as I can here. It's a reasonable commute, and I don't exactly spend a lot of time in the office."

"That's true." She picked up a pen, but rather than writing down the necessary information only ran it through her fingers.

"I'm told there's a bank in town. Nothing along the lines of National Trust, but a small independent bank. Seems to me someone with experience could get a good position there."

"I've always preferred small banks." There was a lump in her throat that had to be swallowed. "Small towns."

"They've got a couple of good schools. The elementary school is next to a farm. I'm told sometimes the cows get over the fence and into the playground."

"Looks like you've covered everything."

"I think so."

She stared down at the pictures, wondering how he could have found what she'd always wanted and how she could have been lucky enough that he would have cared. "Are you doing this for me?"

"No." He waited until she looked at him. "I'm doing it for us."

Her eyes filled again. "I don't deserve you."

"I know." Then he took both her hands and lifted her to her feet. "So you'd be pretty stupid to turn down such a good deal."

"I'd hate to think I was stupid." She drew her hands away to come around the desk to him. "I need to tell you something, but I'd like you to kiss me first."

"Is that the way you get loans around here?" Taking her by the lapels, he dragged her against him. "I'm going to have to report you, Mrs. Wallace. Later."

He closed his mouth over hers and felt the give, the strength and the acceptance. With a quiet sound of pleasure, he slipped his hands up to her face and felt the slow, lovely curve of her lips as she smiled.

"Does this mean I get the loan?"

"We'll talk business in a minute." She held on just a little longer, then drew away. "Before you came in, I'd been sitting here. Actually, I'd been sitting here for the last couple of days, not getting anything done because I was thinking of you."

"Go on, I think I'm going to like this story."

"When I wasn't thinking about you, I was thinking about myself and the last dozen years of my life I've put a lot of energy into *not* thinking about it, so it wasn't easy."

She kept his hand in hers, but took another step away. "I realize that what happened to me and Allan was destined to happen. If I'd been smarter, or stronger, I would have been able to admit a long time ago that what we had could only be temporary. Maybe if he hadn't left the way he did…" She trailed off, shaking her head. "It doesn't matter now. That's the point I had to come to, that it just doesn't matter. Mitch, I don't want to live the rest of my life wondering if you and I could have made it work. I'd rather spend the rest of my life *trying* to make it work. Before you came in today with all of this, I'd decided to ask you if you still wanted to marry me."

"The answer to that is yes, with a couple of stipulations."

She'd already started to move into his arms, but drew back. "Stipulations?"

"Yeah, you're a banker, you know about stipulations, right?"

"Yes, but I don't look at this as a transaction."

"You better hear me out, because it's a big one." He ran his hands up her arms, then dropped them to his sides. "I want to be Rad's father."

"If we were married, you would be."

"I believe stepfather's the term used in that case. Rad and I agreed we didn't go for it."

"Agreed?" She spoke carefully, on guard again. "You discussed this with Rad?"

"Yeah, I discussed it with Rad. He brought it up, but I'd have wanted to talk to him, anyway. He asked me this afternoon if I was going to marry you. Did you want me to lie to him?"

"No." She paused a moment, then shook her head. "No, of course not. What did he say?"

"Basically he wanted to know if I'd still be his friend, because he'd heard sometimes stepfathers change a bit once their foot's in the door. Once we'd gotten past that hurdle, he told me he didn't want me as a stepfather."

"Oh, Mitch." She sank down on the edge of the desk.

"He wants a real father, Hester, because real fathers don't go away." Her eyes darkened very slowly before she closed them.

"I see."

"The way I look at it, you've got another decision to make. Are you going to let me adopt him?" Her eyes shot open again with quick surprise. "You've decided to share yourself. I want to know if you're going to share Rad, all the way. I don't see a problem with me being his father emotionally. I just want you to know that I want it legally. I don't think there'd be a problem with your ex-husband."

"No, I'm sure there wouldn't be."

"And I don't think there'd be a problem with Rad. So is there a problem with you?"

Hester rose from the desk to pace a few steps away. "I don't know what to say to you. I can't come up with the right words."

"Pick some."

She turned back with a deep breath. "I guess the best I can come up with is that Radley's going to have a terrific father, in every way. And I love you very, very much."

"Those'll do." He caught her to him with relief. "Those'll do just fine." Then he was kissing her again, fast and desperate. With her arms around him, she laughed. "Does this mean you're going to approve the loan?"

"I'm sorry, I have to turn you down."

"What?"

"I would, however, approve a joint application from you and your wife." She caught his face in her hands. "Our house, our commitment."

"Those are terms I can live with—" he touched her lips with his "—for the next hundred years or so." He swung her around in one quick circle. "Let's go tell Rad." With their hands linked, they started out. "Say, Hester, how do you feel about honeymooning in Disneyland?"

She laughed and walked through the door with him. "I'd love it. I'd absolutely love it."

* * * * *

New York Times bestselling author

SUSAN MALLERY

invites readers back to her beloved series set in
Fool's Gold featuring three newcomers who find love
when they are least expecting it...

Available Now.

Coming May 27, 2014!

Coming June 24, 2014!

"Romance novels don't get much better than Mallery's expert
blend of emotional nuance, humor and superb storytelling."
—*Booklist*

PHSMFGT0514

REQUEST YOUR FREE BOOKS!

2 FREE NOVELS
FROM THE ROMANCE COLLECTION
PLUS 2 FREE GIFTS!

YES! Please send me 2 FREE novels from the Romance Collection and my 2 FREE gifts (gifts are worth about $10). After receiving them, if I don't wish to receive any more books, I can return the shipping statement marked "cancel." If I don't cancel, I will receive 4 brand-new novels every month and be billed just $6.24 per book in the U.S. or $6.74 per book in Canada. That's a savings of at least 22% off the cover price. It's quite a bargain! Shipping and handling is just 50¢ per book in the U.S. and 75¢ per book in Canada.* I understand that accepting the 2 free books and gifts places me under no obligation to buy anything. I can always return a shipment and cancel at any time. Even if I never buy another book, the two free books and gifts are mine to keep forever.

194/394 MDN F4XY

Name _____ (PLEASE PRINT) _____

Address _____ Apt. # _____

City _____ State/Prov. _____ Zip/Postal Code _____

Signature (if under 18, a parent or guardian must sign)

Mail to the Harlequin® Reader Service:
IN U.S.A.: P.O. Box 1867, Buffalo, NY 14240-1867
IN CANADA: P.O. Box 609, Fort Erie, Ontario L2A 5X3

Want to try two free books from another line?
Call 1-800-873-8635 or visit www.ReaderService.com.

* Terms and prices subject to change without notice. Prices do not include applicable taxes. Sales tax applicable in N.Y. Canadian residents will be charged applicable taxes. Offer not valid in Quebec. This offer is limited to one order per household. Not valid for current subscribers to the Romance Collection or the Romance/Suspense Collection. All orders subject to credit approval. Credit or debit balances in a customer's account(s) may be offset by any other outstanding balance owed by or to the customer. Please allow 4 to 6 weeks for delivery. Offer available while quantities last.

Your Privacy—The Harlequin® Reader Service is committed to protecting your privacy. Our Privacy Policy is available online at www.ReaderService.com or upon request from the Harlequin Reader Service.

We make a portion of our mailing list available to reputable third parties that offer products we believe may interest you. If you prefer that we not exchange your name with third parties, or if you wish to clarify or modify your communication preferences, please visit us at www.ReaderService.com/consumerschoice or write to us at Harlequin Reader Service Preference Service, P.O. Box 9062, Buffalo, NY 14269. Include your complete name and address.

ROM13R

NORA ROBERTS

28594	O'HURLEY'S RETURN	___ $7.99 U.S.	___ $9.99 CAN.
28592	O'HURLEY BORN	___ $7.99 U.S.	___ $9.99 CAN.
28590	SWEET RAINS	___ $7.99 U.S.	___ $9.99 CAN.
28588	NIGHT TALES:		
	NIGHT SHIELD & NIGHT MOVES	___ $7.99 U.S.	___ $9.99 CAN.
28587	NIGHT TALES:		
	NIGHTSHADE & NIGHT SMOKE	___ $7.99 U.S.	___ $9.99 CAN.
28586	NIGHT TALES:		
	NIGHT SHIFT & NIGHT SHADOW	___ $7.99 U.S.	___ $9.99 CAN.
28578	THE LAW OF LOVE	___ $7.99 U.S.	___ $8.99 CAN.
28172	WHISPERED PROMISES	___ $7.99 U.S.	___ $8.99 CAN.
28171	FOREVER	___ $7.99 U.S.	___ $9.99 CAN.
28170	REFLECTIONS & DREAMS	___ $7.99 U.S.	___ $8.99 CAN.
28169	HAPPY ENDINGS	___ $7.99 U.S.	___ $9.99 CAN.
28168	CHANGE OF HEART	___ $7.99 U.S.	___ $9.99 CAN.
28167	CHARMED & ENCHANTED	___ $7.99 U.S.	___ $9.99 CAN.
28166	PLAYING FOR KEEPS	___ $7.99 U.S.	___ $8.99 CAN.
28165	CAPTIVATED & ENTRANCED	___ $7.99 U.S.	___ $9.99 CAN.
28164	FIRST IMPRESSIONS	___ $7.99 U.S.	___ $9.99 CAN.
28162	A DAY AWAY	___ $7.99 U.S.	___ $9.99 CAN.
28161	MYSTERIOUS	___ $7.99 U.S.	___ $9.99 CAN.
28160	THE MacGREGOR GROOMS	___ $7.99 U.S.	___ $9.99 CAN.
28158	ROBERT & CYBIL	___ $7.99 U.S.	___ $9.99 CAN.
28156	DANIEL & IAN	___ $7.99 U.S.	___ $9.99 CAN.
28154	GABRIELLA & ALEXANDER	___ $7.99 U.S.	___ $9.99 CAN.
28150	IRISH HEARTS	___ $7.99 U.S.	___ $9.99 CAN.
28137	PERFECT HARMONY	___ $7.99 U.S.	___ $8.99 CAN.
28133	THE MacGREGORS: SERENA & CAINE	___ $7.99 U.S.	___ $9.99 CAN.

(limited quantities available)

TOTAL AMOUNT	$	_____
POSTAGE & HANDLING	$	_____
($1.00 FOR 1 BOOK, 50¢ for each additional)		
APPLICABLE TAXES*	$	_____
TOTAL PAYABLE	$	_____

(check or money order—please do not send cash)

To order, complete this form and send it, along with a check or money order for the total above, payable to Harlequin Books, to: **In the U.S.:** 3010 Walden Avenue, P.O. Box 9077, Buffalo, NY 14269-9077; **In Canada:** P.O. Box 636, Fort Erie, Ontario, L2A 5X3.

Name: _____
Address: _____ City: _____
State/Prov.: _____ Zip/Postal Code: _____
Account Number (if applicable): _____

075 CSAS

*New York residents remit applicable sales taxes.
*Canadian residents remit applicable GST and provincial taxes.

Silhouette®
Where love comes alive™

Visit Silhouette Books at www.Harlequin.com

PSNR0514BL